LOOP'S PROGRESS

LOOP'S PROGRESS

Chuck Rosenthal

WEIDENFELD & NICOLSON
New York

Published by Weidenfeld & Nicolson, New York
A Division of Wheatland Corporation
10 East 53rd Street
New York, NY 10022

Library of Congress Cataloging-in-Publication Data
Rosenthal, Chuck, 1951–
Loop's progress.
I. Title.
PS3568.08368L66   1986   813'.54   86-4131
ISBN 1-55584-001-9

Manufactured in the United States of America
Designed by Ronnie Ann Herman
First Edition
10 9 8 7 6 5 4 3 2 1

FOR RED AND ELEANOR
AND FOR GAIL

A distinction which we are not able to draw is—
to put it politely—not worth making.
—*J. L. Austin*

What you say about somefin is always less true
than sayin nofin.
—*Willie*

LOOP'S PROGRESS

Fourth of July

KARL KEPT one cannon on the front porch one on the back. The one on the front porch looked like a baby howitzer, about three-feet high and four-feet long, and he kept it pointed slightly left, toward the second story of the brown, wooden flat across the street where the Puerto Ricans just moved in. They were the newest in the neighborhood. He just wanted to let them know. Most the time, during the day, he kept the thing covered with a gray tarp. He wasn't a total jerk.

The cannon in the back looked like something you'd fire a circus midget out of, just a tube on a turret. With that thing Karl claimed he could drop a ball in the Erie Bay, twenty-four city blocks north.

"One problem with that, Karl," I said to him. A lot of people were afraid to talk to Karl because of all his guns, but he liked me, he liked me better than anybody else in my family.

"What's that?" he said. His red and gray hair was coming out from under his wool cap in all directions and he didn't have his top four front teeth.

"What if you miss."

He spit then grinned, held up his right hand that only had the last two fingers. "That."

Fourth of July. The Puerto Ricans put out two flags, one U.S. and one Puerto Rican, but that was good enough. Karl aimed the howitzer so it pointed between houses. Then after supper he got some boards out of the basement and made a ramp down the back steps. Then he brought out a low cart, just some boards on an axle, and made Karl Jr. help him nudge the circus cannon onto it. They pulled the cart out front.

Karl went back in the house and came out with his buckskins on, leather boots, coonskin cap, and waving an American flag. He gave that to Karl Jr., then dragged the cannon down to Big Dick Jinx's driveway and out into the street. He put Karl Jr. out front with the flag followed by his twin daughters, Beema and Maggie. Maggie was a cripple from birth and walked with a bad limp. That's the way they went, up and down the street, with the spooks drunk and hooting and the whites staring and the Puerto Ricans playing loud horn music that sounded like car wrecks. Karl Jr. waved the flag back and forth having a great time, and big Karl waved at everybody.

I was on the front porch with my sister Neda, but Red and Helen weren't letting the two youngest out. My mother Helen thought Karl was crazy and spent a lot of time peeking out the windows to make sure he wasn't doing anything nuts with his guns. She was certain that one of these days Karl was going to come pounding at the door and blow us all away, especially her, because he knew how much Helen hated fat old Sophie, Karl's wife. Through the front window I could see Red in the chair next to the Zenith, newspaper spread in front, but I knew his ears were perked. He was the mayor of the neighborhood and nothing got by him, but he wasn't going to dignify Karl's crazy behavior with his presence either. Red put his flag out and ate a couple hot dogs off the grill and kept quiet and figured everybody else should too.

Karl paraded up and down the street a couple times, then pulled the cannon back up Jinx's driveway and across the sidewalk and in between our two houses. It looked like things were over but he nodded at me and Neda and said, "C'mon Jarvis, I'm gonna blow it. Gonna put one in the bay."

Neda ran inside and that made Karl chuckle. "Should be real interesting," he said. Karl Jr. was grinning like a mouth with no head and Beema and Maggie wobbled their heads back and forth and put their palms out and said, "We're gonna SHOOT the cannon, we're gonna SHOOT the cannon," saying SHOOT every time they put out their little palms. Then Karl and Karl Jr. dragged the cannon into the backyard.

Inside, Red wasn't too happy. He was up and standing just inside the vestibule doorway, all six-two, two-fifty of him, and hot as hot sauce. "He's goddamn nuts," he said. "I ought to call the police."

"Talk to him," I said.

"I aint talkin to him. He's nuts."

Of course it wasn't that simple. Red and Karl were old and bitter friends. Worse than that, neighbors. They owed each other everything.

"Your mother's hiding in the goddamn basement," said Red.

I went down there.

Helen was in the corner of the potato cellar with her hands over her ears. She had my younger brothers Andrew and Joseph with her but when they saw me they ran back upstairs to see the show, though I knew they weren't going to get past Red. Helen had her knees tucked up to her chin. She was shaking.

"He's going to blow us all up, Jarvis. He'll kill us all."

"Now Helen," I said. "If anybody gets hurt it'll probably be somebody between here and the bay."

"I pleaded with Red to do something about him long ago, but you know your father, he doesn't do anything till there's a crisis and then he still might not do anything."

"Well Karl's our neighbor," I said to her. I went up and stooped in front of her and touched her knees. She had a rosary and her statue of the Infant of Prague all cuddled in by her stomach. I patted the Infant on his little crown. "Think he'll come through?" I said.

"Don't get sacrilegious, Jarvis." She clutched the Infant to her breast. "Though you're right, he's on his last legs. He didn't do a thing for Neda's scholarship."

Helen lit a candle every night when Neda applied to art school in Cleveland. The night before Neda got rejected Helen fell asleep in front of the Infant and damn near burned the house down. Red didn't say a thing about it, though he was the one who smelled the smoke and put out the fire. Helen made the Infant stand in the corner for a month after that one, facing in, and she didn't change any of his cute little coats or slips. He was a naked statue for a month.

Helen touched my hand. "Jarvis, why don't we move out of here. We should have moved out of here years ago."

"I'm going to try and talk to Karl," I told her.

Upstairs Red had everybody in the living room. Neda was wringing her hands like Helen, and Joseph and Andrew were hitting each other on the couch. Red had gone back to pretending to read the paper.

In the backyard Karl's dog and our dog barked at each other through the fence and Karl's kids ran around in the weeds knocking into each other like the Three Stooges. Knock. Bop. They were goofy kids. Then Karl came out of his basement carrying a lead ball a little bigger than a grapefruit.

"Thought it'd be bigger than that," I shouted.

"Huh?"

"Said I thought it'd be bigger."

Karl beat his dog and whacked his kids till things got a little quieter. "Shit, how big does it have to be?"

Well I didn't have an answer for that one because I knew how big they were and he knew I knew. "Aren't you worried about the cops?"

Karl put his hands on his hips and grinned toothless. Karl Jr. came up behind him and tugged on his arm. "Hey Dad," he said, and Karl whacked him a good one on the head. "Now I'm talkin'," said Karl. "Hope you learn something before you get too big and kick my ass." Karl Jr. said he'd like to kick his ass and Karl whacked him again. "Kid's got spunk," he said to me.

"Karl, you know how nervous Helen gets."

"Shit, Jarvis, the fucking thing's pointed in the other direction." He furrowed his brow a little bit. "Now Jarvis, you know me. I never hurt a soul in this neighborhood unless they came in to make trouble. Hell, me and Funster are the only cops this neighborhood has. And Red's the mayor. And I don't break any laws either. I got licenses for my handguns and you don't need a thing for rifles, except they can't be automatic. There aint a law in the book about owning a cannon." Karl Jr. had his sisters by the hair and was busy knocking their heads together. The dogs were barking again. "You know, I aint got the only dog here."

I grabbed Honky, Red's white shepherd, by the collar but he bit me hard on the wrist. Karl already had Einstein on the ground with a stick and chased him into his doghouse in the thick of the weeds. Karl never mowed his lawn and neither did we.

"Karl."

"Now Jarvis, you should know me better. It's the Fourth of July and I'm putting that ball in the bay." He rubbed his thighs and smiled and nodded with his lips tight. Then he carried the ball over to the cannon. Karl Jr. helped him as he powdered the barrel, packed it, then powdered and packed it again. He put the ball in and packed that, then set the fuse. I looked back at our house and saw Red at the back window, Neda, Joseph, and Andrew piled behind him trying to see out. Beema and Maggie were still doing their cheer, kicking their legs like they were dancing the can-can. "We're gonna SHOOT the cannon," they said.

Karl lit a big stick match and looked at me. He lit the fuse. It only took a few seconds.

Ba-rooom

Red Before All This

THEY STARTED calling him Redboots because he wore his older sister's red boots to school. Jarvis Joe Redboots Loop. Though in a month or two they dropped the Jarvis. Years later when he was on Midway his wife named his firstborn son Jarvis, and he sat in front of his tent and crumpled her letter and screamed, "We agreed on Michael!" but he couldn't do a damn thing, he was thousands of miles away fighting Japs. You couldn't trust Catholics. His mother had told him that. "Marry a good German girl. A Lutheran. You can't trust Catholics and the Polacks are worse." It took him about five years to forgive Helen, once Helen Pelkowski and now Helen Loop. To forgive me it took him eighteen. He slept with Helen.

His father's name was Luphaus, Joseph Jarvis Whitey Luphaus, but he changed it during the First World War to get work. It was tough being German back then. Krautheads. Victory cabbage. And now it was almost as bad, a depression, the Great Depression, and he had to wear red boots. Every day that winter of 1930 he tromped out of Germantown with his older sister Matilda and walked two miles up the Old French Road to Jefferson Grammar, though usually he ditched Matilda as soon as they got out of the ghetto. It was bad enough wearing red boots.

After school he peddled two paper routes. He had to lie about his age to get the first, saying he was twelve instead of ten, and take a different name, Shorty Wilkey, at a different paper station, to get the other. That's where Richie Rutkowski really made it rough.

The Rutter went to Jefferson too, one grade ahead though he'd flunked. He lived just on the edge of Polishtown so he didn't go to Garfield with the other Polacks and spooks, though that's where he hung out. He had a little gang that he took over to the West Side sometimes to hit on the dagos, and sometimes down to the Bayfront where the spooks were moving in. They didn't come south too often because the Germans were white and didn't have gangs anymore. When the Polacks did come to Germantown they wrecked field shacks and tree houses and beat on Jews.

Rutter waited for Redboots before school and after, always followed by at least three of his gang. He tweaked Redboots' ears and kicked him behind the knees. He thumped his head. He named him Redboots and then everybody in his grade picked it up.

Redboots' dad Whitey Loop was no help. He'd spent too many years keeping quiet about being German and now he sold liquor out of the basement and made do, keeping quiet.

"You can't make friends with him?" said Whitey Loop. He ran his hands over this thinning white hair, then took off his glasses and rubbed the red marks on his nose. "Give him something. Buy him off. Get him a football."

"Mom takes all my money for the mortgage," said Redboots.

"You give her all your money?"

In the kitchen his mother was chopping stew meat. The room smelled like bread. She held the cleaver up to him. "You know what I'd do to your father if he beat me? I'll tell you. The first time he turned his back he'd carry this around in it." She went back to the meat. "When that Polack turns his back you let him know he better either kill you or never turn his back again. What kind of boy are you?" she said.

That was a good question.

The next day after school Rutter was thumping his head and

kicking his butt. Redboots clopped along in his red boots under his red hair and in his red face. At the corner he turned on Rutter and said, "That's it. Don't." Rutter laughed.

Redboots Loop worried through his whole first paper route what he was going to do when he saw Rutter at the firehouse. If he fought him he'd lose. He wondered how much footballs cost. He thought maybe he could wait till dark to get there, but it was February and not getting dark till six now. Too late to deliver. So he didn't make any decisions, he just went to the station.

The day was dry and Rutter and his crowd were out playing stickball against the wall of the firehouse. When Rutter saw Redboots he left the game and followed him inside to the pile of bundled papers.

"I'm telling the station manager," said Rutter. "I'm telling him you're too young to have a route, you creep, and I'm telling him there aint nobody named Shorty Wilkey." He thumped Redboots on the head.

Redboots took out his wire cutters and cut the wire that bundled his papers. He took off the wrapping and walked it to the trash can, then returned and put the papers in his orange bag with black lettering that said ERIE TIMES NEWS. Rutter pushed a hand in his chest. "You little shit," he said.

Suddenly Redboots understood there was nothing to understand. When Rutter walked away he put down his newspaper bag and quietly followed him out the door and back to the stickball game. Rutter stood near the batter, yelling encouragement. The sky was low, dark and purple. Redboots looked at the line of sticks and bats leaning against the wall of the firehouse and picked the heaviest one. He took the bat in his hands and swung it against the back of Rutter's head. When Rutter went down Redboots blasted the head of the bat into his lower spine. After that everybody just called him Red.

Helen in the Past

ESTHER, HELEN'S mother, came to America after her father worked himself to death in the Polish mines, except since there was no Poland then, her birth certificate said she was Austro-Hungarian. She had an uncle who was the monsignor of the largest Polish church in Erie, Pennsylvania, Holy Rosary, where her mother sent her to keep house at the rectory and celebrate holy days with the priests and nuns and have her marriage arranged to Stanley Pelkowski, a furniture salesman. Her mother sent her own wedding dress for the wedding and Holy Rosary had a celebration as big as Easter.

Esther moved with Stanley to a house on the Lower East Side near Holy Rosary where everyone was Polish and Catholic. Stanley went to the furniture store in the morning and drank in the bars afterward. He played numbers, then ran them, then got caught. They busted people pretty good then because the chief of police ran the numbers racket and was a good friend of the mayor, both Irish. The Irish ran everything, the crime and the law. They bent to Yankee money and busted the Poles and dagos who were just doing Irish dirty work. That's just the way it went. Stanley spent six months in jail and when he got out Esther was waiting with his first son, Stan.

Esther had three sons in three years and it was during that

time that she and Stanley built the rabbit cages and the chicken coop, though Stanley preferred wild game and spent weekend after weekend with his friends in the woods south of town hunting rabbit and other small game, so Esther did much of the building herself. At first she thought that's what made her miscarry the fourth child, but she miscarried the fifth too and the doctor advised her to stop having children for a while.

That got Stanley a little upset. He wanted more sons. He needed boys. He was buying out the old man who ran the furniture store, he and two other co-workers, and to make it go they'd need all the cheap labor they could get. He ran his hands through his thick black hair. "You want me hiring dagos or niggers? They'll steal us blind."

"Hire Poles," said Esther.

"They'll want too much money."

"You're too cheap to hire your own people."

"A Pole cannot boss another Pole," said Stanley.

"But he can boss his sons."

"That's a different thing!" Stanley raised his hands in the air. "They help make me rich and then I help them become doctors and lawyers so they don't have to struggle like me, and when I'm old I have someone to care for my body and write my will, and they have someone to bring their children to, to tell them the story of how a family becomes happy and wealthy." He put his hands down and examined them, rubbing the calluses. It sounded pretty good.

But not to Esther. "You don't carry the babies."

"Of course, that's what you do! I can't have babies. *You* have the babies. That's how this works!" Stanley understood a couple things, though now he was mad enough to justify a good drunk so he left. But he didn't get any more babies for a few years.

Meanwhile the war broke out in Europe and Esther received a letter from her mother telling her that Esther's first cousin and closest childhood friend, Edju, had joined the Polish Resistance.

The Resistance! Edju had never resisted anything in his life, other than work. It had been years since Esther heard from Edju. How he must have changed. "Edju," wrote Esther, "I'm proud of you, but be careful, and write."

"Don't worry, Esther," Edju responded. "We're all registered with the Empire. It's the safest place to be, and after the war we will be patriots."

Two months later the Austrians invaded the Resistance's big Vodka-Fest in Warsaw, put them all in the army and moved them up to the front for trench fodder. In the first battle Edju surrendered to the French.

"They're worse than the Austrians," Edju wrote Esther. "The French think that after them comes ten loads of shit, then the rest of the human race. The food is lousy and they make me stay with Serbs and Croats who are good for nothing but farting and fighting. I am a refined individual, almost an engineer. Still, the war is teaching me many languages and the French know how we Poles hate the Germans and Russians, so there is hope."

The French put him in the army and moved him to the front.

Esther got her next letter from a German prison camp. "The Germans get a lot of bad propaganda," said Edju. "They are very clean people and their bad food is very similar to our bad food. And when they heard what the French did to me after capturing me from the Austrians, they were appalled. It's against the rules, you know. I am learning German very quickly and the Commandant here says he is sure there will be a place for me in the German Corps."

At the front.

But it didn't take long for Edju to surrender to the English. "America should enter the war on the side of Germany," wrote Edju. "I think I would like America, and it would be nice to see you and meet Stanley and your boys. Italy would be nice, too, but I hear it is impossible to surrender to Italians before they surrender to you first."

Something in British cunning kept them from drafting Edju, but after he picked up English, though with the oddest of accents, they used him as a clerk in the Foreign Relations Office. "I am an intelligent man," Edju wrote Esther. "I know many languages and I am quite trustworthy when not under pressure."

At least Edju was safe, and his days of surrender ended just in time because America entered the war on the side of the Allies. Esther was glad Stanley didn't enlist. The only thought he gave enlisting was thinking of reasons for avoiding it.

"I'm too old," said Stanley, raising his hands. It had become a familiar pose when he wanted to make a point. "Besides, the Germans are the only ones buying my furniture. What side are the Poles on anyway?"

"The Poles are for themselves," said Esther.

"You mean each Pole is for *himself*. They would rather buy furniture from some cheap dago."

"My teacher says Poland was once a great empire, as big as Rome," said little Stan who now went to grade school at Holy Rosary.

"That's right," said big Stanley. "In the Dark Ages we were something else."

"How can you ridicule your own people," said Esther. She sat in her chair crocheting as Stanley paced.

"A great people!" shouted little Stan. Big Stanley patted him on the head.

"We're like the Jews," said Esther. "No nation, persecuted everywhere. But someday we'll have our own pope."

Stanley held his head. "The pope." Besides smoking and drinking heavily, he'd stopped going to church. "I married a nun," he said.

"You knew where I lived when you met me," said Esther.

"A great nation!" said little Stan.

"That's enough," Esther told him. "Go to bed."

"If my name was Smith," said Stanley, "I could sell furniture."

"And run for governor," said Esther.

Stanley rubbed his chin. "Governor," he said.

"Think of someone other than yourself for a change."

"I'm a Pole," said Stanley. "I think about myself." He raised his arms. It was enough to make him want to get drunk.

That night at the bar Stanley Pelkowksi decided to change his name and his future and his family's future. When he got drunk enough to face Esther he lumbered home, finding her in bed.

"Wake up," he said. "We're changing our name."

"That's nothing to wake up for."

"Mr. and Mrs. Pell," said Stanley. "I'll call my store Pell's."

"Your business partners will love it."

"They will love it!" shouted Stanley.

Esther heard the children stirring. "Now you've done it," she said.

"Stanley Pell," Stanley muttered.

"You can change your name," Esther told him, putting on her robe to go to the children's room. "But I changed my name once to Pelkowski and I'll die Pelkowski. My name is not something for your whim." She left the room.

"My children will be Pells!" Stanley shouted at her back. And they were. And so was Esther, though she introduced herself and signed her name Pelkowski.

Esther had two more children after the war, both girls, and Stanley gave up the request for a platoon of sons. Besides, things started to go well for Stanley Pell. He bootlegged whiskey and made his own beer, he bought out his partners and dressed his family well, he always had money and owned stocks and bonds and some property south of town that was now woods, though he happened to know that Ford planned an expansion plant outside Detroit that was destined for Erie and when that plant came his land was going to boom. He bought apartments down by the bay and collected rent, and sometimes he even sold some furniture. He had three sons, little Stan, Jon, and David, who would take care of the store and then go off to college to become a doctor and a lawyer and a politician, and two little daughters, the last of whom, Helen, had her christening on the same day as the Grand Opening of Pell's Furniture which even the Irish mayor who bought his whiskey from Stanley showed up for and gave Helen a brand new Liberty silver dollar.

Afternoons Stanley drove his Model A out Old French Road to his woods south of town and thought about how good everything was, how good change was, how good money was, and wished he could get Esther to tear down the chicken coops in the backyard that made his house look like a poor farm. Maybe they could even move.

"We need a change," said Stanley.

"Change comes soon enough," said Esther, "without bringing it on yourself."

"We can control change!" shouted Stanley.

"The wind kicks up," said Esther, "or the world turns one degree too much, what do you have? Pffft. Rubbed out. You control nothing."

Stanley knew there was something wrong with that logic, he just didn't know anything about logic. Besides, Esther spent her whole day in the house cleaning and taking care of the kids like a good wife, how could she know anything. Opinions were for men. Look what happened when women started voting. No bars. No liquor stores. The wind didn't cause that. And how did she think he made his money, selling furniture?

"Things may not always be so good," said Esther quietly. "But we own this house, we have the rabbits and the chickens and a small garden. If something goes wrong, we have good neighbors. You want to move, Mr. Pell, move without me."

"Unk," said Stanley. He tried to raise his hands but only got them shoulder high. "I'm going to the store."

"And come home stinking drunk."

Stanley covered his face. "I'm married to a nun."

"Who gave you five children."

"A grandma," said Stanley, putting on his coat. "Grandma."

After that Stanley never called her Esther again. He called her Busha, Polish for grandma, like "boosh," which eventually it was

shortened to, but then just plain Bush like "crush" or "mush."
Even when he loved her and whispered to her that she was a
great and wonderful strong woman and it made him proud, she
was still his Bush, and even the kids started calling her Bush but
she didn't care. Her mother was a busha. She'd be Bush soon
enough.

So if Stanley drank too much and smoked too much and gambled too much, so if his ideas were too big and his head too
small, so, he was a man. Still, now there was money for the
boys' colleges, and if things continued to go well, maybe for her
daughters, Frances and Helen, especially Helen, who learned how
to read on her own just from looking at picture books and could
already add and subtract, even before going to school. None of
the others had done that, even Stanley could see it. Stanley called
her his "little miracle" and put her on his lap and gave her sips
of beer and puffs on his cigar. Bush gave her more chores.

"She's not the center of the world," said Bush.

"Ah," said Stanley, giving Helen a puff of his cigar when she
came in from feeding the animals. "She's going to be a beauty
too."

Edju wrote Bush: "Dear Esther, I'm an engineer. I got my degree
in London. And I'm getting married to a beautiful lady journalist
who was a war correspondent while I worked here in Foreign
Relations. Beautiful Elizabeth. Did you ever think I would marry
someone named Elizabeth? How are you and Stanley doing? I'd
love to show Elizabeth America, whenever you can afford it."

"Stanley," said Bush. "The police are at the door."

Stanley rose from his chair, then put out his cigar, looking calmer
to Bush than he'd ever looked in his life. "Tell them I'll be right
there," he said, heading for the kitchen. Bush followed him. He
put on his coat at the back door. "Tell them I'll be right there,"
said Stanley.

"It's about the store," said Bush.

Stanley nodded profoundly. He had a lot of money in his pocket, he figured he'd just go to a hotel and think things over. Maybe he'd leave town for a while. He needed a vacation.

"You're running away?" said Bush. "They're probably waiting at the back door."

"Ha!" said Stanley Pell. He kissed Bush on the forehead and went out the back door. That's where they caught him. And that's one of the few things Helen remembered about her father, other than he was often drunk, and sometimes, when he had his friends over, he showed off by lighting his cigars with twenty-dollar bills. She remembered sitting on his lap of liquor and smoke, having sips of each after she finished feeding the rabbits and chickens and Bush's two new ducks. She remembered him smelling like a smoked Easter ham. And she remembered his sad face the night he stood between the two police officers in the living room. He looked like an old piece of fruit.

Stanley got off easy. He kept good whiskey and made some of the best beer in town. His biggest buyer sold directly to Mayor Garvey who drank often with the chief of police, the district attorney, and the city judge. It was hard enough on Garvey that he had to get his booze someplace else, and the police chief settled for appropriating Stanley's stock. Still, Stanley got his name in the paper and suddenly had to rely again on his business. He had to make do with Pell's Furniture. Suddenly he realized what a poor location Pell's had, on lower Celebration Avenue, the commercial district on the edge of Polishtown. But he still had his Bayfront apartment houses, though a bit run down, and his land south of town, the land that would make him a millionaire when the city expanded, when the Ford plant came. He just had to work a little harder, but Stanley hated work so he didn't.

He went for walks. He walked in his woods and took his gun, bringing home fresh rabbit and fresh squirrel and sometimes, in season, duck. Helen remembered going out on the back porch in the evening and looking at the dead game, the fur of the rabbits and squirrels listless but soft against their cold, stiff frames, the duck feathers holding the sunset purple then green on the necks of the mallards, the eyes motionless like dark glass marbles.

Stanley no longer ate with Bush and the four younger children. He drank, had a bath, and went down to the store to get little Stan who spent all his time, except for the hours in high school, down on Celebration Avenue keeping the shop in line. Stanley and Stan closed the store together and came home, eating together in the kitchen, talking business.

With Stan in charge Pell's had again begun to make money. Stan studied the catalogues and the big stores downtown and knew what people bought. He knew from the looks on their faces and the way they wandered through the displays whether they wanted help or wanted to be left alone. He knew when they were ready to buy and when they weren't. He found out through conversation whether or not they had a home, what their plans were, if they had money enough to spend seriously. He knew how to sell the most attractive item of a display at cost and make his profit on the rest. And nobody in the store touched the cash register but little Stan.

"Let me take over the store," he begged Stanley as they ate their leftovers on the kitchen table. He had thick dark hair, a flat face, and thin nervous fingers like Stanley. Only his eyes, hazel instead of dark brown, showed him kin to Bush.

Stanley poured them both beer. "Go to school," he said drunkenly. "Be a doctor. Something people need, no matter what."

"I'd be a great manager!" said little Stan, raising both his hands.

Stanley held his head. "You're going to school," he said. Somehow, no matter how well things went, it all seemed more of a struggle than he wanted.

Stanley began throwing parties on the weekends. Each time the biggest event of the night was when he lit his cigar with a twenty-dollar bill. It drove Bush mad and it was one of the few things that gave him pleasure. Then he'd wake the kids and bring them out. He'd get little Stan a beer and they'd joke about the business. Jon grew like a shot and played basketball for Holy Rosary. David had a paper route, an entrepreneur like his dad. Frances sang. Helen showed everyone the Liberty silver dollar the mayor gave her on the day she was christened. Bush let the show end then rustled the children back to bed, all but little Stan who would graduate that June. He'd been accepted at Georgetown. And after that Bush came back to the living room and refilled her glass of whiskey and ate chocolate. She liked the way the brown burn of the whiskey melted over the sweetness and raged into her nose and throat.

When the depression hit it wiped out Stanley's stocks in one day, but he still had his store, his apartments, his land. But even little Stan couldn't sell furniture to phantoms. People had no money. And Stanley's apartments on the Bayfront were all rented to workers now out of work. Stanley's drinking friends, out of work and in need of money, came to him and he lent them what he had till his savings went dry. Little Stan went off to Georgetown in the fall and Bush told Jon that he couldn't play basketball that year so he could help Stanley out at the store.

Bush had prepared for the crisis. She had the chickens, ducks, and rabbits because she hadn't let Stanley tear down the pens. She had her garden, which she expanded, and like every year she canned in the fall and prepared seeds for the spring. She had the money she'd saved from the 10 percent tithe she was supposed to give to the church and that she made Stanley give her on Sundays, except Stanley only gave her twenty dollars and she always kept half. She'd saved all of Frances' clothes and now mended them and gave them to Helen. Jon wore little Stan's hand-me-downs, David wore Jon's. She extracted what she could from David's paper route, though he wanted to quit and help out at the store. Bush felt one son too many already sacrificed to that.

Bush managed all she could manage but she couldn't manage Stanley. In the morning he moped at Pell's with his breakfast beer until lunch when he went down to the Bayfront and vainly attempted to collect some of the rents. But the fathers were out looking for work, or like him, drunk, and the mothers harried and drawn with eyes that made him want to cry. After knocking on a few doors he left the building and lunched on the hill above the docks, watching the oar boats with their long rusty hulls load on the pier and the lake tankers unload petroleum and coal. Then he returned to the store until Jon came and he went out to walk in his woods. He'd just have to hold out. Soon the depression would end, Hoover said it would end soon, and he himself had voted for Hoover because he didn't want to vote Irish, and when it ended the Ford plant would come. His land and apartments would be worth a fortune, and people would buy furniture again. He'd keep a part of the woods for himself. Maybe even build there. He could drive farther south if he wanted to hunt. And the kids would be educated. They'd have degrees, money. His daughters would marry wealthy men. He just had to hold out.

By the time he got home in the evening he was good and drunk. Holding out was much easier then. Waiting seemed the only rational choice, besides, what could he do while he was so drunk? He didn't eat dinner because by then he'd lost his appetite. He let Jon close the store himself, though Bush usually sent David to help. Stanley didn't want to be bothered. He needed rest. Holding out exhausted him. He passed out on the couch and no longer bothered to sleep in bed.

One night Stanley awoke with a familiar but almost forgotten agitation in his loins. He stumbled from the couch and into the bedroom where Bush slept, where he'd made five children with her, where he'd shared his dreams and night anxieties and slept with Bush like a spoon in a spoon. He lay down next to Bush and ran his fingers through her hair. "Bush," he whispered. "Bush."

Bush's eyes opened and Stanley kissed her forehead.

"I'd forgotten how beautiful you were," whispered Stanley.

Bush took Stanley by the wrist and moved his hand from her hair. "If you'd have saved some of those twenty-dollar bills you lit cigars with then you could go downtown and buy some love."

Stanley said nothing. Bush's grip tightened on his wrist. His head got light.

"You think I don't know you used to go whoring when you could afford it."

"Only sometimes," mumbled Stanley.

"I don't care how often. Tell it to Christ on Judgment Day."

Stanley pulled his wrist from Bush's grip. The lightness in his head cleared, but left an ache. His tongue was swollen. He drank Bush's water on the bed table. "You are my wife," he said to Bush.

"I married Stanley Pelkowski, a hard-working Pole, not Stanley Pell the drunk."

"I've drunk and gambled all my life. You didn't complain when things went well, don't complain now."

"You're a man," said Bush. "You worked, you drank, you gambled, sometimes you whored. Now you don't work."

"There is no work."

Bush pursed her lips with a hiss. "There is never *no* work. Hunt. Stop drinking. Repair the coops. You have friends who owe you thousands of dollars. You have apartments filled with people who don't pay rent. Your children work. I work day and night. You do nothing but drink."

"I'm having a hard time," said Stanley.

"Everyone is having a hard time."

Stanley stared at Bush. The love left his groin, the ache left his head, the strength left his arms. He tried to be angry, but it left him too quickly. He sighed. "You are a woman," he said to Bush. "You live in this house. You don't understand. The people in the apartments have no jobs. I can't put them in the street. I can't deny my friends. This will end and I'll get it all back double. I just have to hold out."

"You haven't seen one of your friends since you lent out all your money," said Bush. "And people who don't have to pay rent don't have to look for work. Don't tell me I don't understand." She sat up in bed and met Stanley eye to eye. "Stanley, there is no holding out. Sell the apartments and land to keep the store, or sell the store and find work to keep the land. You're going to lose everything by holding out. Do something."

Stanley went into the dawn, resolute, and got drunk.

One morning a few weeks later, just after Jon left the store to go to the East Side public high school because Holy Rosary could no longer afford to keep its high school open, Roger Strong, a millionaire real estate man from one of the old families in town, came to visit Stanley at Pell's. He wore a fine wool suit and vest, a little derby and a diamond pin to hold his tie. His mustache was trimmed to the corners of his lips. He gave Stanley a cigar and shared a drink from his flask as they sat in one of Pell's living room displays. Strong smiled at Stanley with closed lips and nodded. Stanley kept the cigar in his mouth and concentrated on Strong's tie pin.

"Things are bad everywhere," said Strong.

Stanley nodded. He could bargain with Poles. He knew them. He understood every word they never said. But this type of man he didn't know.

"When things get really tough," said Strong, "then sometimes even the very tough go down. It's not simply a matter of will-power or strength. I'm not condescending. I'm talking straight to you, as a hard-working businessman."

"Those of us with assets will hold out, I suppose," said Stanley. "What we have will be worth more after all this, then we can start over."

Strong breathed heavily and drank. Stanley felt his eyes like X-rays. "I don't think there can be any holding out," he said. "The strong must strengthen their positions." He filled Stanley's glass from his flask and Stanley held himself from sipping the whiskey immediately. "The weakest will go. There's little anyone can do now. This is going to last a long time. But there are some people, Mr. Pell, like yourself, who the community will need later, but who might not make it on their own."

Stanley drank. He wouldn't get anything for free beyond the cigar and whiskey so he finished the glass and Strong filled it again.

"If you're not making money, taxes will take everything. I'm sure you know that. But if you were offered a good price for what you owned, and a job, say staying on and managing Pell's, then you could make a living and have something to start over with when this ended."

"I'm not doing badly," said Stanley.

Strong nodded abstractly, then looked Stanley in the eye again. "It's a time to be practical," said Strong. He looked down momentarily, as if trying to save Stanley's pride, but it was beyond that now, far beyond that. "You're not going to think about it?" asked Strong.

Stanley shrugged.

"I'll send my boy in a couple of days," said Strong. "He runs my store downtown, I'm sure you know. He knows furniture. Maybe you two can talk." He finished his drink, as did Stanley, stood, and nodded again. After Strong left, Stanley drove to his woods and went for a walk. He finished the contents of his flask. He watched the sun lay light on the bare branches of the leaf trees and make blue puddles of shadow beneath the pines. He stood on the hill at the edge of his land and watched the sun become an orange patch on the bay. He remembered his walks in winter when the sun fell from the sky much farther south. The days were growing again. So what if he was a little man. So what.

At home Bush had baked fresh bread. There was duck's blood soup and homemade egg noodles. It seemed he couldn't remember eating so well. His children, he realized, now spoke at the table, freely, without permission. Little Stan was doing well at Georgetown. Jon had been accepted at Penn. David was ready to work at the store and Helen would skip a grade next year at Holy Rosary and join Frances in seventh. Bush said Edju wanted to come to the States. She rubbed Stanley's shoulders and buttered his bread.

"You're hungry for a change," Bush said to him.

Stanley dipped his white buttered bread into his red soup. "Yes," he said to Bush. "Things change."

Furgeson Strong looked like his father only younger. He smoked a cigar. He carried a flask. But he didn't sit down. He walked about the store like a big new rooster. He blew smoke purposefully. Stanley followed him through a living room set, then a bedroom set, then he stopped following. He went back to the cash register, poured himself a drink, and waited.

Furgeson circled, stared, rubbed his face, his chin, his eyes. He stared out the big front window onto Celebration Avenue, hands on his lower back. He finished his cigar. He took a drink. Then walked over to Stanley.

"Things will be different when I'm in charge," Furgeson said to Stanley.

"Some changes," said Stanley.

"Yes." Furgeson lit another cigar, stopped a moment, then offered one to Stanley who decided he didn't smoke cigars anymore. "You don't have any of the recent styles."

"My son kept track of that," said Stanley. Furgeson eyed him. "He's at Georgetown now."

"Well," said Furgeson. "I suppose you've shot for a different kind of customer."

"Yes." Stanley moved from behind the counter and stood in front of Furgeson Strong. "Polish, poor, and stupid."

Strong winced or grimaced or smirked, Stanley couldn't tell. He straightened. "You won't own this place anymore Mr. Pell."

"I own it now," said Stanley.

"Yes," said Furgeson. "But you won't."

"But I do now," said Stanley.

That's when Furgeson Strong got the first inkling that Stanley understood him. He hadn't come to be understood. "I don't understand," he said.

Stanley wrapped his fist around the top of Furgeson Strong's tie. "Get the hell out."

That was the last day of his life Stanley Pell didn't drink. He closed his store. He took what little money was in the cash register and bought hams for the families in his apartments. He watched the first spring ships in the harbor, then went to his woods for a walk, returning home sober before dinner. He washed and shaved. He kissed Bush on the head.

"You've had phone calls thanking you for hams," she said.

"Yes," said Stanley. "Going away presents."

"Some of the Jews couldn't use them."

"It's the thought," said Stanley, sitting down at the table. "The thought."

Bush sent the children out of the kitchen to rewash.

"I thought of my family too," Stanley said. He got up and went out the back door, returning with a ham. He put it on the table, then raised both his arms in the air like the old days, but this time he said nothing. He smiled at one hand, then the other. He let them drop. He and Bush looked at each other with more knowledge than they'd ever asked for.

"Some big decision today," said Bush.

"Yes," said Stanley. "Some big, big decision."

Stanley sold his apartments. He put money in an account so little Stan, Jon, and David would have money for college, even enough to get David started if he didn't win a scholarship. He bought Bush wire and wood for new coops and pens, bought her more rabbits, more chickens, more ducks, some geese, and a dress. He didn't pay the taxes on his land, instead he lent more money to his friends. That's when Bush knew it was over.

Because the girls were going to Holy Rosary for free, she convinced Stanley to give her several hundred dollars for their school, then stashed it with the rest of her emergency fund. She carefully repaired the coops and pens, calculated the reproduction of her stock, then sold all the extra material and stock she could spare. She took on mending from neighbors.

Stanley closed Pell's, except for the basement where he again peddled a little whiskey and brewed his own beer, making just enough income to keep him drinking. He spent his days at the harbor or in the woods, and even when the taxes took his land he couldn't be stopped from walking on it. The only day he missed was the day of the auction. Strong ended up with half of Stanley's land. A grocer named Pelvis Short bought Pell's and kept the name. Stanley moved his brewery to the basement of his home where he set up a cot and slept on the nights he made it home. He didn't live in his house, he haunted it, that's what Bush told him and he agreed. "I'm practicing," said Stanley. He raised his hands about shoulder high, withered and stained with nicotine. He never shaved and never grew a beard. His muscles hung on his bones like rotten fruit.

Autumn came and Roosevelt ended Prohibition on beer. Stanley went for walks in the rain on his old land. He watched the leaves change and caught a cold for Thanksgiving. Helen brought his goose and dressing to him in the basement where he always ate if he ate, the only thing he gave to the upstairs anymore were his coughs and nightmares. He looked like a rag and Bush told Frances and Helen that he wasn't their father anymore. Helen gave him the plate. He gave her beer. She kissed his head.

"Don't kiss me," said Stanley. "Kiss the tax man. Kiss the milkman. Kiss somebody who can do you some good."

"Bush said to come up," said Helen.

Stanley raised his hands about chest high, then brought them back to the plate on his lap. "Have some more beer."

"No," said Helen.

"Okay little Bush," said Stanley. "Go upstairs."

Upstairs Helen and Frances and Bush and David thanked God for what they had left, for Roosevelt who Bush voted for, and for little Stan and Jon doing so well at school even if they didn't have money to come home for Thanksgiving. "Maybe Christmas," said Bush. Stanley caught pneumonia. Liquor was legalized. Little Stan and Jon got to come home for Christmas a week early because Stanley was dead.

Funster

NOBODY CALLED Jarvis Jr., Jarvis Jr. They called me Jarvis and called my dad Red. Red was a good man but Helen always said it took him five years to recover from World War II, to get all the meanness and violence out of him. She said he'd kill almost anything that wouldn't kill him when he got back and there were several nearly dead people in town to vouch for that. Whenever Red got mad Helen left the house and took little Jarvis and Neda with her. Red hated that. It made him feel like he was somebody that had to be feared. It made him pound the doors. He pounded out the basement door, he pounded out the door to the back shed, he pounded out the doors to the bedrooms, the door to the bathroom, the door to the attic. The place didn't have any more doors. If he weren't an ex-Marine he would've cried. What kind of house has no doors?

Jarvis was too little to kill Red so he had to settle for hating him. As soon as Jarvis was old enough to toddle Red popped footballs in his chest, slapped a baseball glove on his hand, chased him around with whiffle bats as big as flagpoles and dribbled house-sized basketballs around his head. From the air football helmets fell like swallows. Every Sunday Red made him watch the Browns beat the Redskins or the Steelers or the Eagles or some other hapless team who didn't have a giant black man named

Brown who could run through anybody. Though one Sunday Jarvis watched the old black-and-white Zenith and saw a team in dark, dark uniforms just as big as the Browns and maybe a little bigger with a little ny on the sides of their helmets. Big Jim Brown kept getting tackled and Red kept cursing somebody named Huff and the big dark team named the Giants beat the Browns.

Jarvis felt good on Sunday for the first time in a long time. He didn't even mind the thought of kindergarten the next day. He went to bed without arguing and instead of thinking about being a dog, which was his favorite thing to think about, he thought about Sam Huff grabbing Jim Brown and Red by the necks and banging their heads together. He thought about New York where giant dark behemoths crawled out of sewers peering westward, to Cleveland.

Red wasn't really that upset about the Browns. They won their share. Red was upset because all his talents were going to pot. He could draw, paint, print signs, play the guitar, and sing too, but he didn't do any of those things, he worked at the Erie Forge. After high school, when things began to pick up just before the war, he applied for the art editor job at the *Erie Times News*. He sent in his drawings. He got an interview. But when the managing editor saw how young he was he didn't offer Red the job, he offered him a scholarship to the Cleveland Art Institute.

"Forget about it," said his mother, Emma Loop. "You've been in school since you could walk. There's a depression. We got a house to pay off."

So he went to work with his father, Whitey Loop, at the forge. He gave most his salary to Emma for the mortgage until he met Helen and got married.

With a little extra money he saved he went partners with his brother-in-law Bif in a little variety store down by the East Bay. That was sometime after the Marines. But Bif juggled the books and got the store in debt and lost all the money so they had to sell the place. Bif also got Whitey and Emma to sign over their house to him, the house Red was brought up in and the one he helped buy. Bif lived there now with Red's younger sister Jelly who had a little tiny leg from when she had polio. He built an extension on the back for Whitey and Emma. Red couldn't even go over there and pound out the doors.

So when things got bad for Red they got really bad. He felt like he was living in a rainstorm of bad. Then Helen fled with Jarvis and Neda to her mother's and that whole side of the family went aflame with how he was such a violent German Protestant bullhead and how his whole side of the family was good for nothing. And then he'd have to show up over there on Christmas or Easter or Mother's Day in front of Helen's family, her brother Stan the chemical engineer, and her brother Jon the lawyer who was some kind of naval officer hero in charge of a dozen ships, and her brother David who just bought a big dairy farm down in Mercer Valley, and her sister Frances who, along with Helen and their mother, worked scrubbing floors after the old man lost his fortune and died during the depression, worked to send Stan and Jon and David to college, and only after that married Harvey Stano who was a bigwig with Pontiac in Detroit while Helen married him, Red Loop, a dumb forge worker who was good for only two things, good for nothin and good for shit.

He could just picture them. They'd sit around the living room and put their right legs over their left knees, then their left knees over their right, bouncing their ankles and drinking Carling Black Label and keeping pleasant long enough for him to leave, unless they could talk about something sneaky like Catholic liturgy which Red didn't know anything about. So when Helen went to her mother's Red left his doorless home, first putting a few dents into the vestibule wall, and went to see Funster.

Jimbo Funster was a little younger than Red, a little shorter and a little fatter. He had a little less hair. Funster's family built the first house in the neighborhood eighty years ago and the main line of Funsters, three or four generations of them, stayed in the house ever since. Funsters saw the woods go down and the barns go up, then saw the fields turn to houses. Funsters saw the working-class Yankees leave and the factory worker Polacks come in. Now the Polacks were dying and the neighborhood getting its first niggers. Funsters had guns.

Red himself hadn't touched a gun since he left the Marines, he had his fists. But Funster stuttered. He looked a little soft.

"They're d-different and I just don't t-trust them. I don't care what anybody says," said Funster.

So he showed Red his shotguns, his twenty-twos, and his very special thirty-ought-six. He showed him the bullets he made himself. Then, with all the guns laid out on the porch railing like Fort Erie, he left Red to guard and brought out meat from his freezer: squirrel meat and deer steaks, wild rabbit, wild pigeons, wild doves. Ducks. Then came time for the frozen trout and bass and fishing poles and a couple beers. "You sh-should come out with me sometime," Funster always invited. "Get you away. It'd b-b-be g-good."

But Red didn't like getting away.

"Well," said Funster, "l-least you should do is get yourself a gun. Neighborhood's getting t-too tough. I worry for my wife and kids."

"There's nothin around here I can't handle with my fists," said Red.

"Y-you can't stop a b-b-bullet with your damned fists."

"When I get too old I'll get a goddamn ball bat."

That was one of those answers that wasn't an answer it was just an answer, and the conversation had reached this point a hundred times, so Red packed back across the street with a couple of deer steaks in hand, meat he didn't eat because he didn't like the taste or smell of wild game and neither did Helen, and went to the closet in the living room, realizing he still had doors on his closets and wondering if maybe he could solve his door problem with a couple easy transfers before winter, and he got out his bowling ball and made himself a liverwurst sandwich with ketchup with his left hand, all the while swinging the bowling ball with his right, all sixteen pounds of it, until it felt so light it was like a part of his arm. Second man on the forge AAAA bowling team, Red was going to make it so throwing that bowling ball down the alley was like skipping stones. Those pins didn't have a chance. In a month he'd be the best bowler on the team, and then the best in the city, just like he'd become the best shot in the Marines, and the best handball player and the best horseshoe pitcher. Everybody already knew he was the best catcher in the Industrial Fast-Pitch League and could hit a softball anywhere in the park including out of the park if the damn parks had fences. Red walked around the house and swung the bowling ball back and forth and back and forth and thought about taking up golf. Then Helen came home from her mother's, Jarvis in one hand and Neda in the other, and Red stood there at the doorway. He didn't say anything, he just stood there and held the bowling ball in front of him and smacked it into his left hand, smack, smack, smack, as easy as if it were his fist.

Funsters and Jinxes

JIMBO FUNSTER had had a particularly bad day. The night before he'd found out that the house on the corner of 24th and German Avenue, just six houses away from his own, had been sold to niggers. They didn't look too bad, he watched them with his binoculars the day they came to look at the place. The man wore a suit. There was a wife and a grandmother and two kids. The little boy, he looked about seven, stayed out front the whole time dribbling a basketball. Funster could still hear that basketball, wump, wump, wump.

He raced over to the Farrels' who were selling the house and moving to Houston, but when he got there he couldn't find anything to say. "Wh-wh-what," stumbled Funster to Farrel.

"I can't do a damn thing about it," Farrel said, rubbing his forehead. "There's all kinds of laws now. Besides, they got all the money they need. If they want it, they get it."

Funster always knew it might happen. If it didn't happen at Farrel's it was going to happen someplace else. There were already four families down on 23rd Street and when he drove by the old Greek Orthodox church the other day he saw the FOR SALE sign was down. Somebody said maybe the Boys' Club bought it, but that wouldn't be much better, he knew the difference between the Y and the Boys' Club. Besides, two houses down Mrs. Flossie was in her eighties and two houses farther the Baggarts were in their seventies, and so were the Spinkses next to Red's. Mrs. Wheedle's husband just died and she and her fifty-year-old retarded daughter weren't going to last that much longer either.

No, all he could do was hope they were different. Maybe they'd be Catholic, Catholic niggers weren't so bad, though Jinx had already spoiled that. Big Dick Jinx rubbed his big chin with his big hand and said, "No fucking way. If he's dribblin a basketball he aint Catholic. I deliver potato chips to that little black Catholic parish down by the bay. They can't play basketball. The Baptists play basketball." Well Jinx knew that stuff. He got all around town in that Buckhorn Potato Chip truck with the deer on the side.

But it wouldn't matter if they were a good family or not. Funster knew it wouldn't matter. Last month at the GE plant he'd got a black on his work crew and that guy wasn't a bad Joe either. He worked pretty hard. And Funster tried real hard to be fair to him too, practiced for days saying "negro" just in case the fellow's race came up, but when it did he got corrected.

"It's not negro no more," the man said to him. "It's black." And even though he went right back to work Funster wondered where he got off telling his foreman how he could be addressed. Funster remembered when his own foreman kicked him in the ass for the slightest lip. Now niggers were telling him how to talk.

So it didn't matter. They were all uppity, and even if the first ones were good, well, they had to be, but if one came, then more were sure to be coming, and the more the worse.

Funster looked around his neighborhood and saw it disintegrating around his Funster house. He saw the streets unplowed and unpaved, lawns unmowed and houses unpainted. He saw trash in the streets. Break-ins. Rapes. Worse still, he thought his son might be hanging out with a faggot.

Stinky Jinx.

Not that Stinky was a bad kid. And sure as hell Big Dick Jinx was all man. But he wasn't home enough. He spent too many days and nights driving around in his Buckhorn Potato Chip truck making a good living and leaving the kids too much to his wife. There was something wrong with Stinky. His voice was too high and he wore his mother's clothes too much. But Funster didn't know what to say to Jinx about it. Nobody did. The only person seeming to do anything about it was Jarvis Loop, who knocked the shit out of Stinky every chance he got.

But Jarvis knocked the shit out of Jimbo's son Funly too, and instead of fighting back Funly ran home to Grandma Funster and hung out with Stinky Jinx. Funster worried about Funly. He tried to remember when he himself started shimmying up trees to get hard-ons. About ten. He'd better get Funly that BB gun. Get him to the woods more. But that night Stinky was sleeping out in a tent with Funly in the Funsters' backyard. There were niggers on Funster's job, niggers on Funster's block, and a faggot in his backyard with his son and Funster couldn't do anything about any of it. So that night he loaded up his .22 rifle and stuffed it under the bed, just like he always told everybody he did but never did, till then.

Jarvis Loop &
Georgie Gorky

JARVIS AND Georgie Gorky sat in Georgie's backyard and counted the rocks that they pretended were gold. Not just any rocks were good for gold, they had to be angular and have little sparklies in them, they had to make you think of ore, and Jarvis and Georgie had long discussions about whether or not certain rocks evoked that particular quality. They had a whole special pile of second-division rocks, tabled because they hadn't been able to come to a unanimous decision.

That morning they'd fallen upon a big pile of hot asphalt in the parking lot of the abandoned Greek Orthodox church with the funny cross on top behind Jarvis' house and scooped up piles of it. Now they wracked their brains for some kind of valuable name for it, because it certainly was a prize and they'd certainly had to steal it and it certainly had to be valuable. That's where Funly Funster found them.

Funly was a short, fat, pudgy-lipped, flat-topped piggy. Georgie Gorky was already making piggy sounds at the back of his throat.

"When I'm twelve my Dad's going to buy me a twenty-two, then you'll be making chicken sounds," said Funly.

"Well I'll get a shotgun," said Georgie.

"I'll get an atom bomb," said Jarvis. That's where the discussion always ended up anyway so he decided to get it there quick.

Funly watched Jarvis and Georgie running the asphalt through their hands like silver coins. "What are you playing in tar for?" he said.

"It's not tar," said Georgie.

"Yeah," said Jarvis. "Not tar."

"Well what is it then?"

"It's valuable," said Georgie. "So just keep away."

Funly put his hands in his khaki pants and walked back and forth for a while deciding how much he wanted to be smart and how much he wanted to have the crap knocked out of him. His tenth birthday was coming up fast and that would leave him only two years away from getting his twenty-two. He'd been picturing that rifle all morning and had already sacked the neighborhood several times in his imagination, taking particular pleasure in lining Mrs. Gorky and Mrs. Loop up against the wall and having Georgie and Jarvis plead with him for the lives of their mothers. Besides, he'd snorfed out several indications that he might get a BB gun on his next birthday just for being ten. He sauntered back over to the valuable substance convention.

"I think it's just going to have to be gold," Georgie was saying. "I can't think of anything else."

"I think it's got to be some kind of solid oil something," said Jarvis. He was a little smarter than Georgie and bigger too, though Georgie was meaner and trickier. "Some kind of valuable oil something."

"That stuff's not worth nothin," said Funly.

Georgie and Jarvis stopped talking for a second and looked up at Funly out the sides of their eyes, then they went back to the discussion like Funly hadn't said a word.

Funly Funster knew he had them on the run. "You guys are dumb. That stuff's not worth shit. They make streets and parking lots out of it. It's the cheapest stuff in the world."

Funly thought he'd been prepared to run but he didn't even get turned around before Jarvis had his arms and Georgie his legs and he was on the ground getting his fat belly beat like bongos, and they didn't stop till he'd oinked out "Oh Susanna" to the rhythm. Funly cried like a baby. "Oink, oink, oink, oink," said Jarvis and Georgie.

"Okay for you," cried Funly when they finally let him up. "I'm sleeping out in my backyard tonight and I came over to invite one of you, but now neither of you are coming because I'm inviting Stinky Jinx." With that Funly rumbled out the driveway and back across the street.

Georgie and Jarvis reconnoitered. Jimbo Funster was at work so they wouldn't have to face him. It'd be Funly's grandma. They went to the back of Georgie's yard and slipped through the fence to the Stuckas' where they chased Stuckas' dog Bosco out of his doghouse in the back of the garage and sat in there, a bit cramped and stinky but a good hiding place. Soon enough they heard Grandma Funster screaming their names in Georgie's driveway, but too, too late. Georgie and Jarvis were hiding on the moon. Mrs. Gorky came out and listened to Grandma Funster recount the pack of lies Funly told her about the brutal attack, but Georgie and Jarvis had whacked up Funly so often that they'd started to gain credibility, half the time adults thought Funly was either lying or stupid or deserved it. The beating wasn't so bad as to make the grudge last till evening, so they wouldn't have to listen to Jimbo Funster stutter at them for an hour either.

The immediate problem out of the way, Georgie Gorky and Jarvis Loop started mumbling to each other about the next. Funly was sleeping out and when the Funsters did anything they always did it with *food*. Sometimes they brought their guns, but they always had *food*. It was the one thing Funly had over them and too many times they'd ended up smacking on each other because Funly came over and invited one of them to eat out or eat over or go to Jimbo Funster's hunting camp or, like tonight, sleep in Funly's backyard, and didn't invite the other. Then they'd have to hate each other for weeks, because if Funly had Georgie sleep over then Georgie had to spend the night talking about the snakes in Jarvis' eyes, and Jarvis had to hate Georgie for being such a creep that he'd sell his friendship and hang out with a piggy like Funly, all for a few pizzas and milk shakes, hamburgers, hot dogs, fried chicken, Pepsi Cola. Pork chop breakfasts.

But Funly blew it this time. This time they were in it together. This time Funly was sleeping out with stupid Stinky Jinx who talked in a high voice and wore his mother's scarves and ran down the street with his wrists flapping. Stinky wanted to grow up to be the Frootie-Pop man and drive up and down the streets ringing a bell. Funly was really stooping low.

Georgie and Jarvis forgot they were in a doghouse. Sweat poured over them and wood crumbled over their heads and dust rose and coated them with truth. Bosco dog whined outside like an Erector Set motor but it did him no good.

"You know that finger-paint set you got for your birthday?" Jarvis said to Georgie. "Good," said Jarvis. "Let's sleep out."

Jarvis and Georgie pitched Jarvis' pup tent with Cowboy Bob painted on the side under the apple tree behind Georgie's garage. Georgie lived right across the street from the Funsters. They didn't have pizza or hamburgers or any of the stuff they knew Funly and Stinky Jinx were having, but they had potato chips, and enough grape Kool-Aid to make them crazy. They had *Mad* magazines and comic books; Fantastic Four, Batman, and Sergeant Rock. They read by flashlight, in the dark, clockless. Apples fell, plop-plop, on the dark ground around them and sometimes hit the tent, boinging them with fear. They didn't know what time it was and they were getting chicken.

"Funly says Jimbo Funster keeps a gun in his bedroom," Jarvis said quietly into his *Mad* mag.

Georgie put down his Batman and picked up a Sergeant Rock, showing Jarvis the cover with the American leading a special troop of international commandos into a German machine-gun nest; a Frenchman, a Briton, an American Indian, a blond-haired southerner, a dago, a Polack, even a spook. Bullets flew all around them but nobody got hit. Sergeant Rock had big white teeth.

"The Germans lost because they couldn't hit anybody," said Jarvis.

Georgie took his small glasses off his small head and turned onto his back. He had black wavy hair and was starting to get his first zits like teenagers. "Funster's never shot anybody," said Georgie.

"Animals," said Jarvis.

Georgie got up and looked out the mosquito netting, but Jarvis could see his hands shaking. "Feels cold out," said Georgie.

Now that Jarvis knew Georgie was scared too he felt better. He put two bottles of finger paint in his pockets and tossed two bottles to Georgie.

It was imperative to be sneaky the whole time. The two of them left the tent and dove for the back of Georgie's garage, then sneaked along the garage wall and dashed to the back of Gorkys' house. Down the driveway on hands and knees. Now they skulked behind the shrubs at the front of the house, the silent, potholed street a sea of streetlight to the Funsters' front yard. No more words. They'd already decided to avoid Funly's house as much as possible, and so the gate at the front of the yard. They'd hit the neighbors' shrubs at the left, then follow them to the barn that was now the Funsters' garage. Then the back gate.

It took forever. They ducked, popped, fell, stumbled, scared each other with their breath. But finally they lay on their bellies at Funly's back gate, panting, peering into the yard for the tent where Funly Funster and Stinky Jinx slept the bliss of premolestation.

"See it?" asked Georgie.

Jarvis pointed past the dirt patch with the rope swing to the clump of walnut and chestnut trees near the sandbox. There sat the green hunting tent, dark and still. He'd never mentioned it to Georgie, but he wondered what would happen if Funly and Stinky woke up during the painting. At least they'd be in the tent. Jimbo Funster wouldn't shoot at the tent. Then, just before opening the back gate, Jarvis remembered another thing, Jimbo's hunting dogs in the barn. He turned to Georgie. "I forgot about the hunting dogs," he whispered.

Georgie thought for a minute, rubbing his chin like his dad,

Gary Gorky. He looked dumb. "Well," said Georgie. "We're next to the barn now."

Jarvis was counting his breaths. The whole idea felt more stupid every second. Maybe tomorrow they could just beat the crap out of the two of them. Why risk their lives?

Georgie went through the gate. He ducked behind the first little walnut tree and Jarvis followed. They squatted there a minute. Jarvis heard the wind in the trees. He didn't think he'd ever heard that sound before and wondered if the wind always rustled leaves. Beyond the back of the yard, over the next block, a crescent moon slept on its back. Jarvis and Georgie crawled on their stomachs to the tent.

Stinky and Funly had the flaps tied down, hooked somehow on the inside. Georgie pulled out his jackknife but Jarvis stopped him. "We can reach in there," he said. "Don't cut anything."

Georgie wrinkled his face. "Shit," said Georgie, right out loud. Something stirred in the tent.

Jarvis and Georgie froze. Inside the tent a flashlight burst, then a voice. "Dad!" Funly yelled. "Dad!" The dogs howled. A floodlight poured from the back upstairs window and Jarvis and Georgie scattered for the nearest trees.

"D-D-Don't leave the tent, Funly!" shouted Jimbo Funster from the window, but from the scream of it Jarvis could tell nobody in the tent was going to do anything but keep screaming. Gazing up at the light he couldn't see anything, but he imagined the blue barrel of Jimbo Funster's shotgun cocked on the window sill.

The dogs kept howling and Funster yelled and stuttered out the window. Finally he managed something. 'D-Don't, d-don't move! I'll sh-sh-shoot!'

That was enough. Jarvis made for the gate. The shot didn't sound threatening at all. It only sounded like a great big firecracker.

Funster couldn't tell how big the thing was he shot but he knew he hit it. Jarvis felt a sharp burst in his leg and fell down, then he didn't feel anything. Then he saw the blood and felt white. Passed out.

Even Funster's mind stuttered when he saw Jarvis Loop in a pool of blood. Red's kid. He'd shot Red's kid. But as soon as Funly Funster found out that Jarvis wasn't dead, just wounded, he felt great. He thought of every whacking and every pink belly he ever took and he was sorry Georgie Gorky hadn't got blasted too. Stinky Jinx looked at Jarvis' white white skin and red red blood and thought a touch of blue would prove quite festive. He kept giggling nervously and pressed his palms together. Georgie Gorky stayed hidden and got clean away.

Franky Gorky

GEORGIE GORKY once had an older brother, Franky Gorky, but one day many Christmases ago that ended. Helen told us the story all the time. Franky Gorky was the nicest kid in the whole universe. Wild animals came up to Franky Gorky and ate out of his hand. Birds waited for him to wake up in the morning before they started singing. Franky Gorky caught houseflies and carefully took them outside instead of hitting them with a flyswatter. He was friendly to other children. He shared his candy and toys. He was respectful to adults. Franky Gorky was the nicest kid in the universe and so he had to die. One Christmas morning when his grandmother arrived, parking across the street because the block was all filled up with Christmas visitors, Franky Gorky ran across the street to greet her, slipped on some ice in the middle of the street, and got wiped out by a drunk driver. That's what happens, Red always said, when people take other people's parking places.

There wasn't a kid on the block who ever really knew Franky Gorky. Even Georgie Gorky didn't remember Franky Gorky because Georgie was still a little tiny kid when Franky bought it. But everybody knew about Franky Gorky because he was the first lesson to every human on 24th Street that no matter how good you are, if you don't look both ways when you cross the street you're going to get rubbed out.

Remember Franky Gorky.

We all sure did.

His parents Greta and Gary Gorky kept his room exactly the way it was that Christmas morning he died. Back when I was friends with Georgie we'd sneak in there, because only on special holidays was anybody supposed to go in there and look at Franky Gorky's picture, he had a face like a horse chestnut, and touch his rosary and smell his pillow. And still, every year on Christmas morning, the Gorkys piled into their car and went off to Franky Gorky's grave and left little Christmas presents for Franky Gorky, that little stinker, as Greta and Gary Gorky had called him, whose taste in toys hadn't changed much in all the years since he died. Then the Gorkys came home and lit a candle in the street in front of their house right on the spot where Franky Gorky got wiped out, and then waited on the curb until a car went by and just like Franky Gorky the candle got wiped out too.

Red & Helen

IT WAS Funster who took Jarvis to the hospital. His wife Betty was hysterical, but his parents just shook their heads like wise old people who'd seen everything. In fact Grandma Funster once ran over her own nephew with a car after a funeral reception, kid almost died, and she totaled his little tricycle, but it got people over the funeral pretty fast. Funster himself was feeling pretty horrible about little Jarvis until he found out the hit was just a flesh wound in the thigh. By the time Funster called Red he was already pretty defensive. What was Jarvis doing in his yard at midnight anyway?

Red felt the same way. If Jarvis wasn't wounded in the hospital Red would have beat the crap out of him. That's what he told Helen.

"Red," said Helen. "That's just crazy."

It was two in the morning and Red had work the next day. He'd have to work all day with hardly any sleep. "He'll be all right," said Red. "He deserved it."

Helen was getting dressed.

"What are you doing?" asked Red.

"Aren't we going to the hospital?"

Red hadn't thought about going to the hospital. Now that he thought of it, it seemed like the right thing to do, but now that he knew it was the right thing and that he hadn't thought of it, he felt resentful and guilty. "He'll be out cold," said Red. "We can see him in the morning."

Helen gave him that horrible pained look that made him feel like a heathen.

"You pamper that kid," said Red. "You pamper him and protect him from everything."

"Well," said Helen. "I didn't do a very good job tonight, did I."

Red went to the closet. Helen thought he was getting his coat, but he didn't get his coat, he got his bowling ball. "I got to think," said Red.

"What do you have to think about? Your son's been shot. He's in the hospital."

Red pumped the bowling ball, slowly, like a dumbbell. He watched the veins in his forearm rise like blue tubes in his skin. His neighbor and good friend just shot his kid. That was something to think about, and he couldn't help it, he felt sorry for Funster.

"What the hell was he doing in Funster's yard?" said Red.

Moments like this Helen felt Red just spent too many years shooting Japs, too much time with other men bent on killing. She knew Red was a roughneck when she met him, that he had a short temper, that he beat people up, but he'd also been kind, sensitive and kind. She thought she could change him. But the war got to him first, just like it got to her brother Jon and made him so crazy he couldn't work, couldn't think, couldn't pass his bars. What did it matter if he commanded ten ships, or a hundred ships? He could take his Legion of Merit and Croix de Guerre and hang them over his hospital bed in the mental ward for all the good they did him.

"Red," said Helen. "What does it matter how it happened. We can deal with that later. Jarvis is in the hospital."

Red didn't say anything.

"I'm getting Neda," said Helen, but when she came back

downstairs with Neda Red hadn't moved, he stood in the middle of the living room with his head down and his eyes closed and the bowling ball raised straight up over his head to the ceiling like the Statue of Liberty.

Helen in the Past Present

RED WAS the mayor of the neighborhood and Karl and Funster the police, not officially, just by some process of spontaneous generation. Big black Mr. Dean Danger lived across the street in the bottom half of the two-porched flat, under the Puerto Ricans. He owned the house. He owned the bar on the corner of 24th and Celebration Avenue, Dean Danger's Grill, the hottest black bar in town, and nobody white ever went in there except for Red or Karl. Red always said you could get anything money could buy down at Dean Danger's, as long as it was illegal, or booze. Dean Danger was the ambassador of the neighborhood and some of us just called him Mr. Ambassador.

Red liked to sit on the front porch of our house and watch the traffic. He did it from the day he moved in and he still did it twenty-five years later, except when he first moved in Helen sat on the porch with him and all the neighbors yakked from porch to porch or went porch visiting, one porch to the other, having a beer and bragging and bitching about each other's kids. That didn't happen anymore. Helen didn't come out because she was afraid of everything, Karl's guns, Funster's guns, Karl's kids, and most everybody who paraded up and down the street between the variety store on German Avenue and Dean Danger's on Celebration. Most people didn't use the sidewalks because they never knew whose dog would be out, except on Sundays till it got dark, when everybody kept their dogs in the yard. On Sunday *every-body* looked like a pimp or a dealer or a whore and we were all too civilized to want our dogs to bite somebody who just came from church, no matter what they did any other time.

But Helen was afraid of them all and Red knew them all by name, kids, pimps, whores, dealers, adults. They said hi and he said hi. Nobody threw litter on his walk and nobody's dog pissed on his lawn. Sisters, white Catholic and black Baptist, came and read him the Bible, it was all the same Bible to him. He gave them beer or Kool-Aid, the beverage of their choice, while Helen huddled up in the bedroom in front of the Infant of Prague.

A few people had thrown trash on Red's lawn and a few dogs pissed on the big maple tree in front of the house or on the St. Joseph lilies in front of the porch when the neighborhood was just changing, just at the very first. But Red swept down from his porch like a tremendous angry wall of anger. He kicked the dogs like lightning and afterwards he was the thunder in dog hearts on 24th Street. They walked the sidewalks until they got to Red's, and when they got there they circled in the street. He swarmed the litterers and gave them a dollar for candy or a drink, then told them if they ever did it again they'd eat the paper they threw and his fist would follow. So he sat on his iron chair in the center of his porch at the front of his house in the center of 24th Street, and I watched him during the years he loved me and the years he wanted to kill me and the years he loved me again and knew what he was thinking; he wanted Helen out there with him.

But Helen wasn't coming out. Red was convinced that Helen had changed since the operation she had after Andrew. I wasn't any trouble for Helen and neither was my sister Neda, but Joseph didn't want to come out for all the life in the world, and when he did, after raising hell in Helen for a day, he came out deaf in one ear, blind in the opposite eye, and he couldn't smell either. Now he's living on government assistance and he's about as handicapped as a hot dog. The doctor told Helen not to have any more kids and that's when I first remember her spending a lot of time at church. She always went every Sunday, but after Joseph she was there every other day and fighting with Red in between about the pill, then about being Catholic and Red being Lutheran, and then Red started cursing the pope and Helen started cursing Red's family and then Red grabbed Helen by the neck and put her against the wall.

I remember the tears in Red's eyes. His face was red and he was crying and Helen choked at him, "Go ahead you goddamn heathen, kill me, you goddamn heathen," and Red just held her and cried and cried. Then he let her go. He took his fist and put it through the basement door or the back door or some other door and Helen told him that was all he was goddamn good for. Red came up to me, his face like a rotten tomato, and said, "I hate that woman, that fuckin woman, and I hope God's Catholic and I get damned to hell." Then he went upstairs. I'd hear him pounding around up there, and then it got quiet. Helen got up from the floor where she fell against the wall and got baby Joseph and me and Neda and made us kneel by the kitchen table with her. We said the rosary for the conversion of Red. "Please God, please make Red a Catholic."

I thought Helen held the numbers then. Red was going straight to hell and good for him.

But when I made my First Communion I sold my soul to God on the bargain that if Red didn't convert I'd go to hell instead. One day, on a drive downtown to buy me shoes, I told him about it. I've never seen Red more philosophical. He stared over the steering wheel and bent his furry white eyebrows at the road. "Well," he said. "Maybe we'll get lucky and the devil will get us both."

I didn't understand.

But Helen started ballooning up with Andrew and things quieted down. Helen spent more and more time on the couch, her face getting puffy and the veins in her legs growing into great purple tubes. Red put them on pillows for her. Sometimes they even kissed.

Late in the pregnancy Helen started having me and Neda in the bathroom with her when she bathed. She'd make us help her undress, then Neda sat on the scale and I sat on the toilet while Helen washed herself, sponging water over her mountainous stomach and huge blue breasts. She'd put our hands over her womb. "See," she said. "It's holy in there. Little Andrew's in there. He's my savior. A holy baby."

"How'd he get in there?"

"That's where babies come from." Her stomach pulsed under our hands. Helen smiled like she did when she prayed. "Everything is going to be different soon," she said.

"Different than Joseph?" I asked.

"Much different," said Helen. "After Andrew, everything will change in some way."

I started to dread being in there, watching Helen bathe with that holy look on her face. I tried to imagine being in there where Andrew was. Was Red ever in there?

Andrew almost killed Helen. The quack who delivered Joseph had packed Helen with wadding because she bled so much after Joseph, then he sewed her up and forgot to take it out. Andrew had to turn around in the womb, kick out the wadding, which catapulted across the operating room and hit a nurse in the chest, then turn around again to get his head out. He came out purple as a grape with a caved-in chest. Still, in Helen's book it was a miracle. She was supposed to die if she had another kid and instead she would have died if she didn't. That's how Andrew became her savior.

After Joseph and Andrew, Red didn't ever want to deal with doctors again. He already had the mechanics and the lawyers and the dentists at the top of his shit list and now the doctors were at the very top. He told everybody in the house not to get sick.

"That's it," said Red. "Nobody's getting sick anymore. Don't break the law, don't get any cavities, and don't get sick. I'm running this house and those are the rules."

"Bismarck," said Helen. "Heil Hitler."

A year later Helen got really sick. She held her stomach a lot and threw up a couple times a day. When me and Neda came home from school Helen was in bed, with Joseph and Andrew playing on the bedroom floor. We helped Helen up, then I watched Joseph and Andrew while Neda helped Helen in the kitchen. She looked bad. Her skin was usually kind of dark, like an Arab or something, and she had deep green eyes and prematurely gray hair like silver. She was pretty. But now she was just gray all over. I brought Joseph and Andrew downstairs and helped Helen set the table, which was unusual behavior for me because usually I took off after school and didn't come around till Red showed up. We sat at the kitchen table waiting for Red with Helen looking like a dead plant.

"I'm going to have to tell Hitler I need a doctor," said Helen. That was the first time I really realized she was afraid of Red.

So we had one of those nobody-eats suppers. Helen didn't eat because she was sick, Red didn't eat because he was mad, and we didn't eat because we were scared.

"Just wait, you'll get better," said Red.

"I won't get better, I'll die," said Helen. She really looked like she would. Neda started to cry.

"Goddammit," said Red. He got up and grabbed his chair. He was in his chair-smashing period. The dining room and kitchen tables and chairs all came from Bush. Every chair was held together by wire and screws and they looked like jigsaw puzzles.

Neda kept crying and told Red that Helen was throwing up all the time.

"Your mother throws up easy," said Red.

"This is different," moaned Helen. "I feel like my insides are coming out."

Red had his big chair in the air now, held in one hand.

"Don't break the chair, Dad," said Neda. "Mom's sick."

Red threw the chair down and it just cracked a little bit. Then Helen got up and went upstairs.

I don't know where Helen got the strength, but she fought with Red right through the night, on her back, over the toilet, she must have really felt sick. Neda cried right along and I sat with the babies playing with my toy soldiers. I was pretty used to the fights, but this one was different. Helen began to cry and she never strayed from the topic. After a while all she said was, "I'm sick, Red," over and over, "I'm sick. I'm sick." Then she stumbled downstairs to the phone and tried to call a taxi, but Red pulled the cord out of the wall. Helen went next door to the Jinxes.

I remember Helen clutching at herself as she walked to the taxi. It was raining and black and the wet yellow cab as bright as a light bulb. Red yelled to her as she got in. "Don't come back! Don't you dare come back!" Then he came in and rubbed out the dining room chairs.

This was the summer before I got shot. Red hadn't hit bowling ball nirvana yet, he still had to get his bowling solace at the alley, blasting pins. It was the summer before the summer without doors. He hadn't settled down yet. Still, the next morning he was up early before work screwing the chairs together, and after work he got Mrs. Jinx to watch Joseph and Andrew and he carted me and Neda off to the hospital where he told Helen, "Don't do it," and Helen said, "I have to do it."

"You won't be a woman anymore," said Red.

And Helen said, "If I don't I won't be a human anymore."

Red's eyes were explosions and Helen looked like a martyr with her gray skin on the white sheets.

"This will cost a fortune," said Red.

Helen looked at me. "He'd rather pay for my funeral."

It sure looked like Helen was right. Red fought with her that visit and the next visit and the morning before the operation and the day after. But the day after that the explosions were gone from his eyes. He came home from work, took one babysitter home, got another, made something horrible for supper from leftovers and noodles for the fourth day in a row, and made everybody shove it down. He piled us into the car and stopped at the first florist and bought twenty-four red roses which he gave to Helen with a hug. "I love you," Red said to Helen.

Helen almost cried. She said "When's the dance?" which she always said to Red after they made up, and I guess right after she had every baby. It went back a long way.

"Come home," said Red.

"Where else would I go?"

"I don't know. I love you. Just come home."

"In a couple days," said Helen. She had color in her cheeks. She kissed me and she kissed Neda.

Red gathered us up and took us to the door. "I'll see you for lunch tomorrow," said Red.

Helen smiled at him. "You still think I'm wrong," she said.

"You're goddamn right I do," said Red.

Helen got visits from her relatives too. Her brother David came up for the afternoon from his farm in Mercer, and her brother Jon with Bush, who he lived with now because he was too nervous since the war to practice law. Jon said, "How are you, little sis," and touched Helen's head, then he went to the foot of the bed and paced back and forth with his hands in his pockets and watched the floor.

"What's the matter with Jon?" Helen asked Bush.

"He's fine," said Jon. "He's just tired all the time. He's tired of being a hero. He's tired of bombs. He's tired of war."

"The war's over," said Helen.

"The war is never over," said Jon. "There's the war of good and evil, right Bush? And the war between the atheists and those who believe in God. Between the Catholics and the Protestants." He looked at Red. "And Communism," he said. "How I cried the day we gave them Eastern Europe. How I cried."

"He's tired," Bush said to Helen.

"Me too," said Jon.

"Me too," said Helen.

Red went over and stood at the foot of Helen's bed in Jon's path. Jon walked into him. "Oh," he said. "Hello Red."

"There's something wrong with you," said Red.

Jon patted Red's shoulder. He was taller and thinner with silver hair like Helen. "We needed everyone, Red. Even men like you," said Jon. "But they were *my* ships. And people tried to blow us up."

"I ought to blow you up," said Red.

Bush took Red by the arm and led him back to Helen. She reached in her purse and pulled out a box of chocolates, gave one each to me and Neda and Red. Helen didn't want any. Then Bush pulled out a bottle of whiskey and poured some into two of Helen's plastic cups and gave Red another piece of chocolate and the two of them had whiskey and chocolate.

"I gave up candy," said Helen. "I made a pact with the Lord."

Bush looked at Helen. Her hair was yellow white and she looked like she was old all her life. "Did he sign?" she asked.

"How could he?" said Helen.

"He never signs," said Bush. "Remember that when you decide to renege."

Helen's oldest brother Uncle Stanley came with his face like a shovel, and his wife Aunt Sylvia with her face like a shovel, and all four of my shovel-faced cousins, just shovels with noses like pickaxes, and they talked about Pope Pius XII opening the letter that the Blessed Virgin gave to the three little girls at Fatima, and how it was going to be opened in 1960 and how it probably said that the Communists were going to take over the world if we all didn't say the rosary every day and stop them in Korea. If we said the rosary every day we'd get a bonus and the Jews would be converted.

"What about the Protestants?" asked Red.

"The Protestants should know better," said Uncle Stanley. He liked to watch the Boston Celtics play basketball. I liked the Syracuse Nats. Basketball was the one sport Red couldn't play well.

Aunt Frances came in from Detroit and picked up Edju in Cleveland where he was a rich engineer. Frances had black hair. She and Helen looked like the ugly and pretty sides of the same face. Edju had one of those shovel faces like Uncle Stanley except he had big ears and just a little bit of hair on the tip of his forehead. He patted everybody on the head, even Red.

"Oh Helen," he said to Helen. "Oh Helen, Helen, Helen." After that he never stopped talking and I never understood a word he said, except the more he talked the madder Bush got. Finally she called him a good-for-nothing.

"I busted my dupa to get you over here," said Bush. "Now you're rich and what do I have? Pffft."

"Oh Esther," said Edju. "Esther, Esther, Esther."

Red's family came around too, but they just brought flowers and kept their mouths shut.

Helen came back from the hospital a new being. She went out and bought herself a brand-new eighteen-inch Infant of Prague and all the bright new clothes he needed for every month, every special week, every holy day of the year. He had white slips and pink slips and lavender slips, red robes and green robes and purple robes and white robes, multicolored capes, fancy booties for his little feet that were crushing that snake Satan. He had silver crowns and gold crowns, little silk mittens for his hands that had to hold the tiny globes of the world with crosses on them. He even had a black-purple satin blanket to hide under during Lent. He had candles galore.

Helen put the Infant high atop the big tall dish cabinet arabesque that used to scare the hell out of me when I was little because I thought the front looked like a big ugly face and always had dreams of it coming alive and chasing me around the room. The Infant stood up there above everything.

Then Helen renewed her campaign for the conversion of Red. Priests started coming over every other day for dinner. Red talked to them about golf. But afterwards Helen had the priests lead the family in the rosary. We knelt there praying our asses off, saving Red and converting Jews and saving the world from Communism all at the same time. Then Helen went to work at the sewing machine and one day after school when I came home I found Andrew toddling around a spitting image of the Infant of Prague and Joseph all dressed up like the Blessed Virgin Mary. Helen got the statue and had Andrew and Joseph march in front of her and they stopped and said prayers in front of every holy picture in the house, a march that got to be lengthier and lengthier since Helen was also into a period of sacred object proliferation.

Of course she always cleaned up before Red came home, but Red was no dummy. He knew something fishy was up. He called a house meeting and cut off half of Helen's funding. He quarantined all the holy objects bought after the Infant of Prague to the dining room and after that we always ate in the kitchen because there wasn't any room for anything but holiness in the dining room once all the blessed junk got in there. He started carrying his bowling ball around.

Now this was before Karl moved next door, and before Mr. Ambassador, Dean Danger, opened his bar. An old tottery couple named Spinks lived where Karl Marksman lives now and they liked to spend their time mowing the lawn and pruning roses. We had the Spinkses on one side and the Jinxes on the other. Back then Helen wasn't afraid of anything, except sometimes for Red.

The Year of
Two Hundred Books

HELEN KEPT buying things for her holy room. She bought pictures of the holy family, blond and red-cheeked with gold halos over their heads. Little Jesus had curly hair and stood on a table with wood shavings on it. Joseph held his legs. Mary knelt. Helen bought silver plaques of the Blessed Virgin and the Sacred Heart of Jesus all burning red with blood and fire with a gold crown of thorns wrapped around. Mary had a red heart too, but it wasn't burning. There were babies with angel wings too small to fly them anywhere. Helen said they weren't angels, they were babies. It was symbolic of babies, after they'd been baptized Catholic of course. When I looked at those pictures I always felt sorry for the babies in limbo who got treated just like good pagans. Helen bought a statue of Mary as Our Lady of the Immaculate Conception. She was all white and stood on top of the world crushing a big snake that bit her foot. Then Helen got holy water from Lourdes, and finally a crutch from the wall there that some cripple left after he got cured.

The crutch did it for Red. He cut off the rest of Helen's funds then started doing the grocery shopping and even the clothes shopping for the kids because he didn't trust what Helen would do if he let her have the money. He figured there was three thousand dollars invested in the dining room, enough for a new car, in fact he kept saying "enough for a new car, enough for a new car," so much he convinced himself he should get one and came home one day with a brand-new metallic-blue Studebaker Rainbow with black-and-white-striped seats and a big blue steering wheel. Helen hated that car. She rolled her head and thought of all the pagan babies we could have bought and saved with that money. That's how the money wars started.

Meanwhile Helen started calling Andrew her savior.

And Neda started to change.

I had to beat the crap out of Funly Funster and Stinky Jinx every day just to keep my sanity, though at the time it was pure impulse.

Red didn't like little Andrew dressed up like the Infant of Prague and he sure didn't like Joseph dressed up like the Blessed Virgin Mary. He hated me because I didn't play sports and I didn't join the Cub Scouts and I beat on all his friends' kids and was starting to hang out with Stubie Stucka who was a known juvenile delinquent, but at least I didn't wear any silly clothes. Red saw what was happening to Stinky. Big Dick Jinx never said anything so Red never said anything, but I saw Red quiver the evening he was out back watering the lawn and old Mrs. Spinks told him how cute she thought it all was with Helen and Joseph and Andrew marching around the backyard all dressed up and sprinkling holy water on the fruit trees. Mrs. Spinks was all Catholic and almost dead so she really got a kick out of that kind of stuff.

Red was supposed to pick pears that evening and usually when he picked pears he put his ladder to the top of the tree and dragged up armfuls of baskets and when they all got full he started throwing pears down to me. He made me wear a mitt and a football helmet and pads but none of them did me any good that night. He dented my helmet. He knocked my left arm off. He put a hole in my chest. I went in the house and got my big silver wooden Prince Valiant shield with the red horse head in the center and just sat there under it, warding off pear bombs like thunder. They came pt, pt, through the leaves then BOOM. Every once in a while I stuck the mitt out and Red knocked it right off. Boy, he had an eye.

"Can't you catch?" he yelled at me.

"No," I said.

Red came down with the pears and made me run around and pick up all the ones left scattered on the ground. He watched me the whole time and when I got done putting all the stray pears in the bushel basket he said, "Wait a minute, stand there, don't move."

I picked up the shield, but he didn't have anything in his hands. Red wasn't much for clobbering a dead target anyway. I guess he thought I looked pretty interesting in my shoulder pads, New York Giants helmet, Prince Valiant shield, and baseball mitt. "Don't move," he said. "I'll be right back."

Red went into the back shed and came out with his cleats, handball gloves, a softball bat, and his bowling ball. He put the softball bat straight in the air and held that bowling ball at arm's length right out in front of him. Then he made me march in front of him and we went all about the yard singing the "Notre Dame Fight Song." Red tapped all the fruit trees with the ball bat, nice and gentle. He was getting in a pretty good mood.

"What other songs do you know?" asked Red. His face was happy and redder than his hair.

All I knew was "Roll Ramblers Roll," the fight song of the local Catholic prep, but Red didn't want to sing that, he was through with Catholic fight songs for the day.

"How about 'Anchors Aweigh'," said Red. "Your uncle Jon would like that."

The only part I knew of that was "Sink the Army! Sink the Army!" but that was okay with Red. We sang "Anchors Aweigh" all the way over to Funsters'.

"W-Why d-d-don't you sing the M-Marine song?" said Funster. Funly stood in back of him looking pretty skeptical, but Georgie Gorky came over from across the street with a hockey stick and a beach ball so Funly got a fishing pole and an old shot put. Stubie Stucka brought a pool stick and put a rusty basketball rim over his head and we marched down the sidewalk singing:

> From the Halls of Montezuma
> To the shores of Tripoli
> We will fight our country's battles
> On the land and air and sea.

Red said we had to say "air" now because the Marines had airplanes in Korea. All the old people came out on their porches and we stopped off while they told Red what a good man he was and Red had to admit it, it was true. "Now isn't this just nice?" said Red. "Isn't this a nice time?"

Everybody agreed. Then we marched over to Stinky Jinx's house where Stinky was on the porch with his Dad, Big Dick, and looking a little glum, probably because he didn't have any sports equipment. But Big Dick found an old pair of boxing gloves and Stinky didn't look much more ridiculous than anybody else with his boxing gloves and his mother's scarf, besides, when we got done marching on our side of the block Big Dick went into his Buckhorn Potato Chip truck and brought out a big gold can of potato chips and a case of cherry pop from his basement. We were really having a good time there on Stinky's porch.

Just then Stubie Stucka got into a little scuffle with Funly Funster over a handful of chips, because Stubie was the biggest and Funly was the fattest, and Stubie let Funly have it right in the stomach. Funly lost all his pop and chips, both the ones he'd eaten and the ones he hadn't. Funly rolled onto the floor and gagged. He always got overdramatic when somebody beat him up, not like Stinky who just cried and ran home. Stubie got up to kick Funly in the ribs when Red grabbed him by the neck. Once he got him turned around he let him go.

Stubie was a tough kid. He had short blond hair and both his parents were drunks. He carried a knife on his belt and liked to vandalize graveyards and churches and wreck tree houses. His older brother was in Korea and both his sisters were pregnant but living at home. He was tall for his age too. "Keep your hands off me," he said to Red.

"Then keep your hands to yourself," said Red. That was one of Red's favorite lines before he belted somebody, but I'd never seen him hit anybody other than me who wasn't grown up.

Stubie went for his knife but Red grabbed his wrist and took the knife away. "You stole my knife," said Stubie.

"You can have it when you leave," said Red.

Everybody was pretty quiet, even Funly, until Stubie said he'd placekick Funly's stomach into the next yard if Red didn't give him back his knife. Funly started gagging again.

"Stubie," said Red. "If you touch Funly I'll flatten you."

"You can't beat up a kid," said Stubie. "I'll sue you."

"Stubie," said Red. "Keep your hands to yourself."

"Okay," said Stubie, and he turned around and buried his foot in Funly. Funly howled and Red brought his knuckles down on top of Stubie's head. Stubie kind of teetered a little bit like the last bowling pin. When he tottered around enough to face Red his eyes looked like they were hiding a lot of nothing. Red put his fist up to Stubie's face. When Stubie finally got aware enough to focus on it Red popped him in the nose. Stubie Stucka was out.

"Jesus," said Big Dick Jinx.

"If you can't win the little ones, you won't win the big ones," said Red.

Funly was already feeling good enough to eat and grunting like a tickled piggy, but the rest of us figured we were in worse shape than ever. Georgie Gorky was already checking his pockets for something to give to Stubie when he walked him home. But when Stubie came to he seemed like a happy kid. He had pop and chips and even played a game with Red where Red hid his hands behind his back and put a quarter in one and nothing in the other. When he put his fists out Stubie had to guess which one had the quarter and if he guessed wrong Red slapped him on the head. Red slapped the shit out of Stubie and Stubie only won fifty cents. I played, but quit after two slaps. When Stubie left he told Red he was going to get him back some day, but when he saw Red after that all he wanted to do was play that quarter game.

Things broke up and Red and me went back to the house. We put our equipment back in the shed and went inside. Helen sat on the couch in the living room watching the old Zenith with Joseph and Andrew and Neda, who sat in the corner of the couch eating a Mars Bar. That's the first time I noticed Neda was getting fat.

"You *must* be out of your *mind!*" said Helen. She raised her arms over her head.

Red grinned like a snake and sat down next to the Zenith, his favorite spot. He never watched TV, he only watched people watching TV. "What," said Red.

"Parading around."

Neda was melting chocolate in her palm and spreading it on her face.

"Stop that," said Red.

"Everyone in this house is crazy," said Neda, which would have been wrong if Neda hadn't been spreading chocolate on her face.

"We just had a little fun," Red said to Helen. "Everyone else has been parading around. Why can't I parade around?"

"Don't make fun of the Lord," said Helen. "He'll curse you."

"I'll curse Him," said Red.

Helen put her hands over Joseph's and Andrew's ears and brought their heads to her breasts.

"That operation made you crazy," said Red. He sat up in the chair. Their voices were getting louder and it was getting harder to hear Lawrence Welk on the TV. Neda had her face and arms covered with chocolate and was working on her legs.

"Where'd she get all that candy?" I asked. "How come I never get any candy?"

"Because you're creepy," said Neda. "You can't do anything. You can't play anything. And you're stupid like Red."

Red jumped up and ran over to Neda on the couch. "Who said you could call me Red?".

"Don't touch her!" Helen screamed at Red. "Don't you dare touch her."

Neda stuck out her tongue at Helen, then Red. "Poop," she said.

Red slapped her and Neda ran upstairs to the bedroom howling.

Red went over to Helen who was well shielded by Joseph and Andrew. "Who said I was stupid?" he said.

Helen said nothing.

"Who said I was stupid?"

But Helen wasn't talking.

"I don't have big degrees like your brothers. I don't have big jobs. I'm just a big damn brute who works in a forge. Is that what you're telling your kids, Helen?"

Helen pulled the boys onto her lap. "I don't have to," she said.

Red got quieter and redder than I'd seen him in a long time. He didn't say a goddamn thing. He just went and sat down. He sat through Lawrence Welk and he sat through Ed Sullivan and when I went to bed he was still sitting as quiet and red as a stalled firetruck.

Next Saturday morning Red dragged me out of bed and threw me in the Studebaker Rainbow and drove downtown to the public library. "I want books," he told the librarian.

"What kind of books?"

Red hadn't thought about what kind and I could see by the way his jaw tightened that he was starting to feel stupid.

"You want stories?" the woman said. "Novels?"

That's what Red wanted.

Red started out with mysteries but he lost interest in them pretty quick. He moved on to historical novels but that didn't last long either. In a few weeks he was reading stuff like *The Catcher in the Rye* and *War & Peace,* and not too long later *A Passage to India* and *Madame Bovary.* Every week Red carted me off to the library, though

Neda came too because all she did was read and eat donuts and cookies and say nasty stuff anymore, and I'd wander off to the juvenile section and come back with a book about airplanes or planets or horses, something I could look at the pictures in because I never read them, and Red brought home a stack of literature like *The Sound and the Fury* or *Crime and Punishment* or *Women in Love*, and plopped down next to the Zenith and read while we watched the tube.

Red read. Red read and read and read. We watched "Leave It to Beaver" and Red read *The Idiot*.

And Red kept a notebook. Every time he finished a book he closed it and looked into the air for a minute or two, then got up and went over to the secretary near the front door. He opened the lid and pulled up a chair and crouched over a notebook. I saw it just once because he didn't like anybody watching him. If you came in the room he'd huddle over his notebook and tell you to go watch TV. He had the title and author of every book and underneath he wrote pages about what happened and what he thought about it. Red was sure acting strange.

And Neda was acting strange. I thought she'd get so fat her arms and legs would disappear. Her parts were becoming indistinguishable. She looked like a walking ham. If something didn't try to eat her she tried to eat it. She walked around saying stuff like "shit," "fuck," and "bleah." I even went to Helen about it. Offered to help with the dishes just to get an audience.

"Notice anything strange about Neda recently?" I said to Helen.

"Don't say anything nasty about Neda," said Helen.

"Neda's going to bust open," I said. "Can't that happen?"

"No," said Helen.

"Knockwursts bust open."

"Only if they're cooked too long."

I could see this was going to be a battle of wits.

"There's never any candy or cookies in the cupboard," I said. Helen started handing me pots. "Neda steals them all the day you buy them and what she doesn't eat she hides. She stole my pocketknife and tried to trade it in on donuts."

"She reads a lot," said Helen.

"So does Red."

"I'm not so sure *he* understands it," said Helen. We were on silverware now.

"He keeps a notebook."

"I know."

"You think Neda's like you because she's so smart." And she was. She was the smartass of her grade. My teacher kept calling Helen about me because I did good on some intelligence test but ended up in all the stupid learning groups. "Red hates me and you like Neda."

Helen put her hands in my hair. "I love you," she said. "I love all my children." She kissed me on the forehead. "Want to say the rosary with me in front of the Infant?"

"No."

But sometimes I said the rosary with her even though I hated her and me when we did. But I'd see her there all hunched over and alone in front of that statue, mumbling the rosary, and it made my heart hurt, so I'd kneel down with her and she'd put her arm around me, my face against her breast and her dress smelling warm and calm and maddening, like her underwear and dirty clothes behind the bathroom door, and I'd forget that Red read too much and Neda ate too much and Helen prayed too much, and who really gave a shit about any of it anyway as long as they left me alone.

Still, that was the quietest year for a long time to come. When Red didn't read he lugged his bowling ball around. He stopped playing softball and handball, though he still pitched horseshoes and he bowled almost every other night. On Friday nights he bought cartons of Pepsi Cola and bags of Buckhorn potato chips and let us all stay up and watch "Cimarron City" until eleven o'clock. Red didn't drink Pepsi and he didn't watch "Cimarron City." He sat next to the TV and read *Look Homeward, Angel*. Before Christmas he stopped working at the forge and got a job selling porcelain enamel at Eriez Enamel through a contact he made during a bowling tournament in Cleveland.

Red bought himself a suit and wore a white shirt and tie to work every morning. He carried a briefcase instead of a lunch pail. He gave me fifty cents every Sunday to shine his shoes. He kept reading. Neda kept eating. Helen kept praying. Next door, the Spinkses died. One for Christmas and one for Easter. Across the street Mrs. Flossie bit it too, and her flat went up for sale and everybody that came looking was black. Mrs. Wheedle still took care of her retarded daughter, but she had to go in the hospital for a while and when she came out she couldn't use the toilet anymore and carried all her waste around in a little sack under her dress. Helen went over there once a week with the Infant stuffed into her big brown picnic basket that she usually filled with candy for Red on Easter. She put a votive candle in there too, along with the Infant, and a bottle of Mogen David Wine. She always came back feeling really happy and then she'd get sick. Red was right, Helen puked easy, and that didn't change after the operation.

Now Funster was keeping his telescope on one tripod and his rifle on another. Since shooting me he'd put an infrared periscope on his rifle so he didn't shoot anything he didn't want to. He had sandbags about two-and-a-half-feet high on the roof of his front porch and began digging a ditch in his backyard for a bomb shelter. Me and Stubie Stucka dug a ditch in Stubie's backyard too, but his old man came in drunk one night and fell in, so it was back to burning shacks and wrecking churches for Stubie, except for when he came around and got smacked up a dozen times for a quarter from Red.

A white family looked at the Spinkses' house.

Edju came to visit.

Edju had a hairline like a spear. He had chubby hands and a chubby belly and a skinny nose like a pickax, just like Uncle Stanley and Aunt Sylvia and all their kids. He spoke Polish, Russian, German, French, and English, but no one ever understood a fucking thing he said. Everything came out ooo-ooo, you, ooo, very, so-so. He had a World accent. His English wife translated and she sounded like the queen. She hated being called Aunt Elizabeth so we called her Aunt Elizabeth. We called Edju, Edju because he wanted to be called Uncle Ed.

Edju always wore a hat, big brim dipping over his right eye.

"Oooo, so very ooo-ooo," said Edju when he came in the door.

"So good to see you," said Aunt Elizabeth.

Edju and Red shook hands. Edju kissed Helen, though Helen was always careful around Edju because Edju never repaid Bush for bringing him to the States and now he was rich.

"So, so, so," Edju said to me. He moved on to Neda. "Oooo Neda so very you so very you."

"Such a beautiful little girl," said Aunt Elizabeth.

"I'm fat and disgusting," said Neda.

"She reads a lot," said Helen. "All the time."

"So does Red," said Neda.

"Oooo, Red, so very, very," said Edju.

"There's plenty of time to exercise," said Aunt Elizabeth.

"Bleah," said Neda.

"Ooo, Jarvis, you so, so very very big, hmmm, big boy, hmm so," said Edju. He rubbed his chin and tilted his head.

So we all packed into the Rainbow, Red and Helen and Aunt Elizabeth in the front and Edju in the back with the four kids and we went to the zoo and counted the flies on the lions' faces and stared at empty bear cages and sleeping raccoons. There was supposed to be a chimp but it just died when somebody threw him a tennis ball and he ate it. They had a lot of animals that had just died. Neda tried to feed the deers dirt. I stuck my finger through the fence and got bit.

Then we went to the public dock and watched boats. Edju bought everybody ice cream sandwiches, the kind that they put a real slab of ice cream, strawberry, vanilla, chocolate, or neapolitan, between two wafers. Edju got neapolitan. Neda put her ice cream in her nose. Helen got gas and farted all the way home.

When we got back Elizabeth went into the kitchen with Helen

and Red, but Edju pulled a wooden fold-up chess set out of his travel bag and tried to teach me chess which was a disaster. Every time I made a move Edju put my piece back and spoke to me in Worldese. Then I'd move it again and he'd put it back, which went on for a long time until Stinky Jinx came over.

Lately I'd been teaching Stinky to play football in the backyard. It was too narrow to do anything but slam straight into each other back there and I had a great time blasting Stinky to bits, his mother's scarf waving, his borrowed helmet launched, his body spread like an X. But it turned out Stinky knew how to play chess. That was the first time it hit me that Stinky was a human being. He and Edju sat there ooping and booping like a circus organ every time one of them made a move. Apparently Worldese came to Stinky instinctively. Big Dick had made Stinky get a crew cut, which went real bad with the scarf, but Stinky could sure play chess and match ooo-ooo very so-so's with Edju. Stinky got beat and told Edju he had a delightful time.

"I never have a delightful time playing football," said Stinky.

After that Edju went into the kitchen with the adults and things got real quiet, so something big was coming down. Then Edju and Aunt Elizabeth got ready to leave. Neda called Edju Uncle Ed as he went out the door and he stopped and gave her five bucks.

It got to be August again and again the pears were getting ripe and one day Red came home from work and opened the drawer he kept his journal in and took it into the holy room where Helen was praying. He put it down next to her. "You think I'm stupid," he said to Helen. "Read that."

Helen got up from in front of the Infant and ran her index finger over the notebook. "Joseph and Andrew are old enough for a babysitter," she said. "I'm going to look for work."

Red didn't say anything, but Helen didn't find a job and I've never seen Red pick up another goddamn book. Just before Thanksgiving Red got laid off from work and then nobody had nothin.

Going Down-down

RED DIDN'T take getting laid off bad at first. At first he took it pretty good. He thought he'd take himself a little vacation. Collect unemployment. Play golf. His taxes were paying for Eisenhower to play golf, now they could pay for Red to play golf. On his off days he bowled, except for Fridays when he had to go downtown to stand in line for his unemployment check, then he came back bitching about standing in line and determined to find work.

But there wasn't any work.

Red had done pretty good selling porcelain enamel. When he took us for Sunday rides he could point out a building or gas station every mile where he'd sold the shiny enamel front. "See that," Red said. "I sold that. Guy wanted to put neon up there. I said to him, 'How long you think neon's going to last? Porcelain is cheap. It's shiny, easy to clean. You don't got to pay a fortune to keep it lit.' Now he's happy. Look how nice that looks. Don't that look nice?"

It sure did. I loved to look at those gas stations, square and white and shining like new refrigerators. Red got made sales manager. Then his boss died. Red didn't get along with the boss's son.

"It's all stinking politics," said Red. "I'm the best goddamn salesman they ever had."

But even I noticed that the new gas stations weren't using porcelain enamel anymore, and after a few months Eriez Enamel folded. So Red was never going back.

He went back to the Erie Forge where he got his first job, but the forge was laying off, not hiring. Soon Red wasn't golfing or bowling on Wednesdays either because that was the day he had to go down to the Welfare Office for his food dole. Then his unemployment ran out and he didn't golf or bowl at all. He walked around with his bowling ball or sat next to the TV where he couldn't see the screen or sat on the porch. He walked around the house looking for dust. He bitched at Helen, he bitched at me, he bitched at Neda the fat genius who had begun a career of crime in order to maintain her candy fix, he even bitched at Joseph and Andrew who were too young to know a damn thing.

"Why don't you steal something halfway decent," Red told Neda.

"Go to hell," said Neda. "Get a job."

Neda wasn't getting any fatter, she was working off too many calories perusing the stores. But she got nastier every day. And Red never touched her. She could tell him to stick his head up his ass and he'd never do a goddamn thing. But if Neda said something nasty to Helen, even the slightest bit, then Red lit into her. It didn't take Neda long to learn that either, being a genius. She'd come rolling out of her room a couple hours after her last candy bar and ready for a good beating. That's when she went right for Helen. Neda was a smart girl but she was nuts.

The worst of the bad days were the ones when Red came home with his public assistance dole. Red came in, his arms full of boxes and bags, his face flushed, and put everything down on the kitchen table. We all watched while Helen unloaded the food, package by package; big cellophane bags of rice and white bags of flour, lard and margarine wrapped in pale yellow paper that Helen had to open to see what was what, round cans of coffee and cylinders of spam, silver cans of fatty chunked beef that looked like dog food, boxes of powdered milk, loaves of two-day-old bread that Red got ten for a dollar, tins of thick sweet peaches or watery beans, oblong slabs of neon orange cheese. It was good to see that food every two weeks because we always ran out of it two or three days before the next batch was due.

But it didn't make Red happy. After it all got put away he brooded at the table, his hands in front of him like mallets. He'd been happy to get the food. Anybody could see that. But after it got put away there wasn't anything for him to do but think about how he didn't have work and how the food would run out too soon and how humiliating it was for him to stand all morning in line, him, Red, who could do anything he set out to do, but couldn't get a job.

A few insurance companies approached him about sales, but Red hated insurance and insurance salesmen ever since a storm blew over the cherry tree in the backyard and the insurance company refused to pay damages because they said it was an act of God. That was before Helen was in such close touch with the heavenly emissaries, so there was no way to check up. The insurance salesmen were right up there with the doctors, lawyers, dentists, and mechanics. Red would rather starve.

So every public assistance day we got something and we lost something, because Red just sat at the table waiting for somebody to speak or move and no matter what anybody did it was going to be wrong. Red could connect a burp from Neda to every slovenly thing he'd ever witnessed in the house and every transgression ever committed by Helen's relatives and ancestors. In those moments the world was unified in one big festering welt of badness. Helen learned to position herself between Red and the dining room, which cut him off from the rest of the house and usually saved most the doors and the dining room chairs. But while we were on welfare Red punched out the refrigerator twice, the oven once, took out the plumbing which was due for a fixing anyway, and went in the backyard with an axe handle and took it to the prune tree. We lost the prune tree during the recession but it lasted longer than any of the machines.

Joseph was the first to canonize Wednesday by saying Red went down-down instead of downtown, so every two weeks we had Down-down Day.

Willie Experiments
wif Deaf

I WAS feeling pretty depressed that Down-down Day's Eve. I went over to Stinky Jinx's but he was playing dolls with his little sister. Funly Funster was making bullets with his dad Jimbo, and Georgie Gorky had gone off to burn shacks with Stubie Stucka. That Georgie Gorky–Stubie Stucka alliance was boding ill. I thought about getting myself a gun or a knife. Maybe Neda could steal my knife back for me.

I wandered past Stubie's to the old mansion on the corner where the three old maids lived. They had an old brick house surrounded by a small field that they never cut down, and lots of trees too, peach trees, cherry trees, apple trees, horse chestnut trees. It was a good place to play, especially since they didn't want anybody in there. Me and Georgie and Stubie had a good time stealing fruit and building shacks and yelling back at the old maids when we got caught, and once Stubie even led an expedition inside the house when they were all away. We didn't really have anything specific in mind and we didn't get too far either because an old man chased us out of there with a BB gun. Got Georgie right in the buns, which served him right after getting away free that night in Funly's yard when I got shot. Stubie sterilized his switchblade with a match and took the BBs out of Georgie's ass, then put iodine on the bleeding holes. Georgie cried and then Stubie punched him out for being a baby.

None of the old maids were on the front porch so I took the farthest path from the house down to the orchard. I must have been about sixty feet from the fruit trees when I noticed something hanging from a tree. When we were younger sometimes Stubie put sacks of treasure in the trees, which was a secret way we kept the midget-spirits away from our stuff when we pretended the field was the dark side of the moon. That's when we were getting along with the ice giants who lived there too, but not with the fire giants who lived on the other side. But the closer I got to the orchard the more it looked like somebody human was hanging from the rope.

So I got cautious. I sat down in the high grass and watched for a while, but nothing happened. I didn't know if that made me feel better or worse. The wind came through the trees and the thing swayed a little bit. I remembered the last time I noticed the wind I got shot in the leg. Still, maybe I was seeing things. When I was little I saw all kinds of things when I went to bed; faces floating in the air, clothes hanging from hooks or doorknobs looked like people all the time. So I stood up. Nothing happened. I walked forward a little bit. It sure did look like a body, one not too much bigger than mine, and black. I looked behind me and across the street. I could see the sandbags piled on Jimbo Funster's porch roof and his tripod telescope that he kept track of the black people on the block with. Funly and Jimbo were leaving the next day to spend a week at the Funsters' hunting cabin.

I tried to be optimistic. I'd never seen a dead person outside a funeral parlor.

So I walked into the orchard. It was a black kid all right. He had on a green flannel shirt, khakis, and two different colored hightop sneakers with an orange shoelace in the black one and a black shoelace in the white. Up close now the face looked blue. Then he opened his eyes.

"Who said you could watch me," he said.

"What?"

"I been watchin you watchin me and I want to know who said you could watch me." He said it real slow like he wasn't in any hurry to get it out at all.

"Who said you could watch me?" I said.

"That is a good question," he said. He licked his lips. "I guess I was here first."

We didn't say anything to each other for a while. He closed his eyes, opened them, then licked his lips again.

"What are you doing up there?" I finally said.

"I am makin a dollar a minute."

"A dollar a minute. How are you making a dollar a minute?"

He blinked again. "I am not," he said. "That was a joke. I am experimentin wif deaf." He raised his arms slowly and grabbed the rope, then pulled himself onto the limb. He pulled the noose over his head. "I do not get paid nofin, but if you ask me, I will tell you it is important work."

"You seem to hear okay to me," I said.

"My name is Willie."

"How can you hang yourself and not be dead?"

"I can fall from this tree and land on my head. Deaf is not interested in me. I am interested in deaf, though my mother has told me that deaf has no personality, it is just blackness."

"You talking about dying?"

"Not exactly," said Willie. "I would say I have been dying several times, myself, but that was not deaf. You, yourself, do not fink about deaf, I can see."

"I almost died once."

"Maybe before you were born you knew somefin."

"I almost died last summer. I got shot in the leg." I pulled down my pants and showed him the scar where Funster plugged me, which was still pretty big and red. I saw his eye whites then, and he dropped to the ground, whop, like a sack. He showed me his wound in the same place. It was a lot bigger. His whole thigh was covered with purple-white wrinkled skin. He said he'd been thinking about deaf while meditating on a shotgun shell with a match. He'd just finished up and brought the shell down from his forehead when it went off and shot up his leg. His left hand was scarred the same way and he was missing two fingers.

"That is why I look a little clumsy sometimes," he said. "Because I used to be left-handed."

I tried to tell him about Funster again.

"You only fought you were dyin because you were scared," said Willie. "You can't be scared if you want to learn anyfing. You haf to be cold and analytic like the scientists in movies." He grinned at me and nodded toward Funster's. "Maybe I should go over there. Though I no longer want to be shot in the limbs. There is no deaf in the limbs, or maybe they have their own deaf. I have been finkin about blood and many of the organs. Also maybe the brain."

"I don't know," I said. "The nuns tell me the body dies without the soul. No soul, no life."

"The soul is a blackness like deaf," said Willie. "I been finkin there has to be deaf in you already. No deaf, no soul."

"I don't know," I said.

"Well how come you belief the nuns?"

I didn't say anything.

"Maybe you should be finkin instead of beliefin."

"Well how do you know about this blackness?"

"I do not. That is why I am experimentin."

Well there I was facing Down-down Day and there was Willie thinking about deaf. It seemed everybody I knew was smarter than me and nuts too. "Do you do any thinking about anything else, other than deaf?" I asked him.

"Yes," said Willie. "Some. But deaf is my specialty."

So I figured maybe he'd know what I should do on Down-down Days. He listened with his crippled hand on his chin.

"I cannot be specific," Willie said when I was done, "because I have not personally examined the situation. But for me there is deaf. After that there are only two fings, experiments and tools. You haf to decide, what is the experiment and what is the tool."

I grunted.

"One has to be finkin all the time because one is human," said Willie. "But we can fink what we want. Myself, I am finkin a lot about deaf."

Willie walked me home, but for the life of me I couldn't figure out what was the experiment and what were the tools involved in Down-down Day. So the next day I sat in the kitchen after all the food had been put away, waiting for Helen to step into the line of fire and thinking and thinking just like a human when the doorbell rang. Red got up from the table and went to the door. Then he called for me. There stood Willie at the door, looking kind of pale.

"You know this kid?" Red said to me.

"Yeah," I said.

"May I use your telephone?" said Willie.

"Why?" said Red.

"Because," said Willie, and he took his crippled hand away from his belly and let the blood flow through his shirt. "It seems I haf been stabbed in the stomach."

Holy Willie

 "WHO DID this?" asked Red.

Willie sat up straight in his chair in Helen's holy room with the pictures of curly-haired Jesus, angel babies, plaques of the Sacred Burning Heart of Jesus, statues of the Blessed Virgin crushing that snake Satan with her feet, the crutch from Lourdes, and a million other things, all watched over by the Infant of Prague dressed in his cute silk robes atop the dish cabinet arabesque in front of which Helen said the rosary every day for the conversion of Red, the Jews, and the Communists. Willie breathed through his nose so slightly you couldn't see his chest move, rotating his head like a human lighthouse.

"Fis is an interesting place," Willie said.

Helen smiled slightly. Neda was looking at Willie with narrow eyes, like he was a future candy bar.

"Call the police," said Red.

"I would prefer if you would call my mother," said Willie.

"Maybe we should call an ambulance," said Helen.

"I would not prefer an ambulance," said Willie.

"You have to go to the hospital," said Helen. "You could die."

Willie's eyebrows twitched when she said that.

"Is this an experiment with deaf?" I asked Willie.

"Not at first," said Willie. "But it would appear to have become so." He looked directly at me. "What kind of experiment is in fis room?"

"It's a communications experiment," I told him.

Willie rubbed his chin with his crippled hand. "Fis is an interestin room."

Red had his hands on his hips now. He walked up to Willie. "You are bleeding all over my house. I want some information."

"Later Red," said Helen. She told Neda to watch Joseph and Andrew. "Get the car, Red. We'll take him to the hospital."

Red put newspaper in the back seat of the Studebaker Rainbow. "Goddamn kid'll bleed all over my car," he said.

"Myself," said Willie, "I prefer being on the newspaper rather than in the newspaper."

"That's very funny Willie," said Helen from the front seat. I'd introduced everybody on the way to the car.

"Lately," said Willie, "I haf been finkin that pain and humor are very close." Helen had given him a big towel that he clutched to his stomach.

"Willie does a lot of thinking," I said.

Helen looked back and smiled. I could see she was worried.

"Seems to me he should do some dodging," said Red.

"I have been finkin that very same fing," said Willie. "But at the moment I was preoccupied wif the larger questions."

"What bigger question is there than saving your own goddamn life?" said Red.

"That was exactly the question I was finkin about."

That was enough to cool Red for a while, and eventually Willie told us that he got jumped by Tony Blanion, a West Side hood who was a friend of Stubie Stucka's when he wasn't his bitter enemy. Red knew Blanion and thought he was a punk.

"We should call the police," said Helen.

"The police will not do nofin," said Willie. "When I get better I will haf to go and hit him on the head wif a hammer."

"That's not the way to solve a problem," Helen said. She looked at me real hard. But I could see Red's eyes in the rearview mirror and they were clear and blue and not very disapproving at all.

Willie didn't have to wait long in the emergency room, and as he left he asked Helen if he could come over and visit her room.

"Certainly Willie," said Helen, and she touched his cheek.

"That is a very interestin room," said Willie. "And I am very interested in your experiments."

When Willie got out of the hospital he started coming over all the time. First he'd visit with Helen and have coffee and he always brought her some sweet rolls or cake and the two of them talked about the unseeable dimensions. They never argued, they just talked. Once I asked Helen if she was trying to convert Willie and she thought that was pretty funny. In fact, as I thought of it, she wasn't trying to convert Red anymore either, not in any overt way, not since the Year of Two Hundred Books. No, she and Willie talked philosophy. They talked about whether death was the Great Blackness or the Great Brightness, whether birth was the beginning or the middle, they talked about whether or not they could talk about the nature of the soul. The only disagreement they had was when Helen called Willie's experiments prayers and Willie called Helen's prayers experiments.

Afterwards Willie went out to the backyard with Red and me where Red prepared him for his coming fair-and-square revenge on Tony Blanion. We borrowed Big Dick Jinx's boxing gloves and Red started teaching Willie how to slip punches, throw jabs, and set his opponent up for the big haymaker. Red relied heavily on the big haymaker. He didn't think any fight should last longer than one minute, mostly because he'd never been in one that lasted longer than that.

"I do not know," Willie said. "Myself, I would like to introduce him to the Great Blackness."

"*You* be the Great Blackness," said Red.

"Myself, I would prefer to hit him on the head wif a hammer."

But Willie, being a philosopher, was committed to a certain degree of open-mindedness, even though he knew that it would eventually lead to his demise, which he explained to us after one of the training sessions over Kool-Aid.

"If you do not listen to anyone, someday you will miss somefin that is going to kill you, and if you listen, then you will hear what kills you."

"You got to approach every situation like this," said Red. "Am I going to be dealt with or dealt to? I don't have to tell you which is better."

"Fis is why I would prefer the hammer," said Willie.

"You got plenty of time for the hammer. It takes too much thinking to get close to somebody with a hammer."

Like I said, Willie was open-minded. So Red called Mr. Blanion one day and told him his kid had stabbed Willie and now Willie was better and was going to fight Tony Blanion fair and square right on Blanion's front lawn. We'd be there a week from Tuesday, about ten days away, and Mr. Blanion better not interfere or Red would flatten him.

"Oh yeah?" said Mr. Blanion.

"Yeah," said Red.

At first I thought it was hopeless. Willie had a good enough build, but he wasn't very pugnacious and he was pretty clumsy with his crippled hand. When I sparred with him it usually took me awhile, several good knocks to his head at least, to get Willie going. But being left-handed made him a little tricky to deal with, especially the way he limped deceptively on his right leg. His right jab was a surprise and Red taught him to use the two knuckles he had left on his left hand so that when he twisted his fist at the end of the punch it hit with a lot of force. Red also taught him how to hammer a guy on the top of the head if he came in with his head down and bring his knee up to meet the down moving forehead, which had a lot to do with our strategy, making Blanion make the first move and then stinging him.

Willie got better at fighting, but I was still pretty skeptical. "Even I can lick him," I told Red one night after supper.

"Good," said Red, "then maybe you can lick Blanion too. You might have to do some fighting around here before this is over with."

Red was right as night about that. I spied Blanion over at Stu-

bie's almost every day now. He always brought a couple members of his gang and sat on Stubie's porch along with Georgie
Gorky and smoked cigarettes and drank pop, sometimes beer.
They knew Red was training Willie and they knew Willie didn't
have a prayer.

Actually, I probably wouldn't have to fight Blanion or Stubie.
It was kind of an unwritten law around the neighborhood that
you didn't fight with somebody younger than you if they were
the same race. Blanion kept an assortment of ages in his gang
just for that purpose. Still, I figured I could handle most of them
as long as they didn't gang up. It was Georgie Gorky who pissed
me off, trying to pick the right side at the right time, the little
coward.

On top of it all, something wrong was going on inside me. I
used to get a great feeling when I connected into somebody's
head with my fist. I liked to see the blood and never felt a thing
until after everything was over, then I felt like all the good things
in the world had gone to sleep right inside me. Now I was starting to get jittery, like somebody was scratching me all over on
the inside. And when I was done fighting it didn't go away, it
stayed for hours.

"Willie can't beat him," I told Red.

"You never know what can happen in a fight," he said. "If
Willie gets up enough, but stays cool, maybe he'll take him off
balance, then, boom." Red punched his fist in his hand and it
popped. I looked at that fist and realized no matter what, this
whole business had distracted Red enough so that he hadn't
clouted me for weeks. Maybe after this I could get him reading
again or something. I didn't mind not hating Red and a lot of
times I was proud of him.

So Willie kept sparring with me and he really did get better. It
was getting harder and harder to get punches underneath his
guard and he was hitting me more and more with his counter-
punches. He was talking less and less about his hammer and
getting a quiet look in his eye and a set to his chin that appeared
as nigger-mean as anybody I'd seen. By the morning of the fight

he wasn't saying a goddamn thing. Red patted him on the back and Helen said she'd pray for him though she was of course against the whole thing.

"He could just hit him on the head with a hammer," said Helen. Willie moved one eyebrow.

"He's going to beat him fair and square," said Red.

"You never fought a fair fight in your life," said Helen. "Who ever won anything being fair?" Helen was holy but she sure wasn't dumb.

"Don't put things in his head," Red told Helen. "Come on, Willie." And Willie and Red and me left for Blanion's in the Rainbow.

Blanion's front yard was full of kids, mostly Italians and mostly from Blanion's gang. Georgie and Stubie were there too, on the porch with Blanion and his dad. They were all smoking cigarettes and drinking beer. Blanion's dad waved when he saw us. "Hello, hello," he said. "Which one's the nigger?" Blanion's dad was stocky with wavy gray hair.

"Let's get going," said Red.

Blanion kept right on smoking and drinking. He poked Stubie and then he poked Georgie, then he flipped his cigarette butt over the railing and laughed. He really didn't look so tough, kind of stringy and bony with long black hair that he combed before he came down from the porch. The kids made a circle on the front yard which was mostly dirt and Stubie and Georgie and Mr. Blanion followed Blanion off the porch and stood behind Blanion opposite me and Willie and Red. Blanion kept laughing and joking and waving at everybody and Willie stood next to us breathing through his nose and sweating through his T shirt, his eyes fixed on Blanion like he was going to tear him apart. He was actually more muscular than Blanion and Blanion sure was underestimating him. I thought of the whole revenge thing Willie had going for him and it was then, for the first time, that I thought Willie had a chance.

"Any rules?" called Mr. Blanion.

"No rules," said Red.

Mr. Blanion stuck out his bottom lip and looked at Tony Blanion and the two of them laughed. Willie's shoulders heaved. Blanion stepped into the circle and smirked.

"Watch his fists, not his eyes," said Red. "His fists."

Willie nodded and stepped in, his fists up, his back now all covered with sweat. Blanion just stood there with his hand at his sides and laughed at him.

"Come on," Blanion laughed. "Hit me."

But Willie stood there and waited. He was supposed to wait for Blanion to come after him, then counter. Everybody started yelling for Willie to swing but Willie refused to move.

"Wait for him," said Red, and Blanion laughed and Willie stood there, fists up, refusing to budge.

Blanion started dancing around Willie with his hands down, laughing, sticking his tongue out, putting his thumbs in his ears and wiggling his hands. Willie turned right with him. He held his ground and refused to swing.

Blanion turned around and dropped his pants. Then he stood up and walked right up to Willie. "Come on," he said. "Hit me. Hit me as hard as you can." But Willie held. He didn't say anything, he just held, and by now the whole circle was hooting for somebody to throw a punch. Blanion threw up his hands and walked over to his dad. Willie turned to Red, who motioned him over.

"Next time he comes in, cork him right away," Red whispered. "Just once. Just get him mad enough to come after you."

Willie nodded and went back out. Blanion flopped back in too and started his clowning again. Finally he put his hands on his hips and walked toward Willie. "Come on," he said.

Willie let him have it.

The circle got completely quiet as Blanion fell back. Blood came over his lip. He blinked. Willie held. "Come on," said Blanion. "Try it again. Come on, try it again." But this time he had his fists cocked at his waist and Willie didn't come. Willie waited. He looked strong. He looked mad. He looked confident. He looked bigger than Blanion. And for the first time Blanion looked worried.

Georgie and Stubie yelled, "Get him, Blanion, get him," but even Blanion knew that was what he was supposed to do and that was what was going to get him licked if he tried it. He circled Willie and taunted him, fists at his waist.

"Watch him," Red said. "Watch him."

Willie held.

Now everybody was yelling and Blanion decided to make his move. He turned toward Willie with his right hand so now they mirrored each other with right-hand leads. He came in slowly, his shoulders hunched, his brows over his eyes. He cocked his right fist.

"Watch him," said Red.

Blanion lowered his right fist and slowly raised his left like a hammer. He took a step forward and raised it a little higher. Then he put it high in the air. Willie looked at it. Blanion blasted him with his right.

Willie was out cold. Kids ran all around patting Blanion on the back and Red on the back and laughing and screaming. Mr. Blanion came over and gave Red a beer.

"We're all limited by what we have to work with," said Mr. Blanion.

Red took the beer and went over to Willie who had his eyes open now, though they didn't look too focused.

"I should have taught you how to kick him in the nuts," said Red.

"Now, now," said Blanion's dad. "Can't teach a man how to fight dirty. That comes natural."

Red picked Willie up.

"Glad we could work this out," said Tony Blanion, shaking Willie's hand. "No hard feelings. Everything's even-steven."

Red took Willie over to the Rainbow and put him in the back seat, then me and Red got in the front and drove off.

"Seems like we are leafing a pretty jofial situation," said Willie.

Red grunted.

Willie rubbed his chin with his crippled hand. "Anyway, I can now prefer to hit him on the head wif a hammer."

That ended the fight lessons. Red got grumpy again. He made me apply for a paper route and threatened to have me join the Boy Scouts because I was lazy and wasn't doing anything with my life. Of course by that time Willie had taught me that I didn't have anything to do with my life except deal with my deaf, but there was no dealing with Red on that level. A black family bought the house across the street, the Dangers, and the old man must have been six-eight if he was two-two. He had a pair of twins my age, Revis and Revco, though they didn't look at all alike, and along with Willie and the kid down on Funsters' corner it gave us enough bodies to start a neighborhood basketball team which Willie named The 24th Street Dialecticians. After practice down at the school yard Helen had us all in for Kool-Aid and then the four spooks went off and talked about books.

Grandma Funster died.

Grandpa Funster had been dying for years. Every organ in his body was dead except for him. His heart wouldn't pump, his kidneys wouldn't cleanse, his colon was petrified. Grandpa Funster ran on his appendix. He sat on the porch in the morning and stayed there until Grandma Funster put him away at night. He said things like "damn the torpedos" and "eat picnic church." He was fun to talk to, especially if you wanted advice.

But Grandma Funster had been healthy, healthy, healthy, though now dead. She took care of Grandpa Funster and all the little Funsters, she canned tomatoes, she cleaned house, she prepared meals. She chased me and Georgie Gorky around the block and over fences. She died. She sat up at her funeral. She was so energetic we could hear her bonking around in her coffin even after they closed the lid. She just didn't want to get put away. It was Grandpa Funster who was supposed to be dead and everybody knew it.

Nonetheless, one evening after energetic Grandma Funster

wrestled fat almost-dead Grandpa Funster out of his porch chair and brought him in for supper, then charged into the kitchen and ordered Funly to set the table, she hustled into the dining room and got everybody seated, announced her famous beef stew, pounded back into the kitchen and didn't come out. Jimbo Funster went into the kitchen after a while to see what was the silence and the holdup and found Grandma Funster in the corner upside down with her head in the stew. He said it was horrible taking all those vegetables out of her face.

It certainly was an unusual death.

Too unusual. After the funeral Grandpa Funster started waking up in the morning by himself, getting dressed, and going out on the front porch to sit. And in the evening, around supper time, he struggled to his feet, looking like he was leaning on something in the air, and trudged to the supper table. He even put himself to bed. "I g-guess Grandma b-babied him," Jimbo told Red.

One night Betty Funster fell asleep while canning tomatoes and when she woke up all the work was done.

"She was probably exhausted and forgot," Helen told Jimbo.

"R-right," said Jimbo. "The s-s-strange thing is that Grandpa says h-he's w-worried about Grandma. S-says she's looking kind of pale."

"He's an old man," said Red.

"R-right," said Jimbo.

But Funly was too young and stupid to fall for that kind of reasoning. "We're haunted," said Funly.

Jimbo Funster spent less and less time in the house. At night I saw him sitting on his porch roof behind his sandbags, peering out his infrared periscope toward the corner where the first black family moved in, then swinging the tube toward Mr. Dean Danger's. Both Red and Helen worried about him, and even his wife Betty came over sometimes to worry.

I took the problem to Willie.

"Myself," said Willie, "I am not really interested in the actual State After. I am concerned more wif the transition."

"What about the Dialecticians?"

"Refis and Refco are not mystics," he said. "They are metaphysicians. Besides, I am no longer interested in being shot in the limbs."

Stinky

WE WERE all getting older, even Stinky Jinx. But everyone sure was surprised when Stinky went out for junior football, more surprised when he made the team, flabbergasted when he ended up starting at halfback. I went to his first scrimmage. They'd lateral Stinky the ball and he'd head around the end, scarf flying and hooting like Daffy Duck. Instead of putting grease under his eyes like everybody else he painted it on his eyelids. I guess I never realized it playing in the backyard where he didn't have any room to run and I flattened him like a pancake every time he touched the ball, but Stinky ran like greased mercury if he got any room. I walked him home after the scrimmage.

"Jees Stinky," I said. "I didn't know you could run like that."

"Oh Jarvis, I'm just doing it for Dad. I really should thank you, you've been so much help."

"How can you run like that?"

"I'm so afraid of those guys," he said. "Who knows what they'd do if they got a hold of me."

"You don't like it."

"Golly no," said Stinky. "It's not nearly as delightful as chess. When is Edju coming again?"

"I don't know. He lives in Cleveland."

"I wish I could play basketball," said Stinky. "Then I could talk with those wonderful niggers."

When we got home Big Dick was waiting on the porch.

"What ya think?" Big Dick said to me. "Pretty tremendous, huh?" He whacked Stinky on the back. "I was a linebacker myself, but Stinky's a real thinker."

"He sure is."

"What's that smell?" asked Big Dick.

"That's Mom's Chanel No. 5," said Stinky. "I get so sweaty under all this, and if they ever grabbed me I'd be so embarrassed."

"What a card," said Big Dick. He gave me a bag of Buckhorn chips, a bag of pretzels, a bag of corn curls, a bag of fried pork rinds.

"I have to go in," Stinky said. "Mom might need her scarf in the morning and it has to be hand-washed."

Karl Marksman

KARL MARKSMAN bought the house next
door and moved in at the end of that summer. He drove up in
an old pickup truck covered with bondo and gray primer with
no license and no inspection. He had three kids, four dogs, two
cats, a blue jay, a crow, and a pig in the back with all his furniture, which wasn't much, a table, some wooden chairs, and a
rug. His wife Sophie sat in the front with him and she took up
the whole front seat. Besides that her forehead was sloped and
she only said things like "flubberty-ble-bla." Red wouldn't let
anybody out on the porch so we all had to watch out the side
window as Karl unloaded the truck and Sophie ordered the kids
and animals all around with no distinction between quadruped
and biped, urba-blooba.

"The proliferation of noncommunicative language systems will
be the wreck of this neighborhood," said Neda.

"Maybe you should go out and bleah at her a few times," I
said.

"I'm self-destructive," said Neda. "That woman doesn't know
any better."

"She must be retarded," said Helen.

The cats and dogs poured out of the back of the truck and the
pig waddled over to our maple tree and lay down in the shade.

The crow flew over and sat on the porch railing. The blue jay was in a cage so it didn't get to run around. There was all kinds of barking and screaming and the oldest boy had his sisters by the hair and kept knocking their heads together, bango, then everybody fell down laughing like the dickens. Sophie flapped her arms and yelled, "arble-scrupe-lbl-rabba!" It was good to hear her working in sentences.

Amidst it all Karl looked like the most peaceful man in the world. He carried in the rug and the table and the chairs and the blue jay, put the crow on his shoulder and took the dogs inside, then opened the upstairs window and put them on the porch roof. "Try to get off there, ya dummies," he said. Already there were no cats in sight. He came down and got the pig and took it inside, then got Sophie and took her inside, then got the kids and put them inside. Then he came over and knocked on our door.

We all followed Red. Karl couldn't shake his hand because Red was holding his bowling ball.

"Hello," said Karl.

"Hello," said the crow.

"Cute little bugger, aint he?" said Karl.

"You got a goddamn pig in your house," said Red.

The dogs were barking down at Karl from the roof of his porch. "Now shut up!" yelled Karl, and they did.

"God bless 'em," said the crow.

Karl rubbed his unshaved gray-red face and then scratched the back of his head. He grinned for the first time and showed that he didn't have his top four front teeth. "I see I can deal directly with you," he said.

Red was on the porch now, pumping the bowling ball up and down from his shoulder to the air and looking down at Karl.

"You bowl?" said Red.

"If I have to," said Karl. He looked up at the bowling ball. "For a minute I thought you owned a cannon."

I came out onto the porch and Red was smacking the bowling ball in his palm, smack, smack, smack. Over at Funsters' Jimbo had his telescope trained on us from the top of his porch. The crow regarded me askance.

"Hello," said the crow.

"Hello," I said.

"God bless ya."

"He say anything else?" I asked Karl.

"Sure," said Karl. "Crows are real smart."

"You got a damn pig in your house," said Red.

"Goodbye pig," said the crow. "Goodbye."

"Smarter than me," said Karl. He shrugged. "So the pig goes. Want a beer?"

Over on Karl's steps he showed us all his guns. He had over a dozen pistols and about eight rifles including two M-1s. Between him and Funster we could supply a revolution.

Jon

ONE DAY Jon and Bush came to visit. Neither of them drove so they walked over two miles from Polishtown on the Lower East Side. Helen served them coffee and they all sat around the dining room table in Helen's holy room.

"Edju thinks Jon is crazy," said Bush. Her face was lined and her hair white. She looked old.

"Crazy," said Jon. He was big and his gray hairline was an arrow like all the other males on Helen's side, only Jon's face was oval and convex, not like a shovel.

"He hears voices," said Bush.

"Everybody hears voices," said Jon. "Or how else could we communicate?"

Red watched Jon.

"You have any whiskey?" asked Bush, getting some chocolate out of her purse.

"Only sweet Mogen David and Gukenheimer," said Helen.

"I'll have both," said Bush.

Helen went to get the liquor.

"It's the *kind* of voices you hear," Bush said to Jon. "You talk to invisible things."

"There's a war going on," said Jon.

"Since the Korean?" asked Red.

Helen came in and gave Bush the two bottles and two glasses and gave one glass to everyone else.

"The war between good and evil," said Jon. "Between those who believe in God and those who don't—Communists."

Helen went behind Jon and massaged his shoulders. "He seems all right to me."

"He is," said Jon.

"He refers to himself in the third person," said Bush.

"He does not," said Jon.

Bush poured, drank, poured. "You think the saints are talking to you."

Jon shrugged. "You're jealous."

Bush poured and drank again. "Edju told you I have to go in the hospital," she said to Red and Helen.

"Yes," said Helen.

"A vein in my leg," said Bush.

"You'll be fine," said Helen.

"Who knows?" said Bush. "Doctors are jerks. All they care about is money."

"They don't treat the soul," said Jon very seriously. "If the soul is healthy, then what else matters?"

"My leg, for one," said Bush. She looked at Red. "You see, he's not so bad. He's just got his head in the clouds."

Jon felt for his head, then put his hands in front of him on the table.

"No one wants him," said Bush. "Stanley won't take him. David won't take him. They have families. Frances is in Detroit."

"They could come get him," said Red.

Bush ignored him. "He can't fend for himself while he's like this. Edju wants to put him in an asylum."

"Edju doesn't have a family," said Red.

"Where would we be without family?" said Jon.

"Not outside an asylum," said Helen.

"I'm not afraid," said Jon. "I'm responsible for my men. But there's a bomb on board."

"He was a hero," said Bush. "And a good lawyer. He doesn't

belong in an asylum. I know Edju told you he does. But Edju
had a different approach to war. He didn't suffer like Jon."

Red got up from the table and went to the closet. He came
back and stood in the doorway with his ball, raising and lowering
it from knee to shoulder.

"Red," said Bush.

"You want him?" Red said to Helen. He pumped the bowling
ball. I could see it working on him, how Helen's family always
treated him like dirt, all except for Bush, though Bush never gave
Red a break either, if it was between Red and her family there
was never any choice.

"Is there a choice?" said Helen.

"How long?" said Red.

"I'll be out in two weeks," said Bush.

"Okay," said Red.

"We want him," replied Jon.

Bush patted Jon's hands. The two of them got up and then
kissed Helen, then Bush kissed Red, then Jon came over to Red
and the two of them held on to the bowling ball.

More Jon

GOOD OLD Uncle Jon. He loved to take walks. Only he didn't like to take them anywhere. He liked to keep them in the house. He walked in the kitchen. He walked in the holy room. He walked in the living room. Back and forth. Uncle Jon rubbed his chin. Uncle Jon furrowed his brow. Uncle Jon was far away taking walks in the house.

Red didn't even bowl anymore but he still carried his bowling ball. Things were getting pretty crowded. Nobody went anywhere except on Down-down Day when Red went to get the welfare food. Uncle Jon watched Down-down Day real close, and Red watched Jon real close, so nobody said anything and we got away with a light one.

Then Jon started joining Helen in the holy room. Helen was sending messages and Jon was receiving messages, but whoever was doing the in-between work in heaven must have had his head up his ass. Helen asked for peace of mind and Jon pounded his head on the wall. Helen asked for guidance in her marriage and Jon told her Red was trying to kill her. Helen prayed for Jon and Jon told her she needed a psychiatrist.

"Who are you talking to?" asked Jon.

"The Infant," said Helen.

"You should deal with somebody older," said Jon. "Somebody with more experience."

"The Infant has been around a long time," said Helen.

Jon sighed and shook his head.

"Who's talking to you?" Helen asked Jon.

Jon stiffened. "Helen, there's a war going on. I can't divulge that kind of information."

"I'm your sister, Jon. This is my room."

"If you were intended to hear those messages, Helen, they'd send them to you. That goes for everybody else too. I take my orders from the Man at the top."

"We're all soldiers in the army of Christ," said Helen.

Jon smiled slightly and patted Helen's hands. "I'm a Navy man, myself." He looked deeply into Helen's eyes. "I know what it must be like," he said to her. "Living with a heathen."

"Which one?"

"Why Red, of course," said Jon.

"Red's letting you stay here, Jon."

Jon nodded sadly. "There is no light that can proceed from darkness. Sometimes we find something good in the darkness, but it's by accident."

"Say that to Red and you'll be out of here on your ear," said Helen.

Jon stood up. "I'm not afraid of Red. I'm not afraid of the asylum. I'm fighting a desperate battle, but I am a light that will never relinquish. It's *you* who should worry. He'll kill you someday and there will be nothing but hell waiting."

Helen shook her head. "Poor Jon."

"I know they're trying to kill Mother," said Jon. "That's why Red is keeping me here. But my messengers are protecting her this time."

"You better keep this to yourself," said Helen, and she went down to the basement to look to the wash.

Jon got up and took a walk in the kitchen.

The Dialecticians
Experiment with Deaf

I MET with the Dialecticians in Willie's attic down on 23rd Street. Willie had a little room fixed up in there with a lot of mattresses and cushions on the floor. Willie, Revis and Revco Danger, and Raymon from down the street were in there lying around and sweating.

"I am glad you came," said Willie. "We are going to have an experiment and you are welcome."

I told them about the communications experiment going on in Helen's room.

"Your mama is a good woman," said Willie, "but she does not control her experiments."

"She doesn't really think they're experiments," I said.

"That is exactly what I am sayin."

Willie got out a shoebox with a spoon and a hypo and some white powder.

"It is hot as hell in here," said Revis.

"Yes," said Willie. "At first I fought maybe we could just sweat to deaf, but myself, I would prefer a process not so long and painful."

Willie melted the powder in the spoon, then drew it into the hypo. Revco helped strap down Raymon's arm and Willie put the needle in. Raymon made a face, then gave me a big grin.

Then Willie took care of Revis and Revco. Pretty soon everybody was looking pretty happy.

"Themselfs," said Willie, "they are nofices to this experiment. You should not worry yourself. It is just like goin to the doctor."

"Doctor Death," said Revco. He wasn't usually the talkative one of the two twins. He had a square chin and a straight white smile, skin so black it looked purple. Revis was skinny with a little head and crooked teeth.

"It is true," said Willie. "I could be construed as a doctor of deaf, but that is only a metaphor." He prepared a syringe. "I will not gif you so much that you cannot go home," he said.

I let him put it in my arm.

First I vomited. But after that I thought I had things to tell Helen and Jon.

Willie gave himself a lot more.

"Myself," said Willie, "I am deeply into fis experiment."

Labor Day with
Karl Marksman

THEY DIDN'T give out hamburgers or hot dogs at the Welfare Office so we didn't have anything planned for Labor Day. I'd got to know Karl a little bit, sharing a beer and watching him when he cleaned his guns, so when he found out I wasn't doing anything he invited me along on his family's Labor Day picnic. Karl threw a couple pistols in the glove compartment of the truck, put a couple .22 rifles on the gun rack, put Sophie, Beema, Maggie, and Karl Jr. in the back of the truck with the dogs and the birds, and drove just south of town to a little wooded area between a couple pastures. Karl drove off the road and into the woods and stopped in a patch of clearing.

Everybody clambered out the back of the truck and right away Karl Jr. got into his banging routine with Maggie and Beema. Sophie wandered around errantly for a while, eyes skyward, then plopped down on the ground. The dogs yelped about, biting each other.

Karl got a blanket out of the back and spread it on the ground, then he and I carried the boxes of food over to the blanket. He got the rifles out of the truck, and a .22 pistol that he gave to Karl Jr. while Maggie and Beema were still on the ground.

"Thanks," said Karl Jr. He had a mop of red hair and was a

bit cross-eyed, which made him look a little stupider than he really was.

"Don't mention it," said Karl. "But if I come back here and find a bullet in one of your sisters or any of these dogs, you may as well be thinking of leaving home for good."

Karl handed me a rifle and the two of us headed out.

"You didn't mention Sophie," I said to him.

"By the time Sophie knew she was dead she'd have him torn to bits. He knows that." He shook his head. "Sophie aint the smartest woman in the world, but I aint got one goddamn complaint."

We found a clearing where we set some cans and bottles up and Karl showed me how to load and fire the rifle. I knew Red had all kinds of medals for shooting from when he was in the Marines, so I figured I'd have an eye too, and I was right. In a little bit I was hitting those cans like nothing. We knocked them all down, then walked over to set them up again.

"Red doesn't like guns," said Karl.

"No," I said.

Karl shrugged. "That's what I like about your family. A lot of people don't like me because I'm poor and dirty. Or they don't like guns. Red doesn't like a lot of things about me, Helen either. I know. But they keep it to themselves."

"It's not even that he doesn't like guns," I said.

"It doesn't matter," said Karl. "He could probably kill anything that got within twenty yards of him with that damn bowling ball."

We alternated shots at the cans. In the distance, between shots, I heard the snap of Karl Jr.'s pistol and thought of him back there with his mother, his sisters, and the dogs. To our left a bird circled, and when we finished shooting it descended and landed on Karl's shoulder.

"Hello," said Crow.

"Damn bird," said Karl. "How's everything?" he said to Crow. "How's Bluejay?"

"Bluejay's okay." Crow swiveled his head and looked at me with one eye.

"You know Jarvis," said Karl.

"I know. I know," said Crow. "Hello."

"Hello, Crow," I said.

We walked over to the cans and sat down on a rock. Karl told Crow to get off and Crow jumped down. He stood there looking everywhere, like a crow.

"Farmer that gave him to me told me he was old," said Karl. "But I've had him for years."

"Seems like a smart bird," I said.

"He aint so smart. He don't say nothin that aint been said to him."

Crow jumped back and looked sideways at Karl.

"How long's Red been out of work?" Karl asked me.

I hesitated because I knew Red would kill me if he found out I was talking about him with Karl, especially about him being unemployed. "Pretty long," I said.

Karl nodded at the ground. "I'd be out too if we weren't making all that stuff for Castro."

Karl worked for Bucyrus Erie and the government was paying them to build steam shovels and cranes and graters to send down to Cuba.

"Still," he said, "I drink and gamble most of my money away anyways."

"Why?"

He looked at me real hard. "What do you want me to do, buy a motorboat?" He pulled a pint of Jim Beam out of his pocket and drank, then offered it to me. I tried some but it burned like hell. Karl laughed. "Not your drug yet, huh?"

I wiped my mouth.

"Think I don't know what you do with your little nigger friends?"

I didn't like the way things were going. He was boxing me in everywhere. I stood up and looked back toward where we left his family.

"Now hold on," said Karl. "I just think the worst and go from there. It's just a policy. Come on. Come back here."

I went back and we shared more whiskey. It tasted better that time.

"What you think about being poor?"

"I don't think about it," I said. "I don't give a shit."

"Red and Helen think about it I bet."

I didn't say anything. Crow came up and nibbled at my fingertips. I had some old bread crumbs in my pocket and scooped them out and he ate them.

"God bless ya," said Crow.

Suddenly I was feeling sad as shit. "God bless yourself, asshole."

"Suit yourself," said Crow.

Karl snapped his fingers and Crow took off toward where we left the family.

"Now I'm talkin to you because I can't talk to Red," said Karl.

It was a hot, hot Labor Day, the sun burning a hole in the blue sky. For a second I thought I saw something out the corner of my eye.

"Listen," said Karl. "Let's me and you get some money."

Neda Experiments
with Deaf

NEDA WAS fat and disgusting and had a horrible disposition, but she was the smartest person in the universe. She read novels in French and Russian and was learning Spanish so she could read the South Americans when they started writing. She was going to read everything in the world and no one was going to stop her. She memorized the Periodical Table of Elements. She quoted Shakespeare. She ciphered astronomical figures through her head in seconds. She stole huge cakes and boxes of candy bars from stores, so many that even *she* couldn't eat them all, so made a tremendous profit by selling them at half price at school. She was a first-rate criminal mind, a Lex Luthor in the body of a fat little girl.

She hated me.

She hated almost everything and everyone, especially me and Red, and she always had good reasons.

In school Neda won everything; spelling bees, math quizzes, poetry memorization contests, writing awards, even elections, even though nobody voted for her. Neda was class president. Neda was May Queen. Neda was Catholic Girl of the Year. Every year. She despised it all. She fixed those elections just to spite everyone.

Neda set records for eating in place.

Then she got sick.

Something went wrong with Neda's heart. Like Neda it was up to no good. It was murmuring and it murmured malice.

Neda had a rumor in her heart that things were wrong.

Red was out of work and carrying his bowling ball around far too much. Uncle Jon took long walks in small rooms. Edju was right. Jon was nuts. He thought we were trying to kill him and unfortunately he was wrong. Bush was in the hospital. Helen prayed all day long. And now there was a murmur in Neda's heart that her self was trying to kill her.

"I said nobody get sick anymore!" yelled Red. "Didn't you hear me, goddammit? Doesn't anybody listen to me?"

Neda lay on the living room floor clutching her chest. She said, "Elg."

Jon stepped over her. He was taking a walk in the living room at the time and every time he saw her he looked startled. Neda really bothered his pacing. He stopped each time and contemplated her before stepping over. He rubbed his chin. "Madness," mumbled Jon.

Helen came in and knelt over Neda.

"My heart is a butterfly," Neda said to her.

"Your father doesn't handle crisis well," said Helen.

Jon startled, then stepped over the two of them. "Sick in the soul," he mumbled.

"Goddammit, goddammit," said Red. He flipped his bowling ball from one hand to the other. It was getting so he could handle that thing like a baseball.

"Call the hospital, Jarvis," Helen said to me.

"Don't touch that phone," said Red.

Jon had to step over Neda again, but this time Red cut him off. "Can't you walk someplace else?"

"I'm responsible for my men," said Jon.

"My heart is a bent spring," whispered Neda.

"You're just having a little experiment with deaf," I said to her. I saw it clearly for the very first time. "Your heart is the tool."

"My heart is the breath of a dark tool," said Neda. She certainly was a bright girl.

Red had his bowling ball in Jon's chest. "Okay buster, I've had it with you. Take a walk in the kitchen and take your men with you."

"Jarvis," said Helen. She waved her head toward Stinky's.

I made my move but Red still had a free hand and caught me by the throat.

"Where you going?"

"Grlk," I told him.

"My heart is a stone ship," murmured Neda.

"Your heart is trapped in fat," said Red.

Helen thought Red had his hands full, but when she went for the door he made a sandwich out of her with me and Jon. Now he had time to think.

Neda got up. "Okay," she said. "Forget it. Just forget it."

Those might have been Neda's last words except that now Red really did have his hands full. He and Neda exchanged death glares, though if it came down to pure glare I think Neda would have rubbed him out.

Red unpacked the people sandwich and we all stood there for a second. Everybody was quiet. Then Neda collapsed. Red went over to her and felt her pulse, then he went over to the phone. "Hello," he said into the receiver. "My daughter is too fat for this world."

Neda may have been a genius but we still had to use a wheelbarrow to pack her into the Rainbow, which wasn't anywhere near as pretty or sturdy as it used to be. Helen got in the front with Red.

"Watch Jon and the kids," Helen said to me.

"My heart is a stale soda cracker," whimpered Neda.

"Your heart is a broken pump," I told her.

"Literal asshole," said Neda.

"Watch your goddamn mouth," said Red, and off they went.

The Fall

IN THE fall I hated high school more than ever. Neda had rheumatic fever and had to live on a mattress in the living room. She wasn't even allowed to walk, but that cut down so much on her steal-sit-eat cycle that she was losing weight no matter how much she stuffed. Bush had complications with her leg, so they didn't let her out of the hospital, and Jon had stopped sleeping and spent all his time walking, which Red quarantined to the kitchen and holy room, at least while he was home. Which wasn't so often now. He'd found a job selling toilet paper supplies to institutions for some company out of Cleveland, almost totally on commission. Every morning he got in the Rainbow with his coat and tie and his bowling ball and headed into the world of janitorial supply. He wasn't making any money but at least he was out of the house, though when he did come home he was always mad as hell because nobody wanted to switch brands of toilet paper.

"It's the best goddamn toilet paper in the world," said Red. "How can you convince somebody of that?"

Red drove Jon to the hospital every other day to see Bush, but by now Jon knew that Red was trying to kill them both.

"You're trying to kill us," Jon told him. "You're trying to kill

Mother and me. After all I did to save this country." Then Jon cried.

"Shut up you goddamn nut," said Red.

Helen sometimes tried to mediate, but she knew Red was right. Besides, Kennedy had just grabbed the Democratic presidential nomination and she was plenty busy bending the Infant's ear about the country's need for a Catholic president. "If all the Catholics vote Catholic," she said, "and some of the Protestants are open-minded, we'll win."

In the evenings, twice a week, Karl and I took rides in his truck in the Glenwood Hills district, a rich suburb on the southern end of the city where a lot of the old moneyed families like the Strongs had built their homes after the Second World War, and where the new rich now built their houses with swimming pools and tennis courts on the outskirts. The area was built in a big spiral and the deeper you spiraled the richer it got.

After we got a good feel for the neighborhood we didn't drive around in it anymore. We spotted several places that had a lot of cover around them and accessible windows and we drew maps on how to get to them from the campus of the nearby all-girls Catholic college where we parked the truck. Then we walked through a little grotto that had a big stone altar to the Blessed Virgin and where the nuns spent their evenings pruning bushes and changing the flowers on the altar. Twice a week we said "How do you do" to the nuns until the weather got bad and they didn't come out so much. They loved seeing us and thought we were just a regular happy pair. Hello sister. Good evening, enjoying your walk? We certainly are, this is a beautiful campus. Oh, it certainly is. We even chipped in a few prayers because I'd put in a lot of time in front of statues and knew just how to act.

So we spent some weeks in the bushes taking notes, who came, who went when and how often, as regular as ants. We watched what lights went on when for who and figured out what room was for what and where the bedrooms were and who was in them.

One of the places we cased was Bobby Hansen's, a kid in my

class at South High who was as clean and white as a girl's First Communion shoes and whose whole family played sports, sports, sports, basketball, baseball, football, tennis, golf, except for his younger sister who was, of course, a cheerleader. We hit them the night of South's first City League football game. The whole family shuffled into their Oldsmobile station wagon and glistened off to the ball game to see Bobby.

We gave them a half hour in case one of them forgot their bleacher pillow or something and then slipped into the parents' bedroom window, cutting open the pane near the window lock with a glass cutter. We stayed right with the top drawers. Left everything real neat.

Karl took the parents' room and got mostly jewelry and a little cash, but I got old Bobby Hansen's room to myself. There I was right in the middle of all his trophies and banners and plaques and awards, mostly a bunch of worthless crap, but he kept a shitload of cash, over fifty bucks, right next to his pile of U.S. savings bonds with all the accompanying gift cards from aunt and uncle, mom and dad. Then we were out and gone, taking a nice walk through campus back to Karl's truck. Karl gave me the cash he got, another fifty, saying he'd get plenty more than a hundred bucks from the jewelry. That was the split; his truck, his ideas, his experience, his risk to pawn the stuff. He got the merchandise and I got the cash and that was fine with me. I was looking at more money than I ever imagined existed in one place and my lungs were pumping like after a fight.

I went right out and bought a whole carton of Mars Bars. Ate three. Gave ten to Joseph, ten to Andrew, and one to Neda. If I would have given one to Red he'd have got suspicious and of course Helen wasn't eating candy anymore because she had a pact with the Lord. As it was, Neda thought me just giving her anything was suspicious enough.

"What good is one fucking Mars Bar," she said from her living room bed. She looked just like Jim Bowie before the Mexicans rubbed him out in Walt Disney's Davie Crockett movie. "A point in the sea of space."

I waited one night till Helen was done yakking at the Infant and Jon was taking a walk in the kitchen and made Helen sit down at the holy room table. She had dark eyes and pretty, dark skin like liquid wood. Her hair was silver, not white like Bush's. It hit me kind of straight on right then that she was my mother, not just some ordinary person, not just Helen, but my mother.

I took out fifty bucks. "I know Red won't take this," I said to her. I had my back to the living room door and my elbows on the table and put the money down right below my chest. We sat at the back corner of the table, Helen's back to the Infant. Helen didn't move. She looked at the money for a little bit.

"I've been saving it," I said. "From doing things."

"What kind of things?" said Helen.

"Some things. Around." I looked in her eyes.

"How could you get money, Jarvis?"

I didn't say anything for a while and neither did she. She shook her head slightly.

"I've been doing things," I said. "You need the money. Neda's sick. Red's not making anything."

"It's not your business what your father makes." She sat back and glanced up at the Infant, probably trying to get a message, but that wasn't her specialty. She was a sender.

I picked up the cash and forced it into her hand. "There," I told her. "You're stuck with it now, okay?"

"I don't want it, Jarvis." But she made a fist around it. "I'll give it to the poor."

I got up and headed into the living room. "Okay," I said. "But I just did that."

I spent Sunday afternoons understanding deaf over at Willie's and then walking over to the football field to watch Stinky Jinx tear up the gridiron. The referees made him tuck in his scarf after every play, but the way he tucked it in it came out as soon as he took off with the ball, hooting and scooting like a goddamn loony bird. Anybody came anywhere near him he took off out of bounds, then it took half the quarter to flag him down. The other teams started lining up half their defense near the sidelines just to keep him hemmed in and Stinky's team had people all over the outside of the field to flag him down just in case he got out.

"Hooo-hooo!" said Stinky. "Those guys just want to *grab* me!"

If he scored a touchdown he might be gone for the day. Stinky's coach was thinking of sandbagging the backs of the end zones.

Sometimes I ran into Funly who'd gone out for the team himself, but porker as he was they stuck him on the line and he didn't last. "Boy, I'd like to have my .22," said Funly Funster. "I'd open some holes right up the middle."

"Hmmm," I muttered. At the time, the only holes I could think of were the ones I was shooting in my arms.

"That nigger across the street from you showed the top of his flat to Puerto Ricans," said Funly.

Stinky's team launched their second-most-favorite play; the quarterback dropped back and flung the ball anywhere and Stinky ran under it. "Hooo! Don't you dare!" yelled Stinky as he skipped out of bounds. They rounded Stinky up and patted him on the butt and he patted them back. That looked like his favorite.

I stared at Funly through my eyelids. I didn't know what a Puerto Rican was.

"They were there last night," said Funly. "Dad saw them with his infrared."

"Well, so what."

"They got parrots," said Funly. "We're all going to die from parrot fever."

"Maybe they'll get along with Crow."

"I'm going to plug that fucking bird," said Funly.

"He's keeping the pigeons away," I told him. I liked Crow. I didn't want anybody coming down on him.

Funly grunted. He sure was getting surly in his early teen age. "Grandpa had a fight with Grandma," said Funly.

"You're grandmother's dead," I said to him. "Grandpa Funster's just old, and nuts like half of everybody else in this neighborhood."

"Tell me about it," said Funly.

But Grandpa Funster started receiving war messages. He insisted his ship had a bomb on it. I started having nightmares about being trapped in Funly's kitchen, canning tomatoes. I dreamed tomato worms were crawling up my nostrils. And Uncle Jon began having conversations with an old but nonetheless invisible woman, which led him to discover, of all things, the telephone. So now he could call Bush to tell her he knew it wasn't her trying to talk to him, because she *wasn't* dead, though he was just calling to make sure. Every time I went to the hospital with Red and Helen to see Bush, she was on the phone telling Jon she wasn't dead yet.

"He's nuts, but he loves his mother," she said to us.

Then Red pulled a small flask out of his suit coat which he wore all the time now, his only one, along with a white shirt and tie, because he was trying to build up as much respect for himself as he could (after all he was white collar now, even if he was just selling toilet paper), and Bush pulled an empty flask from between her mattresses and they traded. Red gave Bush a box of chocolates and we all had one, except for Helen, of course, who had a pact with the Lord.

"Red, you're a good man," Bush said, and they shared a drink.

"You'll be out for Thanksgiving and you won't be able to travel to David's or Frances's," said Helen to Bush. "Why don't you have it with us?"

"I don't know," said Bush. "I promised Stanley."

Red gave Helen a bad stare. I knew he didn't want Bush and Jon over for Thanksgiving anyway, but he gave in after a long fight because Helen really thought Bush and Jon wouldn't have any place to go, so Red was going to be pissed no matter what happened and in this case he was pissed because after all he'd done for Bush and Jon they were going to Stanley's for Thanksgiving.

Later that month, as Thanksgiving approached, Karl and me hit another house and I gave Helen money to buy Thanksgiving dinner.

"Give the money to Andrew," said Helen.

"I don't trust him."

Helen stared at me. "When I was on the operating table with Andrew I was in such pain I begged the doctor, I begged God to let me die. The doctor knelt down and together we said the Act of Contrition."

"He needed it," I said. "Not you."

"I won't say this again to you. Andrew and I are bound in some way by the Lord."

"Okay." I gave her fifty bucks and she put it in the pocket of her gray-and-black-and-white-checked house skirt.

Crow

THERE WERE only three bedrooms in our house, all upstairs, along with the bathroom outside of which stood the only heat up there, a small steam radiator that Red painted silver. Red painted all the radiators in the house silver, he said it was the best color for radiating heat. The floors upstairs were all rough wood because Red tore up the linoleum in the hallway and all the rooms one Down-down Day after a fight with Helen. It looked like it was going to turn out to be a productive destruction for a change, but since we didn't have any money and anyway Red seldom got so mad that he *made* something instead of tearing it apart, now we had bare wood up there and if you walked with bare feet you got splinters.

Red and Helen had a bedroom at the back of the house, nearest the bathroom, and Neda had a room, except now Jon stayed in it while Neda slept downstairs in front of the TV. I shared a room with Joseph and Andrew; they split a double mattress and I had a single one, all on the floor. That's where those two spent most their time.

They kept the front window open and pushed the screen out and Andrew fed pigeons or squirrels or cats or whatever could fly in or crawl up the maple tree and onto the porch roof. Andrew was a regular St. Francis of Assisi, which was a little scary

seeing as Helen already had him pegged for sainthood. So that's
how he got to know Crow.

"Hello, Saint," said Crow.

"Who taught him that?" I said.

"Who do you think?" said Joseph. Till that point he'd been
busy looking into space.

Old Crow came right through the window and into the room,
hop, hop, hop. He looked at me sideways.

"He'll do anything for a goddamn corn curl," said Andrew.

Crow hopped onto Andrew's shoulder and had a corn curl.
"God bless ya," said Crow.

"Why don't you leave them pigeons alone?" Andrew said to
him. "I used to have pigeons here all the time."

Crow didn't have anything to say about that.

"I'm trying to teach him to take messages," said Andrew. "But
he's resisting."

"No way," said Crow.

"Then no way on the corn curls," said Andrew. He closed the
cellophane bag.

"Suit yourself," said Crow.

"Birds can't carry messages," said Joseph, "unless you tie them
to their legs. So he memorizes a few ambiguous things. That
doesn't mean he has a brain."

Crow hopped down from Andrew's shoulder and jumped onto
the window sill. "Goodbye, pig," he said, and flew off.

"He's not going to fall for that simplistic psychology," Andrew
said to Joseph.

Joseph shrugged.

Andrew put on his wire halo. It was kind of a transcendental
antenna. "You might be interested in knowing we're in for a tough
Thanksgiving," he told me.

"Red and Helen fight every holiday," I said. Joseph had his
ear and eye covered. "Why does he do that?"

"I can't transmit unless he shuts down."

"Why don't you get Grandma Funster back where she be-
longs?"

"If you ask me she's been a stabilizing force," said Andrew. "Only we can't use the phone anymore. Besides, you know that's not my area." He adjusted the hanger. "But Kennedy's got the election sewed up. That should make Helen happy. Go see Willie. He has something to tell you."

"Willie always has something to tell me."

Andrew appealed to the ceiling. "You want news, or miracles?" He took off the halo. Joseph opened his good eye and ear. Crow flew back onto the window sill and hopped back and forth. "Hello, Saint," he said.

"Forget it," said Andrew. "No info, no corn curls."

Shiva the Destroyer

IT WAS a warm Indian summer day and all the Dialecticians were at Willie's, already deep in meditation when I got there. Somebody had purchased a big hookah with a long hose so now they didn't have to get up to pass the pipe. As a group, we didn't play much basketball anymore. Willie passed me the hose and I gave him fifty bucks in tens. Earned me some wide eyes.

"I know you prefer not to have a job," said Willie. "So it would seem you have transcended some of your cultural falues."

"You'd prefer a Mars Bar?"

"I would not reject a Mars Bar," said Willie.

"Well whatever you need," I said to him, "let me know. The tools for these experiments aren't free." I had another puff on the hookah. It cooled the smoke down tremendously. Willie flipped the bills in front of his nose with his finger. I had more money, about another forty, but after I gave some to Helen and bought a few Mars Bars and pizzas I didn't know what to do with it, and I knew that spreading it around too much would get me noticed.

"No," said Willie. "As you may know, the other Dialecticians do not know where I procure these tools. It is the safest way for the Dialecticians."

"Yes," said Raymon. "We are a very safe group, considering the nature of our organization."

"Yes," said Revis. "And we are not in the streets creating the crime and the violence."

Revco just kept smiling like a dragon.

The smoke had a fist on my brain now and I had to sit back. I noticed that Willie had a hammer near his pillows.

"Lately I haf been tryin to escape the dualisms," said Willie. "To understand that deaf is neither one side nor the other of anyfing in particular." He had the tool box out and that was making all us Dialecticians feel pretty happy. But he stopped for a moment and picked up a book, thumbed for a page, then passed it to me. It was a picture of a Hindu god dancing, lots of arms, and underneath it said, "I am Shiva, the Destroyer. I create."

Willie poked Raymon, then Revis, then Revco. He looked at me, contemplative, rubbing his chin with his bad hand. "I haf been finkin about the dualisms," said Willie. "I haf been finkin about deaf. I haf been finkin about the hammer. All this finkin."

The other Dialecticians were already humming their own realities to themselves while Willie prepared my hypo. I strapped my arm and Willie found the vein and then I started finding that great quiet place in my womb. "So?" I said to Willie.

Willie finished up with himself. "So lately I haf been finkin about Shifa."

Funly

HALF OF Funsters' backyard was now a ditch. Funly spent a lot of time back there now. He and Jimbo had it all laid out; the quarters for his mother and sister, him and Jimbo, the bathroom, the food storage room, the communications room for radio, CB, short wave. "We might have to make some pretty hard decisions about Grandpa," said Funly. "He's old. And he hasn't got out of bed since Grandma Funster left."

Funly was a little taller now and a little thinner, but he still had that flattop.

"It's a little scary," said Funly. "Grandpa keeps talking about war, but he didn't fight in any war. Maybe he knows something's going to happen." He looked at me real serious. "Soon."

"He's just listening to my Uncle Jon's voices," I said. "You want Grandma Funster back, come over to Helen's holy room and get her."

Funly studied the ditch. "I think we'll have to have a turret," he said. "We can't have holes on every side for guns. We won't have enough people to guard, and there'll be radioactivity. We'll have to have some kind of swiveling periscope and a gun like a tank. The unprepared will be the first to try and break in, and if it ends up house to house with the Russians we're going to go down fighting."

"What do the Russians want with this fucking neighborhood, Funly?"

"We'll have to get some way of monitoring the radiation," Funly said, rubbing his hands over his flattop. "And some lead-lined suits, just in case we have to go outside. Do you know what's happened in Cuba? Do you know the Russians got Sputnik?"

"Stinky's team's playing for the championship today," I said. "Want to go watch?"

"Just don't come knocking on the roof of our shelter when it all comes down," said Funly, "because you'll be looking down the barrel of a machine gun. What are you going to do when this planet becomes a cinder?"

The Football Game Burglars
Strike Again in Glenwood

KARL KEPT his gun collection in his basement and when I went to see him he was usually down there fiddling with his guns, cleaning them, building them, something. He'd just joined an organization called the Sons of the Pioneers and they all built their own muskets and dressed up in buckskins and went out on the weekends to refight the American Revolution or the War of 1812. Sometimes a bunch of Pioneers gathered on Karl's porch and got looped and passed out after requisite hooting and shouting, then the place looked like the bad end of a skirmish.

Red wasn't too hot on the Pioneers. Sometimes when things got a bit noisy he came out on the porch with his bowling ball and sat on the railing flipping that ball into the air and down again and up his arm and even over his shoulders like a goddamn Harlem Globetrotter. That bowling ball was getting to be like a tiddlywink. The Pioneers gave Red beer and Red explained to them that this was a family neighborhood and most people would probably appreciate it if they were a little quieter.

If that didn't work Red exercised the option of speaking to the noisiest one with the bowling ball, just kind of tapping it lightly on his chest, though real polite. Red was getting pretty diplomatic as he settled into middle age, mostly because his forearms

were the size of my thighs, his biceps were logs, and he had tree
trunks for legs. I could barely get two hands around his wrist,
which was the smallest thing he had. Besides, Red exuded with
every movement of his giant self that he'd fight any goddamn
thing in the world and any number of them too, and one night
when one of the Pioneers put a pistol between his chest and
Red's bowling ball, Red told him, "You better kill me with the
first shot because you won't get another one," which may not
have been true but was close enough to being true.

Red wasn't too crazy about Karl or the Pioneers but Karl was
Red's neighbor and that was about as mystical a bond for Red as
family was for Bush or sacred mystery for Helen. So Karl pretty
much decided that when Red came to visit the Sons of the Pioneers he wasn't so much ruining their fun as creating more fun.

One night after the Pioneers left and Red went back in the
house Karl took me down in his basement and showed me his
latest project, a thick iron tube welded on either side to heavy
steel triangles.

"What do ya think?" said Karl. "It'll be deadly for a two-mile
radius." He had his hands on his hips and grinned wide enough
to show all the teeth he didn't have.

I rubbed my chin like Willie. I could tell him he was crazy, but
he knew that enough already. I could ask him what he needed a
cannon for in the middle of a developing slum, but that would
be the stupidest question because it was the only one. "Yeah," I
said to Karl. "That's really great."

"This is just a working model," said Karl. "Eventually I'm going
to build myself a little howitzer."

"You aren't worried about the Russians, are you?" I asked him.

"What Russians? Are there Russians moving in on top
Dangers'?"

"No. Puerto Ricans."

"Shit," said Karl. "Parrots."

"I thought you might be teaming up with Funster."

"Funster's okay. Little paranoid. Just a little nuts. But at least
that shelter's got him off the damn roof for a while." Karl sat

down on the cannon. "We can make one more hit before the holiday season, I figure. I haven't seen anything in the papers and that's good, but the police take care of those people, you can believe that. They'll all be heading down to Florida or Jamaica for Christmas and that's when cat burglars are supposed to strike so we won't. We'll sit out the winter. What you think?"

I thought that was a fine idea. We'd only cased about three houses really well anyway and I already had more money than I knew what to do with, more than I could spend, more than I could give away. It just gave me a tremendous feeling to get inside those houses with everybody gone, look in the bathrooms with the saunas and whirlpools and all the plush nifty towels lined up so neat, and the nice perfumy woman's section of the bathroom with lots of pastel plastic bottles with flowery names, the hamper with slips and silky panties. And I liked the rooms with the stuffed animals like rainbows, closets with dresses or suits. Rooms that kids had to themselves. I liked sneaking into those people's lives and watching their stuff and thinking about them coming home to find what I got of theirs, to think about me looking at their stuff, smelling their stuff, deciding what I wanted and what I didn't.

Karl and me liked football families that fall. We parked his truck at the small all-girls Catholic college and walked through the grotto of the Blessed Virgin where we saw the nuns all the time in the summer, and waited in the woods across the street from the big house that looked like it belonged in England. We waited for everybody to leave, with their cushions and their blankets and their thermoses and their plastic bullhorns, all hooping and excited about the last big ball game of the year, and then we waited a little more, just in case somebody forgot their mittens or something. Then we went to the most sheltered bedroom window near the woods, a little girl's room in this case, sliced out a little bit of glass near the window lock, and went in.

We didn't get any money in there, but there was a bunch in the parents' room and the teenage son must have had himself a little job or some expensive habits or something because in a couple minutes we were looking at watches and diamonds and about three hundred bucks. The boy wasn't an athlete because he had a bunch of books in a bookcase over his bed and on the bottom shelf a great big fancy camera, all black, except for some big white letters that said NIKON across the front at the top.

Karl wasn't too happy when I came into the parents' room with that camera.

"No good," he said. "Too easy to trace."

"I'm keeping it," I said.

"Looks complicated."

"No more than a gun, I bet."

"How you going to explain it?" said Karl.

"I'll keep it at Willie's."

Karl shook his head and smiled enough to show his gap.

"Take the cash if you want," I told him.

"Nah, I got over a thousand bucks here now." He shook his head and chuckled again. "We better lay off this for a while. Risk and greed don't mix. That's something for you to remember."

I certainly had become a catalyst for profundity.

Karl and me slipped out the window and walked back to his truck where we shared a few snorts of Jim Beam, then we drove to a bar for a six-pack of Koehler beer so we'd have something to wash it down with. Karl drove down to the public dock and we drank beer and whiskey and watched the big gold crescent moon set over the bay and watched wealthy adolescents drive their parents' motorized sailboats and inboard yachts in and out of port and watched the sailors from the Merchant Marine and the ore boats get in fights and puke on the asphalt parking lot. Teenagers sat on parked cars and whistled at cars full of girls, something I thought of doing myself someday if I ever had a car or ever desired a girl, which I didn't, though Helen one night asked me questions about how come she never found any stains on my dirty sheets, good old Helen. Not that I didn't get hard-ons, I just never came and never thought about it and didn't really give a shit about girls. Cop cars rode up and down the dock, I guess making sure that the teenagers and the rich kids and the sailors all kept separate. I hadn't quite figured out what cops actually did, I never saw them in our neighborhood, though Karl assured me they were the enemies of truly free enterprise or, at the very least, a clog in the way we were presently interpreting things.

"Those are the people *we* pay to keep those kids on their parents' yachts," said Karl. "A regrettable system, but it's the one we got."

"Fuck it," I said.

Karl pointed to the boats in the bay. "That way of making money is the accepted one, and if we play that game we're never going to get any of it."

"Don't give me reasons," I said. "I don't want any reasons." I looked at my new camera. I guessed I'd have to get a book and find out how it worked.

"You work pretty hard at staying dumb for a smart kid," said Karl.

I drank some beer and drank some whiskey. The sky was black except for a halo of gold on the horizon and the faint dust of star sky. Karl started the truck and we drove right up the center of town and through the suburbs and into the country until he parked at the side of the road and we took the rifles from his gun rack and walked into the field. We fired shots into the sky. BLAM! BLAM! We stood there till dawn firing away at nothing.

Because Big Dick Jinx sold record numbers of Buckhorn pretzels and potato chips, he won four tickets to the big Browns–Giants game in Cleveland that would decide the NFL Eastern Conference champion. Me and Red were supposed to leave that morning for Cleveland with Big Dick and Stinky, so when I got home I made myself a cup of coffee and read the Sunday paper, sports and funnies, and waited for Red to wake up with everybody else and drive Helen and Jon and Joseph and Andrew to mass.

Red himself was not in a church-going period, though he was plenty religious in a personal way and when he did go he went right along with Helen to Catholic church because church was church to Red. But with Jon living there and getting messages and Helen having a little brouhaha with the Infant over Neda's rheumatic fever Red began exercising his humanity through negativity. Helen was ill in her heart over my disposal of the One True Church and often tried to make Red make me go on the grounds that he signed a paper when he married her that all his kids would be brought up Catholic. Of course once again Red was caught between respecting God and church but resenting Catholicism, so he was kind of happy I was rejecting it all but clearly upset that I wasn't going to church and respecting God, though unfortunately he wasn't going to church himself which kind of made it hard to get mad at me which made him all the madder.

So Red rolled down the stairs a tornado of emotions, nothing new. He sighed a couple times and got his bowling ball and when he came into the kitchen I gave him the sports page and got him some coffee. Of course doing two nice things for him made him suspicious.

"When you get in last night?" he said to me.

"I was up pretty late with Karl discussing social inequalities and thinking up remedies," I told him.

"You stink," said Red. "You smell like booze. I don't want any of my kids becoming goddamn alcoholics. I already got a daughter who tried to eat herself to death."

"I had a couple beers," I said. I'd forgotten about the drinking and about how good a nose Red had.

"You smell like decay. You got cavities?"

"I don't think so."

"Then it's that goddamn booze."

"Maybe I got a cavity," I said.

"Don't get any cavities," said Red. "I don't want anybody else getting sick around here." Red went into the living room and yelled up the stairs. "You're going to be late." He came back in the kitchen. "Your mother will be late for her own damn funeral."

"The paper's picking the Browns," I said to him. "They said it was close in New York, the Browns should get them at home."

"Not if they wear white," said Red. "If the Giants wear blue and the Browns wear white, the Giants always win. I don't know why they don't wear brown. They're the goddamn Browns."

Uncle Jon came into the kitchen. He hadn't slept for a couple weeks. I'd heard him walking up in Neda's room when I came in.

"Jarvis," said Jon. "I'm going to call Mother and I want you to listen for me while I'm at mass." He went into the holy room and called Bush. "Good," he said into the receiver, "you're alive. Don't worry, Red won't hurt us, I'm keeping an eye on him."

Helen came downstairs with Joseph and Andrew, both complaining they were sick.

"I'm sicker than him, look at the shape of my head," said Andrew.

"What?" said Joseph. "What? I'm getting an infection in my good ear. Things look blurry."

"Why don't you just shut down," said Andrew.

"Shut up," said Red.

We all went into the living room and Jon gave me the phone.

"I'm not dead yet," Bush said to me.

"Jon's going to mass with Helen," I told her. "I'll call back in an hour."

"I want my own voices back," Jon was saying to Helen at the door. "I don't like this Grandma Funster. I think she's Protestant."

Red and Jon glared at each other. "You want to walk to church?" said Red.

"Will everyone shut up!" yelled Neda from her bed in front of the TV. "I can barely hear Oral Roberts."

"Let's get over to Jinxes'," Red said to me when he got back. "They met Stanley outside church and he's going to take them to see Bush and then bring them home."

I called Bush and let her know, then we went over to Jinxes' and Pat Jinx, Big Dick's wife, went over to our place with Stinky's little sister Becca Jinx to watch Neda till Helen got back. Then we

got in Big Dick's car, Big Dick and Red in front and me and
Stinky in the back, and took off for Cleveland on Interstate 90
which was a brand new freeway and already falling apart.

It was a nice day, cool and sunny with big puffy white autumn
clouds coming in from over Lake Erie and Big Dick Jinx with his
big hands and big jaw all excited about the Browns, especially
Jim Brown and Bobby Mitchel who were going to run around the
Giants just like Stinky ran around everybody, and Stinky sitting
in back with me in his crewcut and his mother's scarf beaming
like one of Santa Claus's elves saying, "Actually, I'm kind of excited, I mean, I've been *in* football games but I've never really
seen a football game, I hope the crowd is dressed fashionably,"
and Red in the front seat starting to feel bad because he was
going to the game for free in Big Dick's car on Big Dick's gas and
was going to have to deal with the whole dilemma of beer and
hot dogs in the stadium and feeling more and more pissed about
taking charity, and meanwhile there's me in the back seat with
350 bucks in my pocket and a Nikon camera under the seat of
Karl's truck.

We took I-90 right into Cleveland and got off at the stadium
which sat right on the lake. Red and Big Dick fought over who
should pay for parking and Red finally won. Then we walked
through the lot and into the stadium by the pennant sellers and
the hat sellers and food vendors until we got to the beer where
Big Dick bought one each for him and Red. Stinky got cherry
pop and temporarily I didn't get anything.

Our seats were okay, underneath the second deck on the thirty-
yard line. There were a million colors in the stands and the field
was greener than green, the sky light blue with big puffy white
clouds, the Giants dark blue with little puffy white Browns.

"They're wearing white," groaned Red.

"Ah, it's not the color of the uniform, it's the man that's in it,
right Stinky?" said Big Dick.

"The color means a lot to me," mused Stinky, who was pretty
pleased about the colorful atmosphere but clearly disappointed

with the surrounding fashion. "I'd *hate* to get tackled by one of those blue guys." He looked all around. "And I'd love to see somebody with some flair."

The place was all buzzing and excited until the Giants took the kickoff. Charley Connerly zipped balls to Frank Gifford, Alex Webster ran through gaping holes in the Browns' line, Sam Huff snuffed big Jim Brown, and Bobby Mitchel bobbled passes all over the field. Mostly there was just a lot of ooohing and groaning and bitching from the stands, of which I was one of the leading ooohers and groaners, being only a closet Giants' fan most the time because I didn't want to get on the wrong side of Red. "Look out, Jim Brown just got *smothered*," I groaned. I was groaning louder than any Browns' fan in the area.

Stinky kept having me explain the game to him, not really having much understanding of the stoppage of play due to somebody getting tackled, in fact not comprehending why any of those guys let anybody tackle them at all with all that room they had to get away.

"This isn't what I do!" said Stinky.

"What a card," said Big Dick.

When the score got 14–0, Big Dick began killing his misery with beer and hot dogs, asking Red if we wanted any, and of course Red kept saying he wasn't hungry and of course neither was I, saying I was too miserable about the Browns getting bulldozed. It just bothered the hell out of me the way they were getting plastered all over the field.

Then the half ended with the score 28–0 and everybody kind of milling quietly near their seats mumbling about great comebacks, like Pearl Harbor, said Big Dick.

"Yeah, but the Browns don't have half a decade," said Red. "Besides, they're wearing white. Goddamn Browns wearing white, most ridiculous thing I ever saw."

Red sure was right about some stuff.

And I could see he was aching away about the fact that he couldn't afford any hot dogs and beer to battle this absurdity, and pretty soon he was going to be resenting Big Dick for having money and bringing him here and making him feel like he had nothing and worse offering to buy him things and put him in his debt and worse than that really be a nice guy, too nice to get mad at. That left me. So when Red decided he had to go to the bathroom I went with him, like Willie said, at least I'd see what killed me.

Of course the big metal trough was packed.

"Well let's just take a piss in a stall," I said to him, and Red shrugged his shoulders and said okay and I watched him until he finally picked one, being kind of persnickety about the cleanliness of toilets since he started selling toilet paper, and when he did I went into the one next to him and folded up $150 and slipped it behind his toilet.

"Hey," I said to him. "What's that behind your toilet."

"What?" said Red.

"I think there's some money behind your toilet."

"Right," said Red, "and my shit don't stink." But he put his hand back there and came up with the money nonetheless.

Well Red came out of that toilet looking pretty happy. He patted me on the back and said, "Hey, you were right for a change, yessir, boy, were you ever right."

"Yeah?" I said.

"Yeah," said Red.

"How much was it?"

"None of your goddamn business," said Red. But he softened up again real quick. We stopped at the concession and got a dozen hot dogs with everything, a ton of fries, peanuts, a cherry pop, and *three* beers.

"Hey," said Red when we got back to the seats. "What do you think, I found some money." We passed around the dogs and food and drinks.

"No shit," said Big Dick.

"Sure did," said Red. "Guess these tickets are lucky all the way around, right Jarvis?" Red patted me on the back and we all laughed. Red told the story about how he found the money and even gave me credit.

"Well that's delightful, Red," said Stinky.

By the time the score was 49–0 nobody gave a shit.

Uncle Jon Experiments
with Deaf

I STARTED putting Helen's share of my income under the votive lamp in front of the Infant of Prague and that's where she found the hundred dollars, so between what Helen found and what Red found we were set for a pretty good Thanksgiving. Bush got out of the hospital the Wednesday before and Red picked her up and took her home, though Jon started calling there as soon as Red and Bush left the hospital room and didn't stop till Bush got home and picked up the phone.

"I'm not dead yet," Bush said.

Thanksgiving was going to be the last day Jon spent with us before returning home with Bush after dinner. Bush and Jon couldn't go to Stanley's because he was having Aunt Sylvia's parents over.

Of course Red was happy as a pizza pie that he got to entertain Bush and Jon because nobody else would.

But Helen was really glad to finally have Bush over. Bush's stint in the hospital convinced Helen that Bush was on her last legs and this was going to be her last set of holidays.

"Who knows," said Helen. "Bush could go any day. This could be her last Thanksgiving, or her last Christmas."

Helen hadn't called Red's football bonanza a miracle, she was too intellectual for that stuff, she said that the world was just evening itself out.

"Things work out, Jarvis," she said to me. "The poor suffer one way and the rich suffer another way. If you're good you get your due, and the other way around."

So that's what I'd been doing in those people's houses, collecting dues, keeping those rich people certified members of the human race.

Meanwhile Uncle Jon was upset because Grandma Funster was pleading with him not to leave the neighborhood.

"Who's she going to talk to if I leave?" asked Jon.

"Maybe she'll go home," said Helen. "Who knows, these could be Grandpa Funster's last holidays."

So Thanksgiving Day we all got up and watched parades in the morning and saw Santa Claus in New York and Santa Claus in Philadelphia and Santa Claus in Detroit while Jon listened to Bush on the phone or took walks between Neda's bed and the TV because Helen was cooking in the kitchen and preparing the holy room table for dinner. Andrew took notes and Joseph watched the parades attentively with his blind eye and Neda read, but Red liked parades, especially the giant balloons of Popeye and Mickey Mouse and Bullwinkle, so everybody watched parades except Helen who we all thought was lucky enough to have to cook though Helen herself said she preferred to watch parades. Every time Santa Claus came on at the end of a parade Red pointed and said, "There's Santee Claus, look, there's *Santee* Claus," and laughed like hell, sticking his fingers in everybody's ribs. Neda told him to go to hell, so he tickled her more. Red sure did like Santee Claus.

After the parades Red and Jon went to get Bush, who sat in the living room when she got there and watched the Lions play the Packers while Jon walked back and forth and Red, who Bush made go into the kitchen to help Helen, kept running back into the room every time he heard cheering to see what the play was or see the replay of the touchdown. Then Texas played Texas

A&M, but we didn't get to see the end of it because dinner was ready, besides Texas always smashed the shit out of Texas A&M anyway, it was ridiculous to even play the game.

Bush and Jon sat at one head of the holy room table, right under the Infant, and Red and Helen sat at the other with Helen's chair closest to the kitchen. Neda wanted to stay in bed but Red carried her in and sat her down on my side. Joseph and Andrew sat on the other side. The heads of the table were a bit crowded but politically correct. Red carved the turkey. Helen passed the food. Bush dished out portions for Jon who had grown suddenly ill and didn't want to eat. He kept whispering to Bush and peering at Red, and though Red was determined as hell to have a good time he wasn't having a good time, partly because when Red got determined to enjoy himself he didn't have a prayer and partly because even understanding that Jon was nuts didn't make up for Jon's antipathy for Red right in Red's own home on Thanksgiving. You knew Red was thinking about how much he'd done for Jon, even though Jon hated him, and about how much he didn't want Jon there yet had to feel grateful he was.

"Jon's not feeling well," said Bush.

"I want to go to Stanley's," said Jon.

"He thinks we're trying to poison him," said Neda.

"I want to go to Stanley's," said Jon.

"Stanley doesn't want you," said Neda. "That's why you're here." Neda was fat and disgusting and sick and clear as a bell.

"Stanley wants us," said Jon. "Right Bush?"

"In his own way," said Bush.

"Stanley wants you like he wants a hole in the head," said Neda.

"Stanley could use a hole in the head maybe," said Bush.

That's when Edju and Aunt Elizabeth came in the door.

"Oh hello, so very hello," said Edju.

"Don't get up," said Aunt Elizabeth.

"Sit down," said Helen, getting up, "and have something to eat."

Both Red and Neda scoured the table with their eyes. It wasn't like there was a ton of food.

"Oh no," said Edju. "We're so um very um so, so very full ooh."

"We just had plenty to eat at Stanley's," said Aunt Elizabeth.

Neda chortled like the witch in *Snow White*, her poetic sensibilities obviously aroused. Red's eyes stopped roving the table and he relaxed for about two seconds until he realized how he'd been manipulated and insulted once again. Helen held her hands on her head like she was trying to hold it on. Bush shrugged and put her hands in the air.

Jon catapulted from his chair and grabbed Edju by the lapels. "Take us to Stanley's, Edju. Mother and I are in trouble here. I can't tell you how much."

Now Red stood up. "I've had about enough of this," he said.

"Ooh-ooh, much so much so very matter," said Edju.

Helen got between everybody. She was certainly brave. "Why don't you come back another time, Edju?"

"Ooh so?"

"Red's trying to kill us, Edju," said Jon. "He's been trying since the first day."

"So very no no, so no," Edju said, waving his hands in front of him like fly wings.

"Well maybe we should go," said Aunt Elizabeth.

"Take me with you," pleaded Jon.

"I'm afraid we're taking a cab back to the hotel," said Aunt Elizabeth.

Red left the room and came back, standing behind everybody and pumping his bowling ball and getting redder and redder by the second.

Things were slowly sifting into the living room so all of us at the table got to eat and watch from a distance at the same time, at least as much distance as anybody ever got in that place, considering you could never really be safe. Bush went to the living room closet and got her coat. She was going somewhere no matter what, which was pretty straight thinking, I suppose that's why she'd already spent most her life being old, having a real knack for flight.

"Edju," pleaded Jon. "Take us to Stanley's."

"Oooh-oooh," said Edju. It was getting pretty clear that good old Helen's half of the family thought Jon was nuts, even Edju, Mr. Flexible, and they wanted nothing to do with him.

"I fought," cried Jon. "You don't know. I was responsible. You don't know how I cried when we gave the Russians Eastern Europe."

"I'd say they paid quite dearly for it," said Aunt Elizabeth.

Jon moved to Edju and grabbed his lapels again. "Edju, I fought to save Europe. Tell him, Mother. I offered my life time and time again to save the world."

"And now his family rejects him," said Bush.

"Who are we?" said Helen. "The Russians?"

"Hmm, I have many, so very many countries, hmmm, fight," Edju told Jon.

"They separated us," said Jon. "They kept Mother and me apart. I lived on the telephone. I never slept so I could keep an eye on him."

"Oooh, so who so who?" said Edju.

"Red!" screamed Jon. "Red!"

Red looked at Helen. He stretched the bowling ball out to the length of his arm. Edju looked at Red. Jon began to choke him. "Edju, take us to Stanley's!"

Elizabeth stepped in saying, "Now, now. Now, now," and Jon grabbed her too.

"I can't stay here!" screamed Jon.

"The children," said Helen. She stepped in and Jon brushed her away. Red looked at Bush who nodded. "Okay Red," she said.

Helen tried to step in again but Red removed her. Then he got Aunt Elizabeth out of Jon's hand, all this with just his left hand because in his right he still had that bowling ball pumping like a cat's tail. Finally Red stuck that arm between Jon and Edju and Edju backed away dusting himself off and Jon hung on Red's extended arm. Red put his hand in Jon's chest and pushed him against the wall next to the front door. "I'll take you home now," Red said to Bush.

"No," said Jon. "You'll never get me in that car with you again. Edju," pleaded Jon, but now Edju was hiding behind Aunt Elizabeth and Bush.

Helen stepped to Jon again but he quickly grabbed her by the throat. "You're with him," said Jon. "You're with him against me."

"I'm your sister, Jon," gasped Helen. "I wouldn't hurt you. Red wouldn't hurt you."

"You're lying," cried Jon. "You've been won over and you're lying. You think I'm crazy."

"No," said Helen.

"Yes!" screamed Jon, and he tightened his grip on Helen's throat then flung her across the room. He stepped from the wall toward Red but he never had a prayer. Red launched that bowling ball from a distance of about eight feet, he claimed accuracy from thirty, and it caught Jon right in the chest, driving him through the vestibule door, then the front door, then the screen door, none of which were on too good anyway since Red's door days, and sending Jon sprawling on the porch floor flat on his back, the black bowling ball still clutched in his thin white hands. We all rushed to the porch where Red stood over Jon like a good cowboy after an unfortunate death.

"Back to the goddamn hospital," mumbled Red, retrieving his ball and fumbling with the Rainbow keys.

Helen already had a cloth on Jon's head.

"Oooh Red, so very big, big so very much man, so," said Edju, clinging behind Aunt Elizabeth.

"He was a good lawyer," said Bush. "And a war hero."

Jon's face looked whiter than the porch trim. "My chest," gasped Jon.

"If you need any work on your heart," Neda said to him, "now might be a good time."

The New York Giants
Experiment with Deaf

EVERY YEAR the New York Giants went to the NFL championship game and every year they lost, according to Red. Of course mostly Red liked to remember when the Browns just entered the league with Otto Graham and always won everything every time, but now it was different and the Giants always won the Eastern Conference by beating *somebody* they had to, usually the Browns, then went on to lose in the title game to the Packers or the Rams or the Lions or the Bears (though never the Forty-Niners) and this year they were going to lose to the Colts with Johnny Unitas and Allen Ameche and Big Daddy Lipscomb. Red said the Giants didn't wear blue or even white for the title games, they wore yellow. That was a big joke for Red.

So the day of the championship game came and me and Red jammed in front of the Zenith and made sandwiches and had some beer and prevented Neda from watching a Shirley Temple movie and watched the New York Giants play the Baltimore Colts broadcast from Baltimore, except that Red got up and sat down next to the Zenith and watched me watch the game instead of actually watching it himself, and though the Giants weren't wearing blue the first half they must not have been wearing yellow till the fourth quarter because that's when they started fumbling the ball and settling for missed field goals instead of touchdowns

and making penalties whenever they had a big gain and letting
Johnny Unitas pass the ball wherever he wanted, right up to the
end when the Colts came back and tied the game at 17–17 at the
end of regulation.

And it was Lindsay Nelson or Curt Gowdy or some Famous
Announcer Somebody who said the game now went into sudden
death even though he didn't like to call it "sudden death," he
liked to call it "sudden victory," though I guess it just depended
on who you were for because death sure came pretty suddenly
for the Giants; one pass, then bingo, Allen Ameche jumped over
the line and into the end zone and all the Colts fans ran onto the
field and tore down the goalposts and carried all those lousy Colts
off the field on their shoulders. The whole business made me
pretty sick. But Red patted me on the back and chuckled to himself for being right again for the most ridiculous reason possible.
"Yup, wearing yellow," said Red.

I felt I had no choice but to visit the Dialecticians.

I picked up some minimum library skills during the Year of
Two Hundred Books so managed to find a book that taught me
how to use my new camera which I kept over at Willie's, and
now when I went over there I took pictures of all the Dialecticians; Dialecticians snorting morphine, Dialecticians smoking pot,
Dialecticians debating with the gods, Dialecticians shooting horse,
Dialecticians thoughtfully meditating on their veins, on their ar-
teries, on the edges of knives and the barrels of guns. Us Dialecticians were learning by leaps and bounds and I was putting it
all down on my black-and-white film inside my Nikon camera.
Willie had moved on in his meditations to contracting diseases,
moving through several colds, flus, and infections, and just fin-
ishing up with a bout of hepatitis, though just as he suspected,
disease wasn't bringing him anywhere near where he wanted to
get in his experiments.

"They haf merely made me feel ill," said Willie. He'd already
lost that nice yellow tint he'd had around Thanksgiving. He had
a copy of the *Bhagavad-Gita* next to his tool box.

I took his picture as he shot up. "This whole life-death thing is getting too fuzzy," I told him.

"You should consider yourself lucky," said Willie. "For me it is all too much at the life end. Myself, I would prefer some fuzzy."

Willie got me my fix, though I was starting to worry a little bit about addiction.

"Don't worry," said Willie, which was something he'd started to do lately, answer me before I told him what I wanted to say. "Fis is not yet a dangerous experiment for you, besides, I have already planned our unilateral wifdrawal." I set the camera for him so he could take a picture of me. "Lately," said Willie, "during our most recent experiments, we have managed to haf what I would prefer to call a group hallucination. I fink it may have somefing to do wif deaf, though fings have not yet progressed so far, so it is hard to say. But it is interestin, to say the least, that we share the apparition."

By then I wasn't feeling so bad about the Giants' experiment with deaf. Revis and Revco had experimented themselves to sleep and Raymon was playing with Tarot cards. He showed Willie the card for death.

"The Dialecticians are in dissolution," said Willie. "Refis and Refco have lost perseverance, and as you can see, Raymon has become infolved wif the trapping and not the essence."

Raymon flipped the card at Willie but Willie flicked his wrist and snapped the card out of the air. He put it facedown in front of him. "Maybe fis vision will redirect us," said Willie. "Maybe it is Shifa."

Karl gave me a .22 pistol as a Christmas present. I checked the chamber and when I found it was unloaded I flipped it back in and fired a few clicks at the closest wall, click, click, just like the camera.

"Now you see where I keep my guns," Karl said to me. "I lock them up in the house or I carry them in the truck to take target practice. You don't carry a gun unless you can use it, I mean on somebody, and you don't pull it out unless you're going to."

Click. I took his picture.

Bush's Last Christmas

HELEN WAS pretty sure it was going to be Bush's last Christmas because she'd been on a hot streak. Every time she prayed to the Infant, he came through. She prayed for Neda to get better and it happened. Not only that, Neda was losing weight and there wasn't a thing she could do about it. She read more and she ate more but the tide had turned out, Neda was losing weight and becoming more beautiful every day. It made me sick. It made her sick too. Luckily puberty was approaching and opening up new doors for Neda.

Helen teamed up with the Infant and got Kennedy the Democratic nomination and a late-night closest-ever election victory over Nixon. Pope Pius XII opened the letter from Our Lady of Fatima and as of yet nothing bad had happened. Helen prayed that Bush would get out of the hospital for her last Christmas and the problem with Jon would be resolved, and that certainly all came true. Not only that, it looked like Grandma Funster had abandoned ship with Uncle Jon. The only person taking messages in the house now was Andrew and those came mostly from Crow, who must have felt he was under pressure since the Puerto Ricans moved in with two parrots who Andrew offered the same terms he'd given Crow—messages for corn curls.

Now Red was starting to sell toilet paper. Institutions who'd been using other brands for years began to buy Red's paper, probably because, as Red said, it was the best goddamn toilet paper in the world. We used it ourselves and, frankly, it wasn't so hot, but compared to most the stuff you got in public toilets it was okay. Helen had an interview lined up after New Year's for a receptionist job at the little all-girls Catholic college where me and Karl parked his truck when we went to burglarize homes in Glenwood, which gave Helen a look in her eye that I'd never seen. The Infant scored an extra votive candle and a new dress while Helen sent all his other little clothes, underwear and all, to the dry cleaners. She got a little box for him to stand on so now he stood higher than ever over the holy room, staffed, globed, adorned. Helen and the Infant were hitting the job world.

Of course Helen's whole job thing made Red mad with a brand new ambivalence. Red didn't know anybody whose wife worked, certainly not in the neighborhood, though the thought of more money in the house made him feel pretty good, except that it made him look like he couldn't support his family so had to send his wife out to work, even if it did make him kind of proud of her, getting a job at a college. Still, she should be home taking care of the kids. And it must have been that operation she had that robbed her of her womanhood and gave her the idea she should go out and get a job and neglect her family like she was some young unmarried kid up there with all those lecherous professors and Catholics who you couldn't trust as far as you could throw them, even though Red could probably throw them pretty far. Helen was still pretty and she and Red still made noise in the bedroom so everything was functioning as far as I could figure.

Meanwhile I'd been collecting rolls and rolls of film of Willie and the Dialecticians and Karl, and from the little reading I did I knew that I wasn't supposed to take the film out of a Nikon and send it out at the drugstore. The right thing to do was develop the film and print it myself. Willie told me of a place down by the bay on the West Side, which was where the other black ghetto was, the first being in the center of town and reaching up to 23rd

Street, though some people said it went as high as 24th, which those of us living there knew wasn't true, documented by our own presence and upward mobility, a place down by the bay that offered cultural programs and stuff, and Willie said he knew a few friends who went down there after playing basketball where some artists let them draw or paint or do whatever they wanted for free, some kind of art-missionaries bringing art to the poor.

So I took a bus down to the bay and walked around until I saw a big house of amalgamated garrets and bricks and wood and various shingles of multi-colors and a big sign over the porch that said "CULTURE HOUSE—You Don't Have To Be White Or Rich To Dig Art." Of course everybody in charge in there was white, white like the "Dobie Gillis" show poetry readings with Maynard G. Krebs. In fact there was something playing on the hi-fi in the big front room where I stood, something that sounded like *poetry* with funny music behind it, instead of Elvis Presley or Frank Sinatra or whoever the rest of the white race was listening to.

Then I saw something which is difficult to explain because it was like being a brand-new baby and seeing something for the first time, a female something, slender and white with dark shoulder-length hair and blue eyes like marbles and something else, something that turned me for the first time in my life out of thought, out of sequence, out of self, and into an urge, a vague, warm feeling that everything was right there, the whole world was right there and if I took my eyes off it it would be gone, everything would be gone, everything that ever was or ever could be would be gone, and I didn't want that to happen, I didn't want anything to happen, I wanted everything to stop right there and allow me to review my life up to that point so I could discover what was happening, but once again, as the world will have it, I wasn't getting the cooperation of my environs.

I had never been enthralled by a woman before. I knew what they were, I had my mother and Neda and Bush and aunts and sisters of friends. I understood fucking completely, in the abstract, in terms of visuals, logistics, potential smells. I got hard-ons thinking about slips and underwear and nylons, but none of it had ever been unified before, it was satellite stuff, rampant phenomena, now converged, now sensified, grounded, centered.

My photography teacher.

How I wanted help in the darkroom. I needed help taking film out of my camera and help putting it into the developing cannister, around that very difficult metal coil in dark my fingers had to be guided. I needed help getting it out, drying it, making proof sheets, test prints, focusing the enlarger, remembering what chemicals where and how long and what order. It didn't take long enough.

We came out of the darkroom and she ran a magnifying glass over my proof sheets. "Wow," she said. "You took these?"

That voice kept chanting over the hi-fi to piano music saying slap-bap, bop.

"You took these?" Her hair fell over her shoulder as she stooped over the sheets and showed a little hollow space between her shoulder and neck that made me feel like I was holding a baby chick on Easter.

"What kind of music is this?" I said.

"Are you fronting these for somebody?"

I lifted the camera and took her picture, changed the aperture and shutter speed and took another.

She put down the magnifying glass and sheets and went back into the darkroom, making some noise. "You know if your parents have money you're not supposed to use these facilities," she yelled out.

"I live on 24th Street. My dad sells toilet paper. You guys need toilet paper?"

She came out of the darkroom and put on glasses, wire rims. She was shorter than me by several inches. She wore painter's overalls over a T shirt. "Free?" she said.

"No."

"Well," she said, lifting herself onto the table next to my proof sheets, looking at them again. "We pick it up here and there. Public rooms." She shrugged. "You don't sell drugs?"

"What kind of music is this?" I didn't want to tell her anything about myself. I didn't want to tell anybody anything about myself. Something told me that information was evil, a mistake, something that could destroy me.

"It's a Kerouac reading. You heard of him?"

"No."

"Listen," she said. "Come back tomorrow and we'll print some of these up, then I'll teach you a little something about composition."

So I came back the next day and she wanted to know what I knew about geometry, which was nothing, even though I did fine in geometry in school because the Dialecticians handled all that kind of stuff for me. But I was definitely motivated to learn whatever she wanted to teach me for the obvious reason that I wanted old Kara Ruzci, which was her name, Kara Ruzci, to be clearly won over by my receptivity and genius, besides, this was the first time I ever really *knew* anything, that is knew something which other human beings out in the world would consider normal, basic, self-advancement, operational civilized-person stuff.

No school, so I came in the morning and stayed till evening. Sometimes some black kids came by and she loaned them cameras or I had to share the darkroom, but mostly I got her to myself, and she'd look over my shoulder at my prints or show me something about burning things in or dodging things out under the enlarger. Pretty soon she started letting me come with her to lunch. We'd pick up sandwiches from an Italian family deli where everybody argued with each other all the time, then drive to the dock or way out on the West Side to the peninsula where we parked and ate with the engine and heat on and watched the ice fishermen and ice skaters on the silver frozen bay. After that, if we were on the peninsula, sometimes we went over to the lake side and climbed on the ice dunes and looked at Lake Erie, dark blue and everywhere, which she said was just like the oceans, only the waves were different, Lake Erie's waves were choppy and quick and the oceans had long sprawling waves that rolled onto the beaches or bashed against black cliffs with a big roar. Also the oceans didn't freeze. She wanted to see the Great Lakes freeze.

She took her camera everywhere and took pictures of everything. She wanted me to do that too, but I didn't like taking pictures of bushes or trees or buildings, and she didn't either, really. Most of the stuff she showed me was of people; twins and midgets and gnomes and retards, pictures she took in New York.

"Do you ever want to see the oceans?" she'd ask me. "Do you ever want to go to New York?"

I never thought about the oceans or New York.

She wanted to know about my family too, but I never told her much of anything. I told her a little bit about the Dialecticians.

"You do that stuff too?" she said. We were in the car, eating eggplant parmesan sandwiches and steaming up the inside so much we could hardly see the bay.

"Yeah," I said. "I'm a Dialectician. I experiment with deaf."

That made her laugh. "I'd like to try it sometime."

"What."

"Heroin."

I just clammed up. I'd already told her too much, though I was real happy she was interested in all that too because it kept her interested in me, which I wanted a whole lot even though I didn't know what I wanted to do about it. After that she started smoking pot with me before we'd go back to the darkroom for the afternoon.

One night, just before Christmas, the Culture House had their big Christmas party that started in the late afternoon, so Kara left me in the darkroom and told me I should lock up when I left. Everybody else was leaving to smoke dope and drink and wear their berets and listen to Jack Kerouac poetry records, but she said she wouldn't tell anybody she was leaving me in there so I could stay as long as I wanted. It was nice in there, dark, warm, I had a fix, the place had a radio, I figured I'd camp out.

I was having a pretty nice time when I heard somebody at the front door. I turned the radio down, listened to them come in, heard sloppy footsteps dump their way down to the darkroom, then knock.

Kara Ruzci, drunk as a toad.

It was warm as swarm in that darkroom, and our coats made a romantic bed on the floor under the soft safelight, and Smoky Robinson was on the radio, but the whole thing was more or less a disaster. Kara Ruzci was a drunk lump with one need and the only thing I knew about vaginas was their general vicinity, knowledge enough when all the parts of the body are cooperating, or at least the essential part, but mine was inflating and deflating like it had a leak. Just got a little bit of the tip in during the last promise, which immediately intimidated the hell out of me while meanwhile Kara Ruzci is begging "For Christ's sake stick *something* in there!" and I wanted to be creative but settled for my middle finger which pretty much put her to sleep. I was relieved. I'd had the impression that the hardest part was finding somebody who wanted to do it.

Now I thought about going home because I didn't want to face her conscious self of post-failed sex, but she was lying on my coat, and I started loving her and wanting her so much and all I could think was what a failure I'd been and how she'd realize I was a naive little rodent and have to embarrassingly find ways to be busy in the future or worse ignore it all, so I spent the next couple hours alternately pacing around her in the darkroom and lying down next to her and kissing her cool unconscious forehead and lips, though sometimes doing nothing but lie there whimpering, it must have been me, there wasn't anybody else in the room.

Then Kara woke up. She sat up and said, "Bleah."

"Hello."

She dragged her hands over her face and through her hair. "Did we do it?" she said.

"Maybe."

"Maybe?" She thought that was funny.

"I need my coat," I said. I tugged on it and she lifted her butt. She put her own coat on. "I'll give you a ride."

It was getting cold out. It must have been after midnight. Kara warmed up her green Ford Falcon, then drove parallel to the bay and up Celebration Avenue till she got to 24th. I had her let me out on the corner.

"I'll take you all the way," she yawned.

"Then if Red wakes up I'll have to explain it."

"Okay," she said. She touched my shoulder. "Listen, come by tomorrow because after that we're going to close for a while for Christmas." She touched my hair with the tips of her fingers.

"All right," I said.

But I didn't. Instead I spent the day with the Dialecticians who were still having group visions. I didn't take any pictures. I just sat around on the cushions in front of Willie's space heater and collected residue and waited, but that day nothing showed up.

"Now he probably thinks we are silly," said Raymon, who was starting to more and more look like Red's bowling ball. He looked like a muscle factory.

"No," I said.

"There are many factors involved," said Willie, who had begun to occasionally pronounce all his v's. "Myself, I do not fink observation necessitates judgment." He looked over to me. "You are afraid of somefin and it is not deaf."

"No."

"That is only an observation. Sometimes the whole world is infatuated wif deaf. Sometimes love. But mostly deaf. But among human beings there is little admission of love or deaf. There is always somefin in between for them which has little truf. I am only saying that you are having an experiment right now and it is not wif deaf, so it is the other."

It was a big year for Christmas lights. Funster had red, white, and blue lights on his bunker on the porch roof, Big Dick had lights on his truck, Karl put his circus cannon on the porch for the first time and hung lights on that. Dean Danger put out a reindeer with lights. The Puerto Ricans upstairs hung lights from the parrot perches that were empty now because it was too cold for the parrots. Even Red hung lights along the porch railings. The Gorkys and the Stuckas had lights. It was getting pretty hard to think that Christmas wasn't important, and the world or at least our neighborhood was momentarily not infatuated with deaf but the other.

I started thinking about Christmas presents.

But my money'd got pretty low since the Thanksgiving give-away and all that money spent on camera film and lunches with Kara Ruzci. I needed another strike. But Karl wouldn't go for it at all. We'd finally made the papers with the last one, and the article even pointed out that we hit during football games. Well football season was over, that's what I kept thinking, football season was over.

Karl was working on a new cannon, his howitzer. Crow was down in the basement with him and the pig. The place smelled like the men's room at Cleveland Municipal Stadium.

"Don't even think about it," said Karl without looking up from the cannon. "Next year you'll budget yourself a little better."

"Got a corn curl?" said Crow.

"You got the wrong Loop," Karl said to him. He looked up at me. "Your brothers have ruined that bird."

"Funly said he and Jimbo might put a turret on the bomb shelter," I said to Karl.

"No way," said Crow.

"Your brothers have turned him into a gossip," said Karl. "He knows everything in the neighborhood."

Crow hopped onto my shoulder. "Come on, buddy, cough up."

"I didn't ask you, I asked Karl," I said to him.

Crow looked at Karl then me then Karl then me. He flew over and landed on the pig. "Cough up, buddy," he said to the pig.

"Now don't tell Red about that pig," Karl said. "We're going to eat him for New Year's, Easter anyways."

"I won't," I said.

"I was talkin to Crow."

"I need money," I said to Karl. "I can't wait till February."

"Talk to your little nigger friends. Where do they get money for everything else they do?"

I didn't say anything to him.

Karl turned around and stood up. He had wrenches in both hands. He smiled his gapful mouth at me, his face just a blotch of red-gray beard. "Now Jarvis, do I look like God or Santee Claus?" Red had everybody saying San*tee* Claus.

"A little," I said.

Karl chuckled and shook his head. "Now listen to me," he said. "You go up there now, by yourself, and you're going to ruin everything at best and get caught at worst."

"Okay," I said.

Karl turned back to his howitzer. "Okay. Right."

Nobody hardly had presents for anybody that Christmas, which was better than the last Christmas when nobody had any presents for anybody, but it still felt dumb because what the hell else was Christmas for if not for getting presents, though Helen knew it was for church and Jesus and Red knew it was for visiting relatives, which he hated and so insisted upon. Helen was real apologetic about the present vacuum, she hugged everybody a lot and told them how soon she'd have a job and Red would be selling lots of toilet paper and the bills would get paid and next Christmas there'd be money for presents. She'd even thought that maybe this Christmas something would work out through the Infant, but it didn't, though you couldn't expect him to come through for everything every time. She gave me the biggest hug when she said that.

Red bought Helen a little transistor radio and Helen bought Red a flannel shirt which was too small because nobody could ever buy Red anything that wasn't too small, so Red pouted, getting all red in his chair next to the Zenith and saying "goddammit, goddammit, I told you not to buy me clothes."

The rest of us got stuff like oranges and candy bars, some socks. Neda didn't get a Mars Bar and didn't even bitch. Red went to

church with Helen and took Joseph and Andrew with them while
me and Neda stayed home because we went to midnight mass
instead, except we didn't. I went to an all-night donut shop and
spent the money Helen gave me for church on donuts and coffee
with lots of cream and sugar. Neda met me there not too long
later with freshly fallen snow on her long brown hair. She ate
about a half a donut and didn't put cream or sugar in the coffee
I bought her. She had on lipstick and eye makeup and a dress
with nylons and a look like she understood everything in the
world.

"I just can't hate Helen and Red anymore," she said. "I just
can't hate them. I can't muster it up to hate anybody anymore."

We toasted coffee to God's omniscience.

Neda smiled. "Worship is one way to God, understanding another," said Neda, which I accepted because despite all her changes
I knew indisputably she was a genius. In the spring she'd graduate from grade school and enter the ninth grade at one of the
Catholic girls' high schools in town, because already she said she
was tired of dealing with boys.

"Adolescence," said Neda. "Fuck."

And we toasted to Bush's Last Christmas.

So Neda made Christmas breakfast while the others were in
church, ham, smoked Polish sausage, eggs, toast, a lot of food
considering we hardly got any presents, and I went out and
shoveled the walk just for something to do. When Red came back
he bitched about me piling up the snow all in one place instead
of spreading it uniformly along the sidewalk. Then we ate in the
holy room right under the Infant and Helen prayed for everything and everybody in the whole goddamn world, especially Bush
who was so good and so old and looking worse every day, while
the eggs got cold and felt like pressed rubber in my mouth when
I finally got to eat.

Red worked himself into a pretty talkative mood by the time
we all piled into the old Rainbow and headed for Bush's. He
thought the neighborhood was going to pot. "Goddammit, we
got pigs in basements, cannons on porches, machine guns on

roofs, parrots, now Danger bought the bar down on the corner and you know what's going to happen there."

"No," said Helen. "What?"

"Everything, that's what. You're going to have drunks parading up and down the street."

"Worse than now?" said Helen.

"We got that church behind us and a bar on the corner. That's the worst mix in the world, blacks, church, and booze."

"Don't get down on the niggers, Red," said Andrew. Everybody in the family was calling him Red now except me.

"Don't use that word," said Helen.

"He sounds like Funster," said Neda.

"Funster's not as crazy as you think," said Red. "In fact I'm the only goddamn crazy person in this neighborhood because I put up with it all."

"You're the only one putting up with it," said Helen.

"What's that supposed to mean?" said Red. "What's that supposed to mean?"

"If you don't like it, move," said Helen.

"I'm not going to move. I was here first. *They* should move. There's no respect anymore. I can't even park in front of my own goddamn house, I leave for ten minutes somebody takes my parking place."

"We don't own the street," said Neda.

"It's in front of my house!" yelled Red. "I don't park in front of other people's houses."

"Your father's right," said Helen.

That was a big mistake for Helen, publicly agreeing with Red.

"And how come I had to cart Bush up to the hospital to see Jon every day," Red said to Helen.

"She's old," said Helen. "She can't walk like she used to, and she shouldn't have to stand in the cold and snow waiting for buses."

"What about her own family? What about them?"

They were all there at Bush's, including Jon, fresh out of the hospital, for Bush's Last Christmas.

Which happened to be one of the densest collections of shovel-faced people in the world, because Uncle David and his family had shovel-faces and pickax noses just like Uncle Stanley and his family, and seeing them all there together made me happy that Helen failed to inherit or transmit any of those shovel-faced characteristics to us, though it sure looked like Andrew had inherited his potbelly and sunken chest from Stanley and Jon and David. Edju and Elizabeth didn't make it in but Aunt Frances was there with her family of three sons who all looked like pinheads. There were six billion of us sitting in that tiny living room and every once in a while Bush called a shift out to the kitchen for beer-basted ham, potato salad, khuka, and duck's blood soup, family by family mostly, though one of the aunts or uncles occasionally wandered into the kitchen to make adult conversation, pretty boring stuff.

My cousins were creeps. They were all going to be doctors except for cousin Audrey-Mary Pell, Stanley's daughter who was engaged to the stranger in the room, a little nerd with dark hair and black horn-rim glasses and a dark three-piece suit named Archibald Strong, a son of one of the richest landowners in town. He'd got his hand caught in a faucet or something while getting a drink of water and so had to exercise it by learning card tricks and now that he knew them he guessed everybody in the world loved card tricks and so he did card tricks, card tricks, card tricks while cousin Audrey-Mary told and retold the story of his miraculous and tenacious recovery and all the money they sued the faucet company for, and Uncle Stanley and Uncle David laughed at every trick while crossing their legs and drinking Carling Black Label and saying a-yaw, yaw, yaw with their knees bouncing and Joseph and Andrew across from them with knees crossed and bouncing and going a-yaw, yaw, yaw every time Stanley and David did.

Uncle Jon passed warm Pepsi Cola in short fat glasses around the room, though I myself had moved into the echelon of adult drinking, so Bush came in and gave me chocolate and sweet wine along with my beer even though she had whiskey and chocolate with Red who himself had brought a bottle of Cutty Sark scotch for Jon. Jon looked up and down at the bottle a bunch of times and said, "Hmm, well, thank you, Red," all in the Christmas spirit. He must have figured Red wouldn't try to knock him off on Christmas, especially with his ribs still all taped up, and besides it was Red who picked him up from the hospital and brought him back to Bush's. Red was surely an enigma for Jon, being a Protestant and all yet continually behaving like such a Christian. I'm sure he might even have tried to regard Red as some kind of human being if Red converted and stopped trying to kill him.

Finally we got the mess call and got to leave Archie Strong and his card tricks and Stanley and David saying a-yaw, yaw, yaw and go into the kitchen and eat. Jon and Aunt Sylvia did dishes at the sink while Bush carted food to the table and said, "It's so nice to have everybody here for my last Christmas," which made Helen blush and Neda giggle.

"It doesn't matter," said Bush. "It's been the last Christmas for years."

"Don't say that," said Helen.

Bush raised her eyes upward. "It's always the last Christmas. It's always the last day. Every night I go to bed and wonder if I'm going to wake up. When you watch yourself rotting away every day, it doesn't matter. One day you're here, the next you're not." Bush got the whiskey bottle. "Red," she said, "have some more whiskey, I am."

Red had moved out of his first stage of drunk, which was jovial. Stage two was quiet and you could keep him that way if you got real lucky.

Bush poured Helen and me some sweet port and gave Neda, Joseph, and Andrew some warm Pepsi and we all toasted. "To my Last Christmas," said Bush.

Jon and Aunt Sylvia didn't toast. Jon wriggled the ice and scotch in his glass.

"I encountered death many times," said Jon to the refrigerator. "In the war people tried to kill me every day. I was responsible for my men."

"He was a hero," said Bush. "The French gave him the Croix de Guerre after Normandy."

"A torpedo lodged in our hull and it took us a day to dismantle the charge," said Jon. "We waited a day." He looked at Red. "So I know how to wait."

"You're an excellent waiter," said Bush. "You can wait with the best of them."

"It was harder then," said Jon. "I didn't have my messengers. They wouldn't help me during the war because they were anti-Communist." Jon perused the table. "There's a war on now, you know. Between good and evil. Between those who believe in God and those who don't."

Now Uncle Stanley was in the room with Aunt Sylvia. "Did you hear what Khrushchev said?" said Stanley. "He said they'll bury us. I'd like to see them try and bury us."

"They will," said Jon. "Because they know it's a war."

Red started to crack a grimace. He was moving out of stage two. "We just had a war," said Red. "When's everybody going to wise up?" That was pretty smart. Maybe the Year of Two Hundred Books did something for Red.

"The next one will be the last," said Jon.

"Want to bet?" said Red. "I'll tell you one thing. My kids aint going. Nobody in my family's going to get shot up so we can change enemies. I never met a goddamn Russian. What do I know about the Russians. They eat and shit, don't they? They put pants on and go to work, don't they?"

"They're atheists," said Jon.

"We have to pray," said Helen. "We should say the rosary every day to Our Lady of Fatima."

"How I cried the day we gave them Eastern Europe," said Jon. "How I cried. I fought to save Europe and my country gave it away."

"Because of Communists in the government," said Stanley.

Now all the adults were in the kitchen, including Aunt Frances who looked like Helen only pointier and Uncle Matt who made a lot of money in Detroit for Pontiac.

Frances went up and put her arms around Helen. "Now Kennedy's in and we have a Catholic president," she said.

And all the adults but Red said "Hmmm" to that.

Then we did the unusual thing of the year, we went to see Grandpa Whitey Loop and Grandma Emma Loop who lived in Germantown in the house where Red was born, the house that Red helped pay the mortgage on in high school when he worked as a paperboy and pin setter and after high school when he continued to work at the bowling alley as a maintenance man nights and worked in the forge days. Red didn't have any ownership in the house now, in fact Grandpa Whitey and Grandma Emma didn't even own the house anymore but lived in a little extension added on to the back while Uncle Bif who always wore a shirt with a big "7" on it because he was a janitor for the Seven-Up plant, and Aunt Jelly who had one big leg and one little tiny leg because she had polio as a kid, lived in the front of the house with their daughter Nancy who was a little older than me, though not their son Bif-boy who was in the Air Force somewhere in Sacramento, California. I always figured we didn't go over there much because they were Protestant, especially Uncle Bif who once was Catholic but converted to Lutheranism when he married Aunt Jelly, that poor fucker was as doomed as glue. But as I got older it became clear that things were a little more complicated, having to do with how come Uncle Bif and Aunt Jelly were living in the old house and also something about some store on lower Celebration Avenue that Bif and Jelly and Red and Helen once owned in common, though Red and Helen never talked about any of that at all ever, there were just these little intimations here and there that accumulated after years of cohabitating with them.

Uncle Bif always seemed okay to me. He always had plenty of Seven-Up and always said "Ha" about everything and slapped me on the back and talked to me like I was a human being, even when I was a kid, which made it difficult for me when I was younger, having to realize that old Uncle Bif was marked to spend eternity with Hitler as was Aunt Jelly, despite her little tiny leg, for disconverting him.

Then there was Grandma Emma who looked like a little mountain with a pie for a head, apparently she had a relationship with Red like he had with me, she just couldn't love him for no particular reason whatsoever no matter what he did for her, and that's the way Red felt about me. If I gave Red gold he'd resent it. Grandpa Whitey was retired from being a bellhop and elevator boy downtown at the Hotel Lawrence, which is what he did after he got tired of slaving away at the forge, and all he liked to do was sit in a big recliner and watch TV and smoke a cigar and chuckle and repeat what you said to him like, "Hey Grandpa Whitey, did you like running the elevator at the hotel?" and he'd say, "Heh, heh, did I like running the elevator at the hotel?" and blow smoke in your face. He didn't give a shit anymore. Neda said with a little practice he could have become a great psychoanalyst. "Heh, heh, me, a great psychoanalyst," chuckled Grandpa Whitey. He blew smoke at Neda.

Uncle Bif always kidded Helen about our yearly yuletide excursion into Germantown, welcoming her to the land of the infidels and telling her how much he admired her for venturing into Paganville and Aunt Jelly would always say, "Oh Bif, stop that," and Helen always smiled because let's face it, she knew she had heaven by the throat and hell had Bif by the ass. Cousin Nancy always took me upstairs to her room to listen to records and then tried to kiss me, which I stopped because it was like feeding the bears. But I still went up there with her and listened to a couple records, this time Buddy Holly who actually did some pretty sexy jerky-voice sounds that I wished right then I could play for Kara Ruzci and maybe get her off listening to that yakkety-yak Kerouac.

Downstairs there was a tremendous Christmas tree that took up half the room and underneath were Joseph and Andrew staring at the Christmas presents Uncle Bif had given them, toy trucks. They danced with their trucks. They saw how high they could bounce. They gave each other back massages with the wheels.

"So I fucked up," Bif said to me, pulling me aside. "What do I know about kids nowadays?"

What I liked about Bif was he didn't buy me a present and he didn't apologize.

"Come here," said Bif, dragging me into the kitchen. "Hey Red," he called. "Drag that dying old father of yours in here and let's the men have a drink."

So Red and Grandpa Whitey came into the kitchen to have a drink and left Helen and the other kids in the Christmas tree room with Aunt Jelly and Grandma Emma.

You could see Red got his size from Grandma Emma and not Grandpa Whitey who more than anything looked like a giant midget. Things had been a little tense when we first came but now there was warm kitchen drunkenness and the dark Christmas night passing for the last time until another year while Uncle Bif and Grandpa Whitey and me and Red stood in the center of the kitchen and drank shots and beer and Uncle Bif said Grandpa Whitey and Grandma Emma were going to live forever and he'd never be able to turn their shed in the back into a workroom and Grandpa Whitey said, "Heh, heh, live forever," and blew smoke at Uncle Bif while Red gave a funny wince and faintly, far away, came the sound of a small explosion like a small sound comet in the star sound night with a tail of whistle that grew and grew on the faces of Red and Uncle Bif and Grandpa Whitey Loop and Helen now standing frozen at the kitchen door and behind her the pie face of Grandma Emma Loop and the quiet blank face of wondering Aunt Jelly, because it was the whistle of the bomb that would end the world, a whistle that would begin with an explosion and end with an explosion amidst the quiet recognition of Christmas faces, it grew, it became a scream, the house shuddered for a moment, and then came a loud THUD.

Red scratched his head. He didn't know how to be afraid of things. He was cocked toward the yard where he heard the thud and that's where he headed, followed by me and Uncle Bif, but not Grandpa Whitey who stayed in the kitchen and blew smoke and said, "Heh, thud."

Uncle Bif turned on his garage light from the back of the house and Red led us to the center of the yard where a newly formed crater emitted smoke like a barbecue pit at the center of which was a metal ball about the size of a softball which Red retrieved with a spade and brought into the light on the driveway in front of the garage.

"Well what the hell," said Uncle Bif.

"Yeah," said Red.

"Looks like one of them meteors," yelled Aunt Jelly out the back window.

"It aint a meteor," said Red.

Joseph and Andrew were outside now hopping around with Helen yelling at them from the back door to put coats on.

"It's a globe," said Andrew. "It's one of the Infant's globes."

"Globe-globe-globular," said Joseph.

"It aint no globular," said Red.

"It's just some damn coincidence," said Neda, now outside too along with Cousin Nancy.

"You watch your goddamn mouth," said Red.

Inside Grandpa Whitey Loop never moved from the kitchen where he blew cigar smoke into the yellow air and said, "Heh, heh, little Christmas present," and Grandma Emma never moved from the Christmas tree room where she sat with her arms folded in front of her and said, "Well, what is it?" and Aunt Jelly limped around on her little leg and put her palms up and said, "Who knows, who knows," and Red stood in the center of the room and called for his coat and took one more shot from Uncle Bif and asked Uncle Bif for a box so he could take the found object with him. He knew.

Red took the Christmas meteor to Karl.

"Ah, shit," said Karl. We were at the front door and could hear the ruckus going on behind him.

"You already got plenty of that in your basement," said Red.

"That pig's going to the slaughterhouse tomorrow. I guarantee it." He scratched his head and looked at the ball. "Pioneers were here for Christmas dinner. They didn't know it was loaded."

Red pumped his right arm like he had his bowling ball in it. "You know where that landed?"

"Shit," said Karl. "They had the whole goddamn city."

Karl Jr. squeezed his way onto the porch and his eyes looked like pinwheels. "Hey Mr. Red, you found the cannonball."

I could see that confused Red. He actually liked kids. While his right arm pumped muscle and veins like an oil drill his left hand went out and touched Karl Jr. lightly on the head, tousling his brown-red hair.

Beema and Maggie, Karl's twin daughters, were dancing in unison behind Karl. "Red found the *can*nonball. Red found the *can*nonball."

"This isn't a celebration," Red said to Karl.

"Kind of portentous though, wouldn't you say?"

I could see Red was trying to control himself. He had lots of feelings lots of times but not too many different ways of expressing them. And Karl was more nervous than he was trying to act. The few fingers he had were twitching and his tongue was roving through his mouth over his leftover teeth.

"You tell those Pioneers," said Red, "that if my family's ever endangered again, I don't care if it's a cannonball or a misplaced fart, I'll ram my fist down every one of those son-of-a-bitches' throats."

By that time nobody wanted to look at anybody so everybody was looking at me.

"You have a nice Christmas now, Karl," I said.

"Thanks Jarvis. Give our best to Helen and the kids."

Red was already down the steps.

Red wasn't much of a drinker, that is he didn't do it very often, holidays or a few snorts with Bush, but that night he was pretty juiced up and on his way down so we decided to have a beer to smooth it out. The rest of the family went upstairs, except for Helen who decided to stay up with me and Red but fell asleep on the couch in front of the TV. Red sat next to the Zenith and I gave him his beer and took a chair to his right. We had the light on so I couldn't see much out the big front window but the faded blare of streetlights and their reflection sparkling faintly on the snow.

Red and me just sat quiet for a while, watching Helen sleep. It would have been nice to have a conversation, but I knew Red didn't know what to say, when he wasn't mad at me he left me alone. He didn't know anything about me anymore and even if he did he still wouldn't know anything really. That was all gone. We were long past him being able to know anything about me.

Red watched Helen. His eyes rested on her like soft thoughts.

"You didn't tell Karl you'd smash *him*," I said to Red.

"I didn't have to." He sipped his beer and looked at me. "You think your old man is all fists. I know some things about diplomacy. I got to live next to that guy, like it or not."

"And you don't."

"No," said Red. "I don't like a lot of things, but I can't do a goddamn thing about any of them."

"Like what?" I said, because I really would have liked to hear what Red didn't like and more what he felt he couldn't do anything about. I really did.

Red didn't say anything. He sipped his beer. "Look at your mother," he said to me after a while. He looked like he was going to eat her with his eyes. "Just look at her."

There was Helen, still sleeping. She started to snore. Red's chest heaved a couple times. He burped.

"You stopped reading," I said.

Red looked at me for a second, then went back to Helen.

"I thought you were going to read everything in the world."

"Like Neda," Red said softly. It was almost a whisper.

I didn't say anything.

"I just did it to show her," he said, nodding toward Helen.

"I know."

"Everybody thinks I'm so damn stupid." He said that to the air.

He had me there. When Red was smart he always caught me off guard.

"You think it did me some good?" He smiled. He didn't want an answer to that. "It was just a bunch of fucking and fighting. That's all. Just a bunch of sad stories." He finished his beer and let his arm hang down over the side of the chair. He stared at Helen and we were quiet. In the kitchen the refrigerator came on and buzzed so nice and long we didn't notice the sound until it stopped and gave us back the quiet Christmas night.

Which didn't last long. Outside on the street someone began honking a car horn. There was shouting, another horn. Helen stirred. Red frowned. He went to the window as Helen awoke bleary and said, "Red?" and Red said, "Goddammit, where do they think they are?" He went to the front door and watched there for a while but the noise continued so he went out onto the porch and stood on the edge over the steps with his hands on his hips watching as if that would be enough, but it wasn't.

"Go out there with him, Jarvis," said Helen, so I did and Red said, "Get back inside," so I did, but Helen sent me back out. I stood just outside the door. There were three guys on one car and three on the other, sitting on the hoods and yelling and drinking beer and occasionally reaching in the windows and honking the horns. They were having a wonderful time.

"Hey!" yelled Red.

And, "Hey-hey," they yelled back. "Have a beer."

"I don't want a beer," said Red. "It's Christmas night. My family's asleep."

And they yelled, "Well get them up," and "hey-hey," and "what fuck," and various profanities and horn honks, none of which was pleasing Red too much because yelling and swearing in front of his house was tantamount in his mind to doing the same in his living room, generally earning his single request to desist.

"Okay," said Red. "You've had lots of fun and noise, you're waking everybody up, I'm asking you just once to go."

And someone said, "Ask twice, please ask twice," and someone said, "Fuck you old man," and they honked their horns some more and somebody yelled, "Come on down and stop us," feeling pretty much I guess like they were the rough young cowpoke outlaws fresh in from the range and ready to shoot up a town full of churchgoers and clerks and maybe just this one old sheriff who they could probably scare away or make dance.

Red was pounding his fist into his palm now and mumbling, "Somebody's going to get hurt, somebody's going to get hurt," and even though there were six of them and one of him he sure didn't mean himself. Red had trouble envisioning himself as an underdog. He turned to me and said, "Stay here," and went on down. Already I wished he had his bowling ball with him. He was deadly with that bowling ball and being a bit of an unusual sight it tended to take people off balance, like first-strike bowling ball deterrence.

Now Red stood in the street with his fists cocked just below his waist. The six guys faced him, their backs to their cars. They weren't kids, they were in their twenties, two of them taller than Red, though nobody nearly as broad. One thing for certain, things had already quieted down.

"Okay, here I am," said Red. "That's what you wanted. Now leave."

One of the guys reached through the window and laid on the horn. Red grabbed him by the back of the head, yanked him out, and drove his fist about a mile into his chest. That guy was never going to breathe again without training wheels. Two of them stepped toward him but Red put his palm in the air like a traffic cop. They stopped, and Red brought his right fist down on the hood of the first car, a Corvette, sadly fiberglass, it crumpled like a Twinkie wrapper. It must have belonged to the guy on the ground because the other five seemed to be reconnoitering the odds. Red stepped back. He had his fists up.

But that's when the third car came.

There were four in that car and I was already thinking underneath what Red was thinking upfront that nine against two wouldn't be any better than nine against one, so better that just Red get beat up and later he could both feel noble and resent me.

Red put himself between the gang of nine and the Corvette, like maybe he was going to roll it over on them and end it that easy, which I knew he couldn't do. He yelled "Stay on the porch" to me so I went into the vestibule and got the ball bat he kept there for special occasions and started down the steps with the determination of a glowworm. This all took about five seconds and the last thing I saw as I headed in swinging was Red pumping and blasting like a great kerosene fire before those bodies put the lid on him.

That's when the shots came. First the windows of the other car went, then the door, then the windows of the third car, BAM, BAM, it sounded like the creation of the universe. That stopped everything. Karl stood on his front porch and pumped the shotgun again and a shell flew. "Next I go for the tires," he said, "and then you're going to have to stay here."

By now the neighborhood was in the streets. Porch lights went on, and Christmas lights, it looked like a goddamn festival. I stood next to Red in the middle of those defeated creeps with Red breathing like a bull and looking at Karl like he'd interfered.

"You guys are lucky," said Red.

Karl had saved them.

They backed away and picked up the first guy Red had given Christmas bliss to, then got in their cars and drove off. Big Dick Jinx went back in his house, the Puerto Ricans and Dean Danger went back into their flats, on top of Funsters' roof I saw the little red periscope eye blink out. Red brushed the pieces of smashed car to the curb with the inside of his foot. "People always leave their trash," said Red. "They go by here and leave their trash."

Karl picked up the ejected shells from his blaster and waited on his steps until Red was through kicking glass to the curb. When Red looked up their eyes met, then Karl went inside. That's the way it was with them. And that's the way it always was. Nothing explainable.

Inside Helen was curled into a corner of the couch under the comforter she'd started a couple years ago which she was going to give to Bush whenever it got done, though it never seemed to get done and usually barely got started because as soon as Helen started working on it she fell asleep under it, sometime she'd got it at least that big, and even though it was Bush's last Christmas Helen didn't seem in too much of a hurry to finish up. So Helen sat under the comforter, crochet needles asunder, when Red and me came in, Red saying, "Goddammit, goddammit," Helen already fighting sleep.

"If you don't like it here, why don't we move?" drowsed Helen.

"I aint moving," said Red. "In ten years we'll have this place paid off."

"Then there'll be another recession and we'll have to mortgage it again." She had her head back and her eyes closed and said that to the air like it was as true as blue and she didn't care. "Only it won't be worth as much because we'll be living in a slum."

Red's chest heaved. He went to the closet and got his bowling ball, pumping it feverishly at first, and then slowly, slowly working down to a steady intense pumping. His shoulders relaxed, his chest sagged a little, he pumped quietly until the only tight thing in him was that arm. He didn't even bowl anymore. "It's not going to be a slum," said Red. "While I'm here it will never be a slum."

Bobby Hansen,
Bobby Hansen

CHRISTMAS HAD come and gone, in fact poor old Bush's very last Christmas had come and gone, though the more I thought about it the more I realized that just because it was Bush's last Christmas didn't mean she had to die right away, in fact she had up till next Christmas Eve to die and Helen would still be right, but it was the middle of Christmas week now and I still didn't have any money. I thought about getting something for Red even though he wouldn't like it, maybe a pocket warmer or a glass bottle coated with leather, something he couldn't fail to wear. I thought of getting Helen one of those big white Bibles with gold leaf pages that the pope gave his personal imprimatur. Maybe Neda would like some flowers or Mars Bars, and Joseph and Andrew were probably old enough to appreciate something. And Kara Ruzci. I was thinking about Kara Ruzci again and how nice it would be to drop down to the Culture House with some candy or whiskey or a Buddy Holly album, or maybe even a little experiment with deaf.

But the only place I could think of hitting was Bobby Hansen's. We hadn't cased any new places since our last hit and Bobby Hansen's was our first house, and besides that I knew that Bobby Hansen's family would be downtown at Gannon Auditorium watching Bobby play basketball for South High in the local Holiday Basketball Tournament. So I packed my .22, dressed warm for the hike up to Glenwood, and headed for Bobby Hansen's, working it out that I'd go in through the same window and head right for the big dresser downstairs, just get some cash and get out.

The first problem at Bobby Hansen's was the Christmas lights around the windows, so the place was pretty lit up, and then I had to make tracks in the snow from the bushes all the way up to Bobby's parents' bedroom where I de-lighted everything easy enough by unscrewing one of the colored bulbs and all the rest of them went out just like on Red's Christmas tree that he set up every year on Christmas Eve and made everybody help him only nobody was allowed to help except for standing around holding things and getting yelled at for moving or trying to put something on the tree. It was nice seeing those lights go out, it gave me the feeling like my actions had an effect in the world.

The Hansens had storm windows on, I'd forgotten about storm windows, probably because I hated them so much because every year Red made me help him put on the storm windows just like he made everybody help him decorate the Christmas tree, only Red always decided to put the storm windows on too late into the winter so I had to stand around holding things and freezing to death and getting yelled at for it. After I got through the storm window I saw that the Hansens replaced the old window lock with a new one, high up at the top of the window so I'd have to have a ladder to get at it. It looked like I was shot. They probably had a burglar alarm in there anyway.

So I put the piece of storm window back into the pane and screwed the bulb in and put the Christmas lights on. I felt kind of light-headed. Nothing like failure for releasing the burden of responsibility. I felt so good I decided to take a look around the outside of the house, after all, I wasn't going to steal anything, wasn't going to do anything bad, I was free as anybody to walk around anywhere I wanted.

Bobby Hansen's house once was brick but now they had fancy tan aluminum siding on it. Looked like they had a pool table in the basement, a bar, probably a whole rec room down there. Probably everybody in the family owned a pair of skis. They probably belonged to the new family-plan YMCA down by the Glenwood golf course. Helen was never too hot on the YMCA because they were Christian and not Catholic. But she wasn't too hot on the Hansens either even though they *were* Catholic, mostly because they had bucks and Helen, for all her philosophizing about how everything always evened out, wasn't so happy about how things evened out with her being poor and people like the Hansens having money and looking down their noses at her at PTA and not realizing they should be suffering just as much as she was only in different ways. And it didn't look like the Hansens were going to be suffering tonight.

I was in back of the house now, in the yard between the garage and the back vestibule, when I noticed the vestibule door ajar. Pretty unusual, locking up everything right and left and up and down tight and leaving the back door hanging open, but Karl always said that locks were made to keep the honest out, after all, it was the back door.

So I snooped into the back shed amidst the boots and snow shovels, tried the door to the house, which led to the kitchen, and it was open too. The big dining room with the dresser was the next room over, I had hours to burn and only needed minutes. I had a couple Christmas cookies and drank milk right out of the half-gallon container, which I always liked to do anyway because then I didn't have to find or wash a glass, though if Red ever caught me he put me through a wall. There was a ham in the refrigerator about the size of my chest but I couldn't think what I'd do with a ham so I had a beer instead, sat at the kitchen bar where they probably ate breakfast. Place was as clean as new sheets so I put the empty beer can in the trash. Then I went into the dining room and crossed over to the dresser and opened the long top drawer and began rummaging for money, but I only found things like checks and change and birth certificates and old Sears credit cards; looked like those Hansens had learned their lesson. But they left the back door open.

On top the dresser was a big silver tea set and I remembered that Helen always liked to put extra cash inside cups and things like that so I checked inside the teacups and in the teapot and finally under the tray and that's where the money was, not a fortune, just a couple hundred bucks, but at least enough to keep me until Karl declared open season. It was a wonderful world until that light went on.

There was Bobby Hansen himself with his square head and flat black haircut and weightlifter's body with a big cast on his left leg up to the knee. He looked scared and then surprised and then mad, all pretty quick. He had tight lips.

"Well," said Bobby Hansen.

"Well," I said.

"I know you," said Bobby.

"That's too bad." I said it from the bottom of my heart.

"Loop," said Bobby Hansen.

"No," I said. "Is that somebody you know?"

He smirked a little bit.

"I guess you're not at the ball game," I said.

He pointed to his cast. "Don't you read the papers?"

No I didn't read the papers and it was completely irrelevant anyway because there I was and there was Bobby Hansen and it looked like I had done everything wrong. He sure had been quiet with that cast on. And now he was smacking his fist into his palm and running his tongue along his teeth. Bobby Hansen was going to be a hero on top of everything else, even with his cast on, and though I hated him he was much bigger than me and I wasn't much of a fighter. The situation was humiliating. Bobby Hansen started to limp toward me with his fists up so I had to pull out the gun.

I don't know what I'd do if somebody pulled a gun on me but I always figured if I pulled one on somebody else all they'd have to do is walk up and take it away because I couldn't shoot anybody, though I'm not everybody and people sure do shoot people all the time, so Bobby Hansen must have thought that I was one of those people who could, or at least might, because he stopped. You certainly can kill somebody with a gun. It felt good being back in charge, though it only took me a few seconds to realize that all I'd done was tied the score at the end of regulation; I was experimenting with sudden deaf.

At least Bobby Hansen wasn't going to beat me up. I thought of putting the money down and heading out of there, but Bobby knew me and there were all those other unsolved burglaries. Even if I convinced him not to tell on me that would probably only be temporary.

"Well," said Bobby Hansen, trying to be cool in front of my gun.

"Well," I said. I guess he did okay in school but I never did respect him much for his intelligence. He wasn't going to out-think me, after all, I was a Dialectician and I had the gun, though the longer nothing happened the worse things got for me because Bobby Hansen wasn't really the one who had to do anything or even should do anything if he was smart, but Bobby Hansen wasn't smart.

"I think I'll just have to call the police," said Bobby Hansen.

That was dumb. If Bobby Hansen was smart he would have just stood there and then I would have just stood there and then he could have just stood there some more and I'd have just stood there too until somebody else came home, and then faced with the alternative of running or becoming a mass murderer I'd have run and in a few days been in jail and that would have been that. But Bobby was dumb. He wasn't the kind of guy who would back into the title, no, he had to win it himself. He couldn't take the gun away and beat me up. I might shoot him accidentally if he tried that, though I guess he figured I wouldn't shoot him in the back, which wasn't all wrong.

Bobby turned away and started limping to the phone and that's when I remembered what Red did when Helen went to the phone when he didn't want her to, he pulled the thing out of the wall. So Bobby limp-lumped past me and over to the phone in the sitting room, still amazing me with how quiet he could be on that big cast, probably because the rugs were so thick and expensive, and I followed him, though not too close, and when he got to the phone I followed the wire to the wall, waiting till he picked up the receiver, and when he did I gave the cord a good yank.

It didn't come out. Must have been held in by cement or something, but when Bobby saw me yanking on the cord he yelled and jumped toward me. And that's how the gun went off.

Jarvis' Appendix Is in the Wrong Place

WHAT HAPPENED there at Bobby Hansen's house that night had a big effect on me, but that would be a different story. Things pick up and leave off, they go up and don't come down, like Karl's cannonball.

Willie once told me that when you get to the end, that's where you start, though he denies he ever said it, and that's where I am. Willie and the Dialecticians are in Willie's attic. Funly's on his porch roof with Jimbo and Stinky's hooting in the azure sunset somewhere, faster than sound. Kara Ruzci's in her darkroom, ghosting images. I'm ready to start with them.

But I'm not there with Red and Helen yet, nor myself. I'm still working my way to the beginning.

Red and Helen
in the Past Past

RED WAS no dummy and to his mind he'd been an adult for a long time. He never wasted a goddamn second because he didn't have any to waste; he peddled papers in the morning before high school and peddled papers in the evening after high school and after that went down to the Kronenburger Club on German Avenue, where the Germans used to live at the turn of the century before they moved south and made a little Germanburg up on Marvin Avenue where Red was born, and set pins at the bowling alley. He gave all his money to his mother Emma and she gave him back an allowance of two dollars a week. That gave him enough to buy a pad and some charcoal pencils, that gave him enough to buy a used guitar, and that's what he did at night when he went home and on weekends, he made sketches and learned chords, except sometimes on Sunday afternoons after church he went over to the field on Holland Street and played football. The one thing he wanted to do and couldn't because he had to work was play high school football for South High who had the best football team in all Pennsylvania and New York and Ohio and probably the world and even the starters for South High who came over to Holland Street Field on Sundays couldn't bring Red down when he had the ball, and even Lank Ward who ran the ball for South High and last spring high-jumped over six feet (and everybody knew it would be half a century before anybody else did that) kept telling Red to go out for the team, but Red couldn't because if Red didn't work then the Loops would lose their house, and Emma didn't even like him playing on Sundays, but that she gave him, that was the one thing she gave him.

Then it was going to be Red's senior year and Red was thinking. He didn't know much about girls but he knew they liked athletes, and though maybe he was the best athlete in the whole city, nobody knew it, and nobody was going to know it as long as he had to keep working, so Red saved up some more of his two dollars a week and when he had enough he stopped playing football on Sundays and went downtown and took dance lessons; if he couldn't blast the world into submission he'd finesse it into submission, but only on last resort.

So even though it turned out that South's Homecoming game against East was the biggest game of the year, both were undefeated and just the week before while the whole Great Lakes were covered with mud, East High had beaten Niles, Ohio, in Erie Stadium in the rain while South had gone down and roughed up Massillon, Ohio, so everybody knew that South and East were playing for the championship of the world and not just Erie, PA; and even though South beat East 13–12 that fall of 1938 in the greatest football game to ever be played beneath the sky and everybody from South and East would be at the Homecoming dance, including sports writers and college scouts lauding and hanging on all the football players, Red knew that he would go to the dance alone and pick out some beautiful girl and dance her into adulation.

So Red went to the Homecoming dance and walked into the gym immediately recognizing that the band was playing swing and walked over to the side of the floor where it looked like all the undated girls from East High stood and started asking them to dance, and if they didn't want to dance that was okay with him he asked somebody else. Even Lank Ward came up to Red during the night and said, "Christ, Red, you sure can dance," and Red said, "You're goddamn right I can," and Lank said, "But your taste doesn't seem too discriminating," and Red said, "They're girls, aint they? They got dresses on, don't they? I'm dancing, aint I?" or at least one of those, at least he thought one of them, besides, Red wasn't planning on getting married, he was just dancing. And that's when Frances and Helen Pell came to the dance.

And that's when they saw Red with his old shoes and used suit and strawberry hair and cheeks like a lumpy end of a heart with shifty hips and fast legs and shoulders like borrowed from a buffalo, arms willy-nilly and akimbo, dancing, dancing, dancing, he wasn't even dancing with anybody, and now getting as much awe-at-a-distance attention as any of the football players. And it was Helen's *first dance*. She had on her first pair of high heels that she'd been practicing dancing in since the moment she got her ankles stiff enough to walk in them and the dress that Frances wore last year to Homecoming and weddings and other events until it got too much for one girl to continue to wear, and nylons and makeup that she bought herself with the money that Bush let her keep as allowance from what she made working nights with Bush in the Strong Building downtown, scrubbing floors, the rest of which Bush sent to Stanley and Jon and David so they could have money to finish their grad degrees in chemistry and law and business, and when Frances left her saying there was always somebody drunk at these dances and she was going to stand around by the football players Helen stayed and watched Red. She watched Red dance. And Red never stopped dancing, not the whole night, and girl after girl he asked to dance and some did and some didn't and he danced with some and sometimes he danced by himself, and that was the night destined for them to meet each other, that was the night, but they didn't. Every time Red saw Helen he thought she was the most beautiful girl in the world and so he couldn't ask her to dance. And even when it was lady's choice Helen didn't ask Red to dance because he was the center of attention and asking everybody to dance but her and besides she just didn't dance that good, but their eyes met, their eyes met for the first time that night and nothing happened.

They met downtown at the Arthur Murray Dance Studio above the drugstore kitty-corner from Perry Square because after that night Helen decided she needed to know how to dance. And that's when Helen walked up to Red and for the first time said, "When's the dance?" and Red said, "Now," because he didn't know what else to say, he didn't even understand the question. After that day neither one of them ever went back to the Arthur Murray Dance Studio, they spent their extra time and money on each other, which didn't make anybody in either of their families very happy.

One Saturday after Red finished an afternoon shift at the Kronenburger Club setting pins and had an evening to himself so planned on walking down to the East Side with his guitar to play "The Yellow Rose of Texas" and "When Jimmy Rogers Said Goodbye," which he'd just learned that week for Helen, he went home and went in the kitchen and put his percent of the week's earnings on the kitchen table behind his mother, Emma Loop, and headed through the living room to the stairway to get his guitar so he could practice one more time when Emma said, "Hey, come back here."

So Red went back into the kitchen. Emma was at the counter cutting stew meat with her cleaver.

"I'm going to need a little more money this week," said Emma Loop.

And Red said, "As long as I'm going out with a Catholic Pole you're going to need more money."

And Emma Loop said, "That's right," and kept on cutting meat. Emma Loop didn't talk much but she communicated.

Red emptied his pockets and put the rest of his money on the table. There were lots of things he didn't know much about, he admitted that to himself, but he'd done plenty of work and contributed plenty to the house and did lousy in school because he never had time to do anything but work, and he didn't go out for any sports because he worked, but now he was eighteen and liked a girl and liked her on his own time and that was his business goddammit, he was old enough to do lots of things including work at the forge, which is where he figured he was going to end up, or even fight in a war, which he figured might happen too the way things were going in Europe, besides, he had some money saved in his bedroom.

So he went and got his guitar and got ready to leave but when he went back into the kitchen Emma Loop said, "Your father needs help with the storm windows." She cupped red meat in her hands and threw it in a pot, though with a little more force than usual, Red noticing an extra flick in the flip of her wrists which caused hot oil to jump up and sprinkle her forearms. That made her mad. At Red.

"I'll help him tomorrow," said Red.

Emma Loop went back to the cleaver even though there wasn't any more meat. "Do you know what those Catholics will put you through?" she said to Red.

"Helen's different."

"It's not up to her. You think she doesn't have a family? You think she doesn't believe in her church?"

Red wasn't thinking about family or church, he was thinking about "The Yellow Rose of Texas" sparkling like the dew. He didn't come to America on a boat like Emma and never had to rely on other Germans for anything or fend off Irish, Italian, or Polish Catholics throwing beer bottles and blaming him for World War I, he'd had his singular war with the Polish and Rutter Rutkowski, whom he'd belted with a ball bat years ago, still spoke with a slur because of it. Now he knew a girl who was so smart she skipped a grade in school, and so nice that she even went down to the Kronenburger Club and watched him set pins till he got off, and so pretty that all the other workers there kidded him constantly and envied him completely; and she told him he should send his drawings to magazines and newspapers and art schools, or become a country singer or even sing at weddings around town, or go to college in business and get a job with a big company, and when he sang her songs he saw the flush come to the dark skin of her cheeks and saw her dark green eyes fill with the hint of tears, and when he touched her she trembled and clutched his chest and made him feel like the world had been made for him to protect it, and that there was something deep inside him so peaceful and calm, some deep thing that only Helen Pell brought out, something he had never felt before and never wanted to feel with anyone else again; and family and church had nothing to do with any of that. Besides, Whitey didn't need help with the storm windows. Whitey'd just make him stand around and hold things.

"I'll help him tomorrow," said Red.

"Don't leave," said Emma Loop. She shook the cleaver at him.

"I'll help tomorrow," said Red and turned for the door.

Emma Loop threw the cleaver.

And it stuck in the woodwork of the back door. Red watched the quiver of the blade and the quiver of Emma's lips.

"Don't come back," she said. "Don't you dare come back."

Bush was always a little distant with Red, though while he waited for Helen she served him sweet wine and chocolate which he ate at first because he didn't want to turn down anything though by now he'd started to like it. "As far as I'm concerned," she told him, "I tell the neighbors you're a good Irish kid." This was the first time he got the joke which on top of everything else he felt made him feel stupid and if there was one thing Red didn't like to feel it was stupid.

Bush looked at Red real close and got out the whiskey for the first time. "You don't look so good tonight," she said. She liked having Red come around because Stanley was dead and all the boys were in college, and even if Red was Lutheran he was clean and he was big and he treated Helen good and he wasn't so dumb as his size and muscles made him look, and if he wasn't going to be a doctor, well, so what, he was Helen's first boyfriend, nothing lasts, and he didn't have relatives in Germany so his people weren't killing her people, besides, they were killing Jews anyways, not Catholics.

Red liked whiskey and chocolate even better than wine and chocolate. "I'm fine," he told Bush.

"So your family's going to make trouble for you about seeing a Polack. So whoever told you things were going to be easy."

"Nobody," said Red. But nobody ever told him they wouldn't either.

Red took Helen to the New York Lunch on lower Celebration where on Saturday nights you could get six hamburgers for a quarter so Red got a dozen and Helen ate one of them. Red wasn't used to giving up one of his hamburgers, but he liked Helen a lot and preferred when she let him know right out that she might eat one or two instead of saying she'd just have a bite or two of his because it was important for his stomach to know just how much it was going to get. After eating he felt better and told Helen that Emma threw her meat cleaver at him, and when Helen asked why he told her for the same reason Bush told the neighbors he was Irish.

"Bush doesn't tell the neighbors you're Irish," said Helen.

"Right," said Red. He wondered about french fries but didn't think he could afford them.

"Don't worry," said Helen. "It doesn't matter. We love each other."

Red said, "Right." He looked at Helen. "She told me to never come back."

"Right," said Helen. "Then who's going to help her pay the mortgage."

This Helen was no dummy. Red took her back to her house and played "When Jimmy Rogers Said Goodbye" and "The Yellow Rose of Texas." He sang everything he knew and then he sang it all over again. Afterwards they sat on the couch in the living room and Helen put her head on his chest and Red felt that deep, deep calm and knew he could go back home and Emma wouldn't say anything, he'd just wake up in the morning and have his coffee and oatmeal and hold storm windows for Whitey.

That spring Helen helped Red gather up the best of his drawings and submit them in support of his application for a job as an art consultant for the *Erie Times News,* which Red didn't think too much of as an idea, not that he didn't think he was one of the best artists around, he just didn't think being good at something had much to do with anything, and the proof or disproof of that just gave him less faith in the human race, which was just the obverse of Helen who despite her unerring faith in God and various sociocosmic principles of balance could always see what kind of fruit was in the jello, even if she didn't eat the stuff, which in later years is what she did, served it up and didn't eat it. So while Red applied for the art consultant position Helen took the local Catholic Women's Scholarship Exam which funded two scholarships to each of the three Catholic women's colleges in town, even though the scholarships usually went to girls who went to the Catholic prep schools affiliated with the colleges; but Helen had skipped a grade and ranked second in her graduating class and she certainly was Catholic. She won the sixth scholarship.

Meanwhile Red got an interview with the *Times* and Helen told him "See" and Red said "Ah" and went to the interview in his only coat and tie and sat in front of an old bald guy with glasses who wore a suit worse than Red's who said, "Boy, you're talented," and "Cripes, these are good," and Red was thinking how all that was true and feeling happy about how Helen helped him pick out all the right drawings, mostly ones of women with their legs showing, and feeling more and more confident, and he said, "You're goddamn right they are," and the bald guy scratched the side of his head where he had some unkempt hair and said, "But you're so young," and Red said, "What's wrong with that?"

"How come I didn't notice you were so young?" said the art editor.

"I don't know," said Red who already figured he was on the

outs. "Seems to me you should have known that before you dragged me in here."

Then the old art editor scratched his head and left the office and came back after a while and said, "You have to have a college education to apply for this position. We assumed you did, even though you don't have it written down here."

"Along with my age," said Red.

"Listen," said the art editor. "You're very talented and we'd like to have you but you're too young and you don't have an education. But we have a training agreement with the Cleveland School of Art and Design. We'll send you there for two years, then you can come back here and finish your education locally while working for us. When you graduate you can be an art editor."

"How am I going to live in Cleveland for two years?" said Red.

"You won't," said his mother, Emma Loop, who had biceps like lamp legs. "Who's going to support you while you're running around painting pictures?"

"I'll get a job in Cleveland."

"Who's going to support us?" Red's older sister Matilda had already married and moved a block away and his younger sister Jelly had a little tiny leg.

Red used the argument Helen gave him. "In four years I won't have a job, I'll have a career."

"Four years," said Emma. "I could be dead in four years. That editor will be dead in four years. In four years you could make a lot of money at the forge. Whitey got you a job. What's the newspaper offering you, a promise in four years."

Whitey was by the radio, having a cigar.

"You got me a job at the forge," said Red.

And Whitey nodded. He looked like he would have been big if he wasn't little.

"I want to be an artist." Red really hadn't thought about being an artist, he just wanted a nice job at the newspaper, but the dramatics of the situation made him put things in concise terms.

"An artist," said Whitey Loop. He blew smoke much like he

did when he got older and became Grandpa Whitey Loop, only now he was younger and the depression was just ending and he still gave a shit about a few things. "What's an artist?" Whitey Loop was certainly enigmatic, in a simple kind of way.

Red didn't have an answer to that so he went back to Helen who had told Bush that she got the scholarship to Villa Maria College and Bush said, "Great, can you trade it for money, maybe some ducks? It won't get you a husband, it's an all-girls school."

"I love Red," said Helen.

"Good, maybe he'll pay for your books."

"I'll get my own job, I'll pay you rent. If I want to go, I'll go."

"Pffft," said Bush. "What do I got? Big muscles? A barbed wire fence?"

So Red told Helen he wasn't going to go to Cleveland, he'd graduate and go to work at the forge. He was the only son and owed it to Whitey and Emma to help pay the mortgage on the house that he'd lived in all his life.

"Oh," said Helen. "That's a lot of crap." Because she thought that underneath Red's big giant self of muscle lurked something very scared. But Helen decided not to take the scholarship to Villa Maria College because they already had problems enough being Polish-Catholic and German-Lutheran and she didn't want to make it worse by being more educated, besides back then Helen thought she could change Red, she thought she could reach down in and find whatever he was scared of and get him to wring its neck and then go out and do *something* with at least the same determination he had when he was mad or when he *didn't* want to do something, if he could just want something that bad he could do anything, and she'd give up anything to see him do it. Helen would do anything for Red except die, she drew the line at death, and good thing.

So Red went to work at the Erie Forge, which like every other factory in town was producing more and more and hiring more and more, and Helen kept scrubbing floors with Bush until Frances got married and moved to Detroit with her husband and then she got Frances' job as a teller at the First National Bank, though that didn't last long because she was so smart and competent that soon she was a loan secretary and then an administrative secretary to a vice-president. England gave Czechoslovakia to Germany and Germany took Poland and Austria in the bargain, which made Helen's brother Jon so upset he cried, missed a law exam at the University of Pennsylvania, and dropped out for a term. He came home and did nothing so it was a good thing Helen had such a good job.

Unlike Helen, Red didn't get promotions at the forge, because he was a big strong guy who worked too hard. The foreman told him to slow down and the people he worked with told him to slow down, but when Red slowed down he got bored, so they started giving him the worst jobs like shoveling the hot steel fragments from the pits, but still Red worked like a bastard and finally the Union Dirty Man came up to Red and told him he better slow down.

"What should I do?" Red asked Whitey.

"What should you do?" said Whitey. "Slow down." Back then he still gave a shit about a few things and sometimes offered advice. He would have been gigantic like Red if he wasn't so little. "You got something at stake?" said Whitey Loop.

"What should I do?" Red asked Bush over whiskey and chocolate while waiting for Helen.

"What should you do?" said Bush. "Slow down." She looked older every day. Her hair had gone white and she had to have an operation to pull most her teeth. "This isn't Russia. You don't get medals for working hard or having babies."

"Everybody thinks I should slow down," Red told Helen.

"Then slow down," said Helen. She had on a black dress with a white frilled collar that swooped down to the top of her breasts.

"I can't slow down," said Red.

"Then don't slow down."

Red looked at Helen.

"Give me a sip of your milk shake," said Helen.

Boy, Red hated that. If people wanted milk shake they should get their own milk shake. He'd help them finish it if they couldn't finish it. "I'll have to fight the Union Dirty Man," said Red.

"Can you beat him up?"

"Maybe," said Red.

On Monday Red didn't slow down and when the whistle blew for lunch Whitey told him he was in trouble. In fact Whitey seemed a little nervous and didn't finish his limburger and onion on rye so Red had to eat it for him so it wouldn't stink up his lunch box by sitting in it all day, because Whitey wouldn't throw it away because since the depression Whitey didn't throw anything away, not even trash, you had to take it out of his hands and throw it away for him or eat it.

That's when the Union Dirty Man came up to Whitey and Red and said to Red, "Hey, how come you stole my lunch."

Red and Whitey were sitting on a bench with a big furnace in back of them warming their backs and an open garage door in front of them blowing in cold and snow. Men gathered around now at a distance just far enough to get close in case something started happening, except for three guys who stood behind the Union Dirty Man with tools, wrenches and hammers and such, not that they'd use them, if they did they'd kill somebody, it just added important intimidation and gave the impression that they weren't standing around idle looking for a fight.

"He didn't steal your lunch," Whitey told the Union Dirty Man. "He stole mine."

"No," said Red to Whitey. "I did steal his lunch."

"You did?" said the Union Dirty Man.

Red stood up. The Union Dirty Man was supposed to be the toughest fighter in the whole world. Red had seen him fight before and though he wasn't that big, neither as tall nor broad as Red, he fought like a bull, burrowing in close and punching like an engine.

"When did you steal my lunch?" said the Union Dirty Man.

"When do you want me to steal it?" said Red.

Now the Union Dirty Man realized he was being made fun of,

which didn't happen too often unless the other guy was six-eight and from out of town. He dipped his forehead a couple times like a little rhinoceros. All the men started gathering around now because it looked for sure like something was going to happen and Whitey Loop patted Red on the back and said, "Heh, when do you want me to steal it, you're nuts," and sauntered toward his machine where he cut steel sheets.

The Union Dirty Man began walking toward Red, that was his old trick, everybody was always on the defensive with the Union Dirty Man so he always walked right up to everybody and bounced his chest on them a few times and then if you didn't back down it was too late because he was already in close where he wanted to be. As he came closer Red saw the scars on his fists and on his forearms and his forehead, he saw the veins in his arms, and his chest that looked like a bag of softballs. Somebody yelled at Red, "This'll slow you down for a while," and that's when Red remembered something he hadn't felt since he massacred Rutter Rutkowski; there wasn't any up or down or right or wrong, there wasn't any justice, there wasn't anything, nothing at all but the advance of the Union Dirty Man. Red measured and launched. There was a crunch. The Union Dirty Man stopped and wiped blood from a crushed nose, his eyes dark and inanimate. He lowered his head left, then right, and that's when Red knew he could hit him in the face all day and he'd end up with sore fists. The Union Dirty Man smiled and stepped forward and Red put his fist between his stomach and his chest. There was a loud CRACK and the Union Dirty Man coughed up blood.

The crowd of men was quiet. Over the din of machines Red heard the snow falling behind him. That's when he knew there was nothing he could do to stop the Union Dirty Man except kill him because the Union Dirty Man had even less motivation to fight than Red, he would just fight until somebody killed him and nobody could do that so eventually he won.

Red backed up. The Union Dirty Man charged. Red stepped aside and threw him into the side of the furnace where his head buried into his shoulders with a loud dong. Quickly Red grabbed him by the ankles and lifted him into the air. He thought momentarily of swinging him into a wall but instead put him upside down in a big metal garbage can.

Red stepped back as the Union Dirty Man kicked his way out of the garbage can and Red realized that the fight was just starting. He wasn't fighting a human being, he was fighting a dinosaur. Even if he cut off the Union Dirty Man's head he would keep fighting. The Union Dirty Man came at Red and Red hit him and then he came at Red again and again and again until he became the first and only man to get under Red's guard, though even when he did he didn't have enough left to really hurt Red, he just pounded away at Red's chest and stomach with his head and fists until Red finally hammered him to the ground. Then he got up again. That's the way it went and that's the way it would have gone forever if the back-to-work whistle didn't blow. That's when the Union Dirty Man pointed at Red and said, "I'll see you tomorrow," and walked away. Then the next day at lunch the Union Dirty Man came back with his nostrils steaming and his eyes like dead snakes and began his assault. And he did it the next day and the next day and every day the same way until Red, tired of spending every lunch hour fighting instead of eating his and Whitey's lunch, actually did start to slow down a little at work, though his efforts didn't go in vain either because the union notified the foremen that if ever they fell behind schedule they could call the office for help and the Union Dirty Man would get Red and let him help whoever was behind schedule with all the fever pitch he wanted.

Red started to hate the Union Dirty Man. It got so he didn't even bring a lunch to work. He just left the pits or wherever he was when the lunch whistle went off and walked over to the big steel door in front of the furnace and watched the snow or the rain or the nothing until the Union Dirty Man, looking none the worse from whatever apparent beating Red had given him the day before, came and resumed the fight. Nobody even came around to watch anymore. Workers ate their lunches to the comforting thudding and bonging of Red and the Union Dirty Man working out the eternal problems of labor. Winter changed to spring and Red began to hear the sprouting of tiny green shoots in the trees instead of the falling snow. The feel of the Union Dirty Man's chest and face beneath his fists became as familiar as underwear, and still, every day, the Union Dirty Man came.

Meanwhile, at the bank, Helen was having a crisis of nerve. Every day her boss, the vice president in charge of loans, Frederick Carpenter Strong, brought her flowers or candy or took her to lunch where he slurped cocktails and talked about the burden of being brought up rich, having the way paved for him everywhere, the difficulty of finding meaning in a life like that, of finding challenges. He thought Helen was beautiful and half his age and he was right about both. He thought Helen was the smartest girl to ever work in the bank, and very sweet too, the way she listened intently to him and wasn't intimidated about his being rich, sometimes even joked with him about it, asking him if he wanted to trade problems or jobs sometimes or, when he complained about his wife, saying that she would like to have a wife, that she would like to have four children but not have to give birth, and one time she even told him that her family had been rich once too, but they gave it up because of all the problems, they gave all their money and land to some other rich people who had been rich for years and could deal with the problems more adroitly. That was a good one, he liked that, so he pulled out a small cigar and told her, "Well, the Strong survive," which was a very famous line among the Strongs, kind of an in-family joke that they were usually smart enough to keep to themselves and not unleash upon classes lower than them who couldn't appreciate the densely packed logic of the phrase. Yes she was very sweet and smart, even if a little naive, which was sometimes good because one afternoon when he got too drunk, kissing her, telling her his wife was frigid, she simply didn't understand and so later there was nothing to explain.

But Helen knew a couple things, in fact Helen knew a lot of things, though not in the same way I knew them, or Red knew them, or maybe anybody knew them, actually the miracle of Helen wasn't even so much what she knew as what she subdued, for whatever reason, though as Kara Ruzci might say, that's been the premise of female existence for all history, subduction or self-destruction, though I don't know what to do with that, I can't even take it to the zoo, not even in a story like this, but Helen knew some things, after all, she spent plenty of time in her backyard as a kid with the rabbits and the chickens, besides, Bush was her mother, though she'd stopped talking about some things with Bush, one of them being Frederick Carpenter Strong who was, as Helen's boss, putting her in the precarious position of absolute subjection and delicate rejection if she planned on keeping her job, and the creep probably owned a piece of what was once her family's land.

What Helen decided was that she could solve the problem by getting married. Certainly and conveniently she was in love with Red, and though she hated to put it in those cold terms, sometimes things had to be seen in clear cold terms, in fact, like Bush, Helen thought that was the only way things should be seen, warm and murky was a nice way to feel but no way to see, besides, there was a war in Europe and war in Asia, people were fighting everywhere, including at the forge where Red could use a little break from fighting the Union Dirty Man every day, with a wedding and a honeymoon he could relax, maybe put a little weight back on, even think about looking for a new job, though Helen doubted Red would look for a different job, that would look too much like running, especially since holding his own like he was he got to work as hard as he wanted all over the plant.

Also Helen really was serious about having four kids, though just like she'd told Frederick Carpenter Strong she'd have preferred being on the giving end of the process, so she figured she may as well get started and get it over with. Red's family looked healthy, except for his sister Jelly with that tiny little leg, but she got that from polio, and Red was certainly healthy, maybe they'd even have a kid with blond hair and blue eyes. If they got married Red wouldn't have to pay the mortgage on Whitey and Emma's house anymore and Helen wouldn't have to give Bush money for her brothers' educations.

So Red and Helen got married on the last day of August, the day before Red's birthday, a pretty small wedding because nobody was too happy about it, in the rectory of Holy Rosary, the Polish cathedral, because Red wasn't allowed to get married inside a Catholic church because he was a "goddamn heathen" as Helen affectionately put it, in later years not so affectionately. Red had to sign a piece of paper agreeing that all his children would be brought up Catholic and he'd never talk to them about Luther and when he got back from his honeymoon he'd start catechism classes twice a month that would teach him all about the Catholic church, about how it really wasn't much different from Lutheranism at all except more true, and of course Red signed the paper because religion was religion to him.

So they had a little wedding in the rectory, the same rectory that Bush cleaned every day when she came over from Europe, though afterwards they had a reception at the Kronenburger Club, which was the compromise, and even though none of Helen's brothers came back to town for the wedding, being caught up in summer school and various jobs to support themselves, most of Red's family came to the reception with Emma Loop running herd on all them, not letting them drink too much and telling them this was not a situation to celebrate, good thing Protestantism allowed divorce. Helen's sister Frances came in from Detroit pregnant with her first pinhead and told Helen she could always take the train to Detroit to get away, and Edju came and told Red, "Oooh so Red so big oooh," and Helen, "Oooh so so," and gave them fifty bucks from inside the band of his big-brimmed hat that dipped over one eye, and even the Union Dirty Man came and gave Red and Helen a pair of heart-shaped picture frames to stick their wedding portraits in and told Red, "I'll see you when you get back."

It was a warm sunny Saturday and Red and Helen drove to Niagara Falls, Canada, because Edju told them in so many words that the falls were much prettier on the Canadian side and the Canadians took much better care of their facilities with brick walls and mowed lawns and huge flower gardens and even a big clock at the center of a wishing moat, all made out of flowers, in fact Edju thought the Canadians did everything better than the Americans, the Canadians were civilized people like the Europeans, and Bush, who served as translator for this whole business, said, "How come you don't live in Canada?" and Edju rubbed his thumb against the inside of his index and middle fingers and pursed his lips and Bush looked at Helen and Red and said, "Money."

So Red and Helen borrowed Whitey's black Ford and drove to Canada. They liked the falls and they didn't like the falls. Whenever Red got near the falls he got quiet. He didn't want to talk. He couldn't think. They made him nervous. And the falls made Helen think about babies. So the honeymoon was a disaster of sorts. Red said he couldn't fuck in a heart-shaped bed, though he didn't put it in those words, though Helen hadn't quite worked out what she expected and in general was happy anyway. So I didn't get made till later. I could make up a day but it strikes me as too personal or at least too soon.

Still, it happened sometime during the time Red and Helen made their down payment on the house in the middle of 24th Street between German and Celebration Avenues and Helen went back to work at First National Bank where Frederick Carpenter Strong wasn't bothered at all about the fact that she just got married and Red went back to work at the forge where he spent his lunches battling the Union Dirty Man who now brought Red a red rose every day before they battered the walls of the forge with their flesh, some kind of symbol I guess, that Red brought home to Helen pretty much because he didn't know what else to do with it, though he didn't tell her where he got it from so Helen put it in a narrow white vase in front of Red and Helen's wedding portraits in their heart-shaped frames. Sometime during that time it happened, though I guess I like to think it occurred on the morning in December when Red had the night shift at the forge and President Roosevelt came on the radio and said that the Japs just bombed Pearl Harbor.

Helen cried that morning.

Helen cried and at first she didn't even know why she was crying though later even before Red got home it hit her, it hit her real plain. Outside, the whistles from the factories hooed under the purple Lake Erie sky and the bells from the churches began giant bongings like a great funeral drone and all over the city people put on their coats and went out and stood on their porches and didn't say a word except for a few older women who lost their husbands in the last one and stared at the women like Helen who were going to learn a lot about waiting in the next years, and a few young men were in the streets shouting, ready for war, but most everybody else wasn't ready.

Helen wasn't ready. Things had just begun. And Red came home that morning as tight as a fist and as easily opened and put his arms around Helen and felt her grab down in deeper for that sweet calm than she'd ever grabbed before, and though thinking about the end of all things was thinking in smaller ways than it is now, they were thinking about the end of all things and that's what I like to think I came out of.

At work the next day the Union Dirty Man gave Red a white rose instead of a red one and said, "Well," and Red said, "You can't wait around to be drafted," and the Union Dirty Man lowered his head like a little rhinoceros and Red said, "The Marines."

"The Marines," said the Union Dirty Man, and Red didn't say anything to him but that day the Union Dirty Man fought harder than he'd ever fought before, throwing himself at Red like something launched, Red's fists meeting him like mallets on beef, their bodies wronging the steel walls like funeral bells until the whistle for the end of lunch. The next day they enlisted in the Marines.

But the Union Dirty Man flunked the physical. Flat feet.

Red spent a couple days with Helen making arrangements for her to follow him out to San Diego where a couple days later, after a bus ride in the opposite direction to Buffalo, he got sent

on a train with a whole trainful of Marine recruits from everywhere east of Erie and north of Philadelphia, not nearly as rough-
looking a bunch as the guys who worked in the forge. The train
went back through Erie, though it didn't stop, and Red watched
the train station go by and looked over the bridge down onto
State Street, the main street, and then over the bridge onto Celebration Avenue and thought about what Helen was doing. He
pictured her in the bank office where he'd never seen her and
thought about her sleeping alone that night next to that giant
place where he wasn't and deep inside where he always got that
warm calm feeling he instead felt some kind of naked ache and
that's the only time he came close to crying during the war. After
that, whenever he felt himself getting sad he thought about eating lunch and all the future lunches waiting for him, one lunch
for each day, an endless string of lunches with a whole hour to
eat them. Lunch sure did make Red happy. And it became his
favorite meal, which is saying a lot because meals were one of
Red's favorite things in the world. Later on Red always made a
big deal about supper, wanting everybody there sitting around
the table like a wonderful family, that was important to him, but
supper made him nervous because he had to watch all the food
get divvied up and even if Helen served him first and gave him
the biggest portion he could never be sure there'd be anything
left after everybody else got theirs. And there was just something
wrong about breakfast, there wasn't enough time to look forward
to it, he had to get up and eat and go to work and he couldn't
wake up early just to think about it, that seemed a waste of time,
besides he'd wake up too hungry. But lunch Red could look forward to all morning, which he did with tremendous relish now
that he didn't have to fight the Union Dirty Man, and what he
got was all his and he didn't have to share it and usually lunch
came in the form of sandwiches which he could eat with his hands
in as few bites as he wished. This is the kind of stuff Red thought
about on the train. He didn't think about Cleveland or Chicago
or the plains of Nebraska and Kansas or the mountains of Colo-
rado and New Mexico or even the desert of Arizona with its big

cactuses, they all just went by like so many water buffalos because Red was thinking about lunch and that kept him pretty good until he saw the palm trees in Southern California and it hit him that down there he probably wouldn't be able to find good braunschweiger and probably no liverwurst. Still, thinking about lunch got Red through a lot of tough times, including being woken up at three in the morning by his platoon sergeant to run five miles in his underwear with his gun and then stand outside with his gun over his head until dawn. Except for that, Red didn't mind training camp because he was already in shape, and by the time training camp was done Helen came to San Diego and Red got to see her every night unless he had guard duty.

Everything was pretty good for a while. Helen got a job with the Bank of America in San Diego as secretary to the president and almost every night had some of Red's new friends over for dinner who always brought and left their own place settings so soon Helen had a whole bunch of knives and forks and spoons as heavy as lead with USMC written on the handles. Red signed up for the Marine paratroopers and led his platoon in almost everything, including target shooting where he won a dozen medals because he went through the whole shooting final without missing a target except for two at five hundred yards because the sighting device on his rifle was out of whack. So of course they reassigned him to the carpentry unit where he won all kinds of favors from officers by building them box lockers for their gear, vanities for their wives, and rocking horses for their kids. They got him off mess duty and taught him to pitch horseshoes and play handball. They didn't have bowling alleys.

Red got to be close friends with the chaplain, Captain Chaplain, who was Lutheran and a great handball player. After breakfast Red got to play handball and after lunch, which was Red's favorite part of the day, even if all he got to eat was shit on a shingle, he got to pitch horseshoes. Red could hit ringers almost every time, especially if the guy in front of him hit ringers, that made Red really want to hit ringers. He loved putting ringers on top of ringers and he loved cheating at handball by hitting the ball with his fist. If Red hit a handball just right he could splatter it, but then of course he lost the point.

Chaplain Captain Chaplain loved to hang around the Officers' Club, where all the Marine and Navy officers spent their time relaxing from the pressures of war in San Diego, and make wagers on horseshoe pitching matches and handball games. And because he was thin and lanky with glasses and losing his hair the officers were happy to accept his challenges and then Chaplain Captain Chaplain sent for Red and the two of them mashed the officers and won lots of money. Then Red would give them a rocking horse and that's how Red got to be a corporal, though of course everybody on the base learned pretty quick that Red and Chaplain Captain Chaplain could clean up anybody in the world in horseshoes or handball so the Officers' Club saved them especially for visiting dignitaries, admirals and generals and movie stars and such, who got to spend an extra lot of time going around playing horseshoes and handball as a break from all their war strategy and who usually thought nobody in the world could beat them, especially not a chaplain and a corporal. If there was anything Red liked nearly as much as lunch while he was in the Marines it was putting ringers on top of admirals' and generals' ringers, he liked it even better than smashing handballs with his fist because there was always the chance that somebody might return a fisted handball, even if by total luck, but there wasn't anything anybody could do when you put a ringer on top of their ringer.

Red was having a good time in the Marines.

But in other places in the world things weren't going so good for everybody, in particular, as far as the Marines were concerned, the Pacific Ocean, and in fact every week more and more new Marine recruits came to San Diego and more and more of the Marines who'd been there a while got sent into the Pacific to battle Japs for tiny islands that nobody used to care about. More and more often Helen and Red had Chaplain Captain Chaplain over for dinner in the little bungalow Helen rented off base and Chaplain Captain Chaplain worked hard at keeping his horseshoe and handball partner from being sent out, though he never told Helen and Red, once even managing to get Red transferred to a different unit the day before Red's old unit got their packing papers.

"What the hell," said Red at supper that night.

"What the hell what?" said Helen.

"You're lucky you're Lutheran," said Chaplain Captain Chaplain. He smiled pleasantly at Helen to let her know it was a joke.

This whole business was making Red pretty confused. Pearl Harbor was still pretty abstract for him, he'd never even seen a real Jap, though he figured he wouldn't have any trouble recognizing them once he got out there fighting. He liked being in San Diego during the winter with the warm weather and the palm trees and Helen, but sometimes he felt like he wasn't doing his duty, after all, there was fighting to be done and if there was anybody in the whole world who could fight it was him, besides he'd already proven he could shoot a nickel off a goddamn moving airplane, so why did he end up not getting sent out, though he was real happy he didn't.

"You just don't know," said Chaplain Captain Chaplain. "Sometimes things work out in strange ways and we just have to do our part the best we can. Think about what you do for all the noncoms here by beating all the officers in horseshoes and handball. A lot of people are dying in the fighting now. Maybe you'd be wasted."

"I'd waste them," said Red.

Helen threw a pot holder at him.

Red's old unit got entirely rubbed out.

"Well," said Chaplain Captain Chaplain that night at dinner.

"Maybe I'd have been the difference," said Red.

"It seems so inconceivable that they could beat us at anything," said Helen.

"They have the advantage for now," said the chaplain. "But we're in the right. Things will change, and we'll win."

"What will we win?" said Helen. "I could use a new washer and a dryer."

Chaplain Captain Chaplain eyed Helen. He had to keep reminding himself to stop underestimating her. She shot directly at nothing and always hit.

Red got up and clutched at the air. Any dope who knew the future could see he needed a bowling ball.

"I don't want to be here when he gets sent out," Helen said, but she didn't say it to anybody or anything, she said it to the air.

Chaplain Captain Chaplain touched her hand while Red went out the door.

"You can't keep him here," Helen said to him.

Chaplain Captain Chaplain looked away. He'd learned how to keep his mouth shut but he hadn't learned how to look like he didn't have anything to say. He got better by the end of the war. What he didn't get better at was realizing what people really meant when they said stuff, like Helen probably would never have said "You can't keep him here" if she meant it, if she didn't want Chaplain Captain Chaplain to figure out some way to keep Red in San Diego. If he'd have done his end she'd have worried about the rest, for Red, better mad than dead, and Red felt the same way, though he could never admit it, that's why he got so upset that he didn't get sent out.

"What," said Helen.

The chaplain shook his head. Sometimes he forgot he was young and so did everybody else, because he always ended up in charge of social situations. "Who told you?" he said to Helen.

"I'm the person around here who knows this stuff," said Helen, as if it wasn't obvious to everybody in the camp except Chaplain Captain Chaplain and Red that the chaplain was working at keeping his handball and horseshoe partner in camp. She also knew Red wasn't going to die in the Pacific, but of course a lot of people thought they knew stuff like that and often it turned out they were wrong.

Red came back in the house shaking his head.

"I'm leaving next week," Helen told him. "I'm not going to wake up here some morning and find out you're gone."

"Shit," said Red.

"You have the chaplain," said Helen.

So Helen gave her notice at the bank where they were very disappointed and wanted to know why she just didn't settle in San Diego where it was warm all year and she had a good job and she could be right there waiting at the port when Red got back. But at that time those were the exact reasons why Helen was leaving. Red traded guard duties and got the chaplain to cover for him right and left so he could sneak off base and spend the last days as well as nights with Helen who he suddenly realized once again was the most important person in his life and even handball and horseshoes, even lunch, couldn't replace her.

They made arrangements for Helen to take the train back East and for Red to trade guard duty so he could meet her at the station to say goodbye. Helen spent the week packing her things and shipping all the stuff she'd accumulated in San Diego, like the Marine Corps silverware that was heavy as lead and had USMC written on every handle. At night Red clung to her like a bear and woke up constantly to kiss her cheek and neck. He dreamt he had a fist fight with President Roosevelt who got out of his wheelchair and tried to kick him. Red caught his leg, flipped it, and the president fell on his back. Roosevelt was very embarrassed. He blushed.

In the mornings Red woke up so hard his hips fucked the air. His penis tried to get in anything Helen had available and often succeeded. Afterwards he felt embarrassed like President Roosevelt. But Helen loved to feel herself underneath him, feel him holding back from crushing her with his strength. She knew when Red came back things would be different.

So the night before Helen left they stayed up all night, not intentionally, actually they went to bed early so Red could get up early and sneak back into camp to pretend he'd been there all night, but Red couldn't sleep so Helen didn't sleep so they stayed awake in the bed saying nothing, just looking at each other quietly and touching each other's hair and lips and sometimes Red kissed Helen on the forehead or on the eyelids while the future and doom and hope made everything electric.

That morning after they kissed at the door Helen went back to bed and slept into the late afternoon.

When she awoke the day had gone cold. A storm blew in, and as she took the cab to the train station where she was to meet Red two hours before the train departed it began to rain. Helen waited outside the station at first, but the wind and rain blew at her like a wall so after Red was fifteen minutes late she went inside. After another fifteen minutes she checked outside again, but after the third time she found a corner in one of the huge wooden railroad benches and sat watching the clock, watching the door, and feeling for the first time in her life that something was missing. She got up and took her bags over to the reservation desk.

"Can I help you?" asked the clerk.

"Soon," said Helen. It was midnight and in a half hour she'd have to board the train. She knew now there would be no goodbye. At 12:40 they paged her and she stuck out her hand for the phone.

"I'm not supposed to do this," said Chaplain Captain Chaplain. "No one is supposed to know."

"I know," said Helen, and hung up the phone. Something was wrong now. Finally, at last, something was wrong.

Midway was okay. Red got there after the invasion and spent all his time moving up behind the front lines every time the Marines changed headquarters so he could make whatever needed to be made out of wood for the officers at the front-line camps, which was nothing, the Marines didn't need carpenters, but the War Department said they had to have them. Red was trained in trench reinforcement which had been very valuable in Europe twenty-five years previous. Red spent a lot of time at his tent on constant red alert waiting to make all the stuff that would never have to be made. Sometimes he got off duty and was allowed to retire to his tent and not be on red alert.

Sometimes Red thought about Japs. When thinking about Helen made him sad and thinking about lunch made him too hungry, he thought about the Japs. The only Japs he'd seen were little tiny dead ones all blown up which reminded him of insects, though of course insects, like anything else, could be deadly, but these little Japs weren't so deadly as they were dead. Everybody said they stunk but Red had a good nose and he didn't think they stunk, they smelled kind of good, like something in the autumn air in Indian summer, warm and dry and sweet like the afterburn of whiskey, certainly better than dead Marines and better than a lot of the live ones.

Red tried to think of reasons to kill Japs. Not that he needed a special reason to kill Japs, right about then he felt like he could kill anything, just point him, but Japs just seemed like any other thing out there, a lot of bangs and booms, Marines came back dead, Japs went back dead, letters got sent home, your kid's dead, your husband's dead.

He wrote Helen about it and she wrote back, "Don't worry about it, just don't end up dead. You start thinking about things and end up frustrated and mad. Then you'll go out and try to kill somebody and that's how you end up dead."

Dead, thought Red, what was dead.

"I can't tell you," wrote back Chaplain Captain Chaplain. "We are ants now. God only watches. Great powers battle. You are small. Pray."

Helen was right. That just made Red want to fight.

"Who's going to be in reserve if the reserves fight?" said his commanding officer, Captain Wilforce.

"I don't care," said Red.

"I could use a nice wooden locker if you find the time," said the captain.

Red played horseshoes.

Then one night he dreamt that Helen came to visit him in the tent. She told him she was going to have a baby and then she had the baby and gave it to Red and it looked like a Japanese Guy Lombardo. "Merry New Year," it said to Red.

"It's *Happy* New Year's," said Red. He got up to open the doors and let out all the old bad air and let in all the new good air. Helen grew a lump on her head that smiled at Red. "Forget it," it said.

That dream gave Red the shivers. He could hardly get back to sleep. The next day Red got a letter from Helen and she told him she was several months pregnant.

"Whatever you do," wrote Red, "if it's a boy, don't call him Jarvis."

A few days later the Marines made another advance and most the personnel got moved forward except for troop assistance personnel like Red. A new bunch of troops were to follow and move the camp forward the next day, but they didn't get in that night, they got delayed in some behind-the-lines skirmishes that nobody thought anything about, Japs were always holing up in caves like snakes and coming out behind the lines and then you just had to wipe them out and get on with things. They figured there'd still be Japs on that island fighting after the U.S. had made it a state.

Of course all that reasoning was completely wrong and that night was the night the Japs chose to hit the camp in force. Red got woken up by a dream of wind and bees. The bees started to fart, that's what did it, loud stinking farts that smelled like burning canvas. Red left his tent with only his helmet and gun, just like in boot camp when the sergeant woke him up and made him dance in the moonlight in his underwear. Already the Marines were abandoning everything else in the camp to form a defense line around the supply area, which wasn't so good because that was starting with the last resort.

There was a lot of noise, but mostly noise, Red still hadn't seen a Jap, just some tents in flames, the ground going up here and there like blown-out tires, lots of Marines heading for the defense line in their underwear. It wasn't so scary as it could have been because nobody could really see the thousands of Japanese surrounding the camp, and the Zeros hadn't hit yet, and the Marines didn't know that the air cover they were calling for wasn't going to be there. They didn't know this was going to turn into the famous Midway Underwear Massacre because of all the Marines that were going to be left dead without their boots on, in fact without anything on but their underwear. In fact if anybody in charge would have done one smart thing then maybe the Marines would have made an organized retreat, lost the camp, and saved a lot of lives. In fact that's what Red suggested when he ran into his commanding officer, Captain Wilforce, who had previously explained to Red the importance of reserve units and asked him to build a foot locker. Captain Wilforce was the highest-ranking officer left in the camp.

"We got to get out of here," said Red. "What's closer, our front line or our backup?"

"We're waiting for air support," said Wilforce. Red noticed he had a square head.

That's when the first line of Zeros made their pass. Marines went up like popcorn.

"We got to consolidate and move," said Red. "We're sitting ducks."

Captain Wilforce would have grabbed Red by the shirt if Red had any clothes on. "Get behind that bunker and *defend*, Corporal," said Captain Wilforce.

The Zeros hit again and the Japanese were within mortar range. Red still couldn't see any Japs but in the trees he saw the stars of fire from their guns.

"By the way," said Captain Wilforce, "did you ever finish that locker?"

Just then the Zeros made another pass and Captain Wilforce got divested of selfhood. Now Red didn't have to make the locker, though he had a hunch he wouldn't have had to anyway the way things were going. The Zeros were coming in so close you could see the teeth of the pilots and now for the first time he saw the Japs moving in from tree to tree, getting ready to breach the gap between the jungle and the camp. He knew that if the Marines stayed in the supply depot they'd all be dead. He tried to think of Helen and the new baby she was carrying but it didn't make any sense. Instead he kept thinking of Guy Lombardo.

Red figured it would be senseless to try to break through to the front lines because the Japs were probably engaging the front lines too if they were attacking behind them. So whatever was behind the Marines couldn't be as much as there was in front so probably the best thing to do was head out the side and circle around to the support troops to reorganize an offensive.

So Red went down the line and said, "Come on, we're getting the hell out of here," or "Come on, we're going to attack," whichever he thought was appropriate to the look on the face, and not saying anything about orders but letting everybody assume he was in charge, and about half the men came and about half stayed. When the Japanese made their move to hit the bunker Red led an attack out the side right into the Japanese, which partially protected them from the surrounding fire because there they were in the middle of all the Japs, some of whom Red finally got to see face to face, they mostly looked scared or mad, and not really very yellow, actually more brown. Everybody was on top of everybody right in the middle of the little gap between the jungle and the camp so soon there wasn't even much gunfire, mostly bayonet fighting that might have reminded Red of the *Iliad* had it happened after the Year of Two Hundred Books and you could picture the Greeks fighting with bayonets in their underwear. In fact the whole business got pretty impersonal. Red would have killed anything that got between him and the woods, and he did. A lot of bodies got left in that little gap though most of them weren't Japanese.

Still some of the Marines got through and headed for the back lines, but when they got out of the Japanese pursuit Red stopped them and told them that as many as wanted could keep going but he thought it was their obligation to go back and harass the Japanese and keep them in disarray until the Marines could organize a counteroffensive. Of course nobody had any clothes on so nobody knew anybody's rank and everybody figured Red was in charge, which was okay with Red, he always figured he should have been in charge anyway. So only a couple guys went back, because somebody had to, and the rest followed Red back toward the camp where already the Zeros had stopped strafing and there was only the occasional spatter of automatic gunfire cleaning up the last few Marines who stayed to die in their underwear.

But Red felt pretty good. He wasn't dead. And he'd been figuring pretty much from the start that he'd end up dead. Now he'd just as well have it happen facing the Japs as running from them. And he didn't want his sweat to dry. So they headed back. Red figured he'd spread the Marines out in as thin a line as possible along the edge of the jungle and start pecking away at the Japs in the camp. It would keep them from moving the supplies or attacking the front lines from behind. They wouldn't think that the few Marines who got away would turn around and attack, so they'd have to figure they were under attack from the vanguard of the counteroffensive. Also they'd be caught on the defensive in a stable position, something they weren't used to. It all made pretty good sense to Red.

Some Japanese had already started cleanup on the outskirts of the jungle and they had to take care of them. That was the first time he got to think about any of it. Red got the feeling like it was already over, that he was already dead, and he sat behind a bush watching the brown men with strange voices forage through the foliage looking for someone like him to kill, and he held them in sight sometimes for minutes at a time, following them, thinking about the medals he got for hitting targets in boot camp in San Diego, thinking about them as targets and thinking that there was no future, there was no future, and knowing that all there was between the Japanese soldier and the end was the pressure of his finger, and then the lightning.

And when they came to the edge of the jungle again and began firing on the Japanese and heard the cry of their voices as they hit the barriers that he had lain behind not too long ago in the night, he thought of his dream of bees, and a little story he had to read in grade school about a colony of ants invading a beehive, about the ants dying on the legs of the bees, but slowly,

slowly overcoming them, pulling the legs off the bees and advancing methodically toward the queen. So when the Japanese did what he did not expect and left the barriers of the depot and advanced in swarms toward the edge of the jungle, he did what they did not expect and moved into the opening. He could see bullets. He felt explosions in his flesh. He advanced like an engine, his blood pouring like hot black oil. And then he was among them and they beat on him like a thousand Union Dirty Men, clinging to his arms and legs, tearing at him with the blades of their bayonets until there was nothing left of anything, nothing at all, he could barely hear the roar of gunfire behind him or the drone of planes in the sky.

They didn't find Red's body in the field between the jungle and the camp. It was all in pieces. It was somewhere else. It was gone. It was just one of those things. He walked into the camp two days after the Marines took it back. All that was left of his underwear was the waistband and the new officers were plenty suspicious except that Red's dog tags seemed to confirm things and he sure didn't look Japanese, besides the survivors of the escape and counterattack said, yeah, that was the guy who led them and that was the guy they saw go down amidst a thousand Japs in the middle of the field.

But he aint even an officer.

Well what the fuck, everybody was in their underwear. Or dead. Or both.

"Where you been the last couple days?" asked the interrogating captain.

"I don't know," said Red. True as Asian flu.

Some kind of Sacred Mystery. Worse, the more the accounts of everything gathered it looked like Red deserved a medal.

"What do you think we should do with you?" asked the captain.

"Put me in the front lines," said Red.

They shipped him to Hawaii. The Marines never admitted that the famous Midway Underwear Massacre ever happened. They didn't lose any ground, just a few thousand casualties, many without uniforms or dog tags, so by the time they gradually gathered all the information, day by day, it looked like it took a long time for all those guys to die.

Back in Hawaii they made Red a sergeant and put him to work in the mess hall as an assistant janitor where it didn't take Red long to see how inefficient everything was, besides the fact that all the assistants worked like bastards while the guys in charge stood around and watched, so Red, just off his recent bout of being in charge without really being in charge, went up to the head janitor and said, listen, you know how good I work, why not put me in charge and then you can go off and do what you want and come back at the end of the day and I'll report to you and if you don't like the job I'm doing well you can just take over again, and then Red went around to the head cook and the head supply man and the head distribution man and told them all the same thing and soon Red was running everything. Then he put the most reliable people in charge and told them they'd stay in charge as long as they followed his rules and worked along with the people under them, if they did that he'd cut them all in on half of all the supplies they saved under his system, which he did, and the Marines were happy and gave all the credit to the officers who were supposed to be in charge of Red, so they were happy, and the guys who Red appointed were happy because they got some responsibility and made out like bandits, and the meals at the mess hall improved, especially lunch, and that made everybody happy, and Red, who checked up on each separate department twice a week for a couple hours, had a four-hour day, four-day week, so he was pretty happy too, in fact he spent almost all his time playing handball and horseshoes with Chaplain Captain Chaplain who got transferred to Hawaii too. There was even a bowling alley. Not only that, the weather was great.

Helen couldn't get her job back at the bank when she returned to Erie. Frederick Carpenter Strong wasn't too bothered that she'd left the bank, and he wasn't too bothered by her wedding ring, though a little more bothered by hers than he was his own, and it certainly would be convenient having her husband in the Pacific, possibly even dead, but that little baby in her belly bothered him. Couldn't have a pregnant woman, not even on the job. That's the way it was at the factories too.

Red sent his paycheck back and Helen got temporary work with a typing pool and before Helen got too pregnant to work Bush helped her rent the house and move to the special war housing for wives of soldiers built way over on the east edge of the city by the railroad tracks that ran from the docks downtown to the big factories like Hammermill and GE. Everything had a certain gray hue to it over there. The air had a different kind of stink every time the wind changed. In the morning, every day, Helen got up and washed the grime off the windowpanes and sills outside her little apartment at the end of the long row of small one-story apartments, each separated from the other by a thin wall. Out the front window and out the back were other long rows of originally white apartment barracks, now already gray, and across the sidewalk at the end of each row, more. And in every apartment was some woman, usually young, often pregnant, some a little older with kids already, some woman whose husband was in the Army or the Marines or the Navy or the Air Force and who might not come back.

Bush came over almost every afternoon. Stanley had his PhD in chemistry and was working down in D.C. for the War Department and David enlisted in the Army and was now in England. Of course Frances was in Detroit so it looked like Bush wasn't going to have any family around until Helen came back from San Diego and Jon flunked his physical when he tried to get in the Navy. Then he flunked the bar exams. Now Jon was home feeling very nervous about life. He took a lot of walks and thought about jobs.

Bush worked nights cleaning offices. She took a nap in the morning when she got back, then made breakfast for her and Jon before going out to feed the chickens, ducks, and rabbits and clean the pens. Then she walked down to Pell's Grocery that a Polish Jew owned now and bought food for the day. She and Jon had lunch, she got supper started, then walked over to Helen's, three miles up Ash Street and over 18th until it crossed a long bridge over the train yards and became Buffalo Road, and walked and walked until she got to Helen's barracks where she and Helen drank Mogen David in Seven-Up and played double solitaire.

"You shouldn't walk so far by yourself," Helen told Bush.

"You shouldn't be pregnant without a man around," said Bush. Bush was unbeatable at solitaire.

At home Jon was worried. He was losing weight in his hands. "I can't keep them in my pockets," he told Bush. "They float right up."

"You shouldn't do everything for him," Helen told Bush.

"If he did anything I'd never stop hearing about it," said Bush. Her hair was silver-blond and she looked like she was once the most beautiful girl in the bakery shop. She was almost sixty.

Sometimes Helen's neighbor, Dee Delco from right across the way, came over to play three-handed pinochle. Dee was brought up in Birmingham, Alabama, but moved to Erie with her husband Derk after the depression because they heard the mills were paying better in the North, which was wrong, but they didn't have money to get back. Derk was in the Marines too only Dee didn't know where because his work was so secret, she figured he was probably in Japan under the Sun Emperor's bed waiting for the right moment. "He's real good around beds," said Dee. Her view of the Civil War was that it was imminent. She was a month or so more pregnant than Helen.

Dee thought herself a pretty good cardplayer but Bush sure beat her butt in three-handed pinochle.

"How do you win every time?" asked Dee.

"Think about it," said Bush.

Which Dee did, but all she could figure was that Bush was a better cheat, which was hard to believe.

Helen didn't care who won at pinochle and she didn't cheat. Pinochle kept her mind off her belly and Red. You could only clean the grime off the windows so many times, only spend so much time shopping, having coffee at Dee's, only so much time sleeping, only so much time preparing breakfast, lunch, and supper, eating it, and cleaning up. At night she was studying Latin so she could understand mass and she was thinking about taking up French. So the afternoons were something extra to do. Only she didn't like Bush doing all that walking by herself. Next winter it would be dark in the late afternoons when she had to walk home.

"You could fall. If you broke a hip or pelvis at your age you might never recover," said Helen.

"That's right, honey," said Dee.

"That's what I need," said Bush. "To live longer."

"Don't you want to see all your grandchildren?" said Dee.

"I look like somebody who needs to see more," said Bush. She trumped and took the hand. "When they put a man on the moon, do you think they're going to give me any credit?"

"Honey," said Dee. "We're not talkin about the man in the moon."

"I'll tell you something," said Bush. "This three-handed game is for the birds."

Jon threw his hands up over the whole thing.

"Listen," said Bush. "Where do you walk in the afternoons?"

"That's a question," said Jon. His years of law school were showing.

Bush got up on a chair and dropped a coat down over Jon's hands. "You're walking with me to Helen's."

Bush held on to one hand while they walked and the other one floated. When they got to Helen's they tied his elbows to the back of a kitchen chair and when his hands floated up it put them in perfect position to hold the cards. He and Bush became pinochle partners and played like they knew each other's every card and every thought.

"Honey, we got to get a system like theirs," Dee said to Helen over morning coffee.

"Then we wouldn't have an excuse for losing," said Helen.

Dee poured more coffee. Her nails matched her red hair. "Helen dear, you got a bad attitude."

"Red has hair like yours," said Helen, "only a little lighter."

"Dyed, sugar."

"Think of the pressure they have on them, having to win all the time," said Helen.

That's when Dee gave Helen a lecture about winning, which didn't do much good as far as I can see. Helen had a more transcendental view of the world back then and always. Still Dee told Helen that winning was the only thing outside revenge that had any value in the world. Why she remembered times when Derk had to go to work every day and fight for his life just to keep his job. Derk would fight anybody. Derk was a good man. She never knew a time when she was within two feet of Derk that he didn't get the most amazing hard-ons since the invention of hard-ons, and she'd seen plenty of hard-ons as a girl.

Derk didn't even get in the Marines the first time he tried. He tried to join the Marines to fight for his country and they wouldn't let him because he had flat feet, so Derk started standing on billiard balls, got to the point he could pick them up and toss them to himself with his arches, turned his feet into something like a ballet dancer's and got into the Marines. With Helen's attitude she could never get in the Marines.

"That's true," said Helen.

After a week of pinochle Jon got a job in the mornings teaching kindergarten. He liked it okay. He spent most the time taking the clothes off and then putting the clothes back on the kids, he made them take lots of naps and when they were awake they played lots of games that involved keeping their hands in the air. The only problem was that Jon was starting to feel light-footed in his left foot. He fought all morning to keep it down, but when he got to Helen's in the afternoon he let it hang out from the table and float. Sometimes he stood for hours on one leg looking like a logo for Indiana University or a symbol of the planet Uranus, maybe Neptune.

Dee got a letter from the Marines that said she might not hear from Derk for a real long time. His mission was Top Secret, she told Helen. Helen found out Red had been sent to Hawaii. Dee made Helen learn a system of signals to tell each other what was in each other's hands and what to play next but it didn't work, Bush and Jon still always won.

"I don't understand," said Dee.

"Pffft," said Bush. "Till now you've been playing children."

Dee was getting bigger every day and she and Helen talked about naming their babies and of course Dee wanted a boy and was going to name him Derk for his Derk Dad the Top Secret Marine, and of course Helen didn't care what she had, especially since she was planning on having several more, though at times she kind of hoped it might be a girl, just to take all the firstborn-son-of-returning-Marine pressure off the little tyke, so didn't think she'd name the baby Jarvis no matter what, besides Red was sending her letters saying "Whatever you do, don't name him Jarvis."

Well Derk Delco Jr. got just about due, then he got due, then he got overdue. Helen sat up nights with Dee Delco drinking Mogen David in Seven-Up and sitting by the telephone for Dee so she could call the hospital at any moment while Derk Delco Jr. decided to come out, then decided to stay in, then decided to come out, then decided not to come out. It hurt like hell. He was a goddamn little sadist cracker just like his dad and apparently just as secretive.

Dee talked and talked about Derk Delco. He was a dandy. He might look like a baby rhinoceros but he was a cute baby rhinoceros, he always brought Dee candy or roses or sometimes just a single rose, and sometimes out of nowhere, even after a hard day at work when his hands and face looked like they'd been banging on meteors, he'd come home all dressed up in a suit and tie and take Dee out to a movie and dinner, and when they'd get back home Derk Delco made Dee feel like she was the only woman in the world who had anything between her legs and afterwards he'd stick his nose up under her breast and that's how they'd sleep. He didn't make her get up with him in the morning to make his breakfast or lunch, though of course sometimes she did because if she didn't he wouldn't make himself lunch, often he didn't have time for lunch, and on weekends sometimes he got up early and washed the car and then brought her breakfast in bed, usually accompanied by a Bloody Mary or André champagne, and then they'd go out for a drive in the country in that shiny washed and waxed car, or go down to the dock and watch the boats; that was the only thing Erie, Pennsylvania had over Birmingham, watching boats.

It was easier in the afternoons because Bush and Jon were there, and it felt good to have Bush, who went five for seven with babies, all at home, there even if all she did was play pinochle and act unworried. Jon said he was now getting light-footed in his right foot too and between games he often got up to stand with his arms and left foot high in the air, then leapt off his right foot and let it rise as he floated momentarily above the floor before lightly touching down again on his right big toe.

"Honey, you sure are agile," said Dee.

"He played a little basketball at Duquesne," said Bush.

"Not true," said Jon. "They only wanted me because I was tall and thought my ignorance of the game would make me more coachable." He leapt again, raised his right foot, floated, floated, boy he could float, then touched down again. "I've tried to teach the men, but none of them can do it. And they're very light men."

"What are you talking about, honey?" said Dee.

"On the ship," said Jon. "Where do you think I spend my mornings and nights?" He leapt, pirouetting slowly like a suspended panda bear.

"That boy should reproduce," Dee whispered to Helen. "All that ability."

Bush dealt and Helen tied Jon into position. That morning she'd got a letter from Red that made reference to some big deal on Midway, but then a big part of the letter was censored, which is what happened every time Red wrote about Midway, the only part that didn't get censored was when he wrote about not remembering what happened to him for several days. Helen thought about Derk Delco's Top Secret mission and suddenly felt like she knew something, she just didn't have any knowledge on the other end of it.

Dee squirmed in her chair. She looked like a dead pear. Maybe a little paler. "Sure wish Derk Jr. would make up his mind," said Dee. "That little honey wants to stay undercover like his old man."

Helen put her hand on Dee's. "He's got to come out sometime," she said.

"Or not," said Bush.

Jon pushed away from the table and for a moment he floated above the floor, chair and all. "Sorry about that," said Jon when he came back down. He and Bush both had straights in spades.

That night Derk Delco Jr. made his decision.

He wasn't coming out.

"Feels like a piece of lead in there," said Dee.

Helen called the hospital and a cab. She figured they'd be opening Dee up to get Derk Delco Jr. out now. She held Dee's hand in the cab as Dee rested her head on Helen's shoulder. When Dee looked up her face looked inverted.

So when they got to the hospital they took Dee away and made Helen wait in the waiting room where she looked at all the old magazines about how to make up your face and what rotten people the Germans and Japanese were, degenerate races for centuries. A man came in who smoked a lot of cigarettes and looked at her big belly and finally said, "What are *you* waiting for?" and Helen said, "The same thing everybody is waiting for," and the man said, "What's that?" which Helen took as a rhetorical question seeing as she'd already given him a rhetorical answer. Every once in a while a nurse came out and smiled nicely at Helen and told her everything was going fine. Then she'd tell the man with the cigarette that everything was going fine and then she'd leave.

"I guess everything is going fine," said the man with the cigarette.

"Or not," said Helen. She was feeling kind of negative. She looked at the guy with the cigarette and wondered why he wasn't off fighting somewhere. Seemed like the appropriate thing now-

adays. She thought of her barracks apartment and her coffee in
the morning with Dee and about cleaning the grime off her windowpanes and windowsills and saying hello to all the women
who walked by with children in them or around them. She felt
the movement in her belly.

Those apartment barracks were okay. The women all helped
each other out with plumbing or carpentry or painting or whatever and when they were done they talked about their children
or said how much they missed their husbands, lots of nice things
to say about them in general but, except for Dee who really seemed
to think that Derk Delco Sr. was the sweetest thing since chocolate rhinoceroses, when the women got specific they were usually bitching. It was hard to figure out what they really missed.
That's what Helen was feeling. She felt like she missed Red but
she couldn't figure out what she missed. Maybe sleeping with
him, except that he took up the whole bed and sweated.

The nurse came out and told Helen she could see Dee soon
and told the man with the cigarette everything was going fine.
The man tried to smile at Helen and that's when Helen realized
that the difference between men and women was that men didn't
know anything about pain.

That explained the whole state of affairs.

The nurse came in again and told Helen to come into the next
room where there was a doctor with a bald head and a chaplain
with a white collar that went all the way around instead of showing just a little white square at the throat like Catholics.

"The baby was stillborn," said the doctor. He looked at Helen's
belly.

"I baptized him," said the chaplain. He looked at Helen's belly.

Everybody was looking at Helen's belly.

Helen put her hand on her belly. "Does Dee know?" she said.

"You can see her in a minute," said the doctor.

"She's doing fine, considering," said the chaplain.

Helen looked at the chaplain, who obviously didn't know what
the hell he was talking about.

"Do you want me to come with you?" he asked.

Helen went in alone. She held Dee's hand and Dee cried. They didn't say anything for a long time, though sometimes Dee touched Helen's stomach.

"Can you tell Derk?" whispered Helen.

"No," said Dee.

"You can't reach him?"

Dee put both her hands on Helen's. "He already knows." She smiled slightly. "He and Derk Jr. are working on the same project now." She put her index finger to her lips. "Top Secret."

Dee got more philosophical about pinochle, sometimes she and Helen even won. Every day she asked Jon, who was gaining weight in his extremities now, though losing some in his head, about his men.

"They're good men," said Jon. "They eat their snacks. They take naps. They urinate efficiently."

"That's real good, honey," said Dee. "Myself, I think I'm through with men."

"You're young," said Bush. "You have plenty of time for more mistakes."

Dee smiled. "You're a real card, honey," she told Bush.

Communication had never been better. Except between Helen and Dee. Helen got bigger and bigger and Dee got quieter and quieter and pretty soon when Helen went over to Dee's in the morning after wiping the grime off the windowpanes and windowsills Dee wasn't there. She left a note saying she had to shop or clear up some administrative matter about Derk Delco Sr. downtown, though after a while she didn't leave any notes, she just showed up in the afternoons and played cards, though even then she barely talked to anybody but Jon.

"So what are your boys really doin everyday, honey?" Dee'd ask.

"Top Secret," said Jon.

"I can understand that," said Dee.

And then one day she didn't come. Helen went over to Dee's and went through the unlocked door to the kitchen when nobody answered her knocking and calling. She found a note on the table.

> Good luck Helen, honey, had to go on a mission.
> Top Secret.
>
> —Dee

And that was it for Dee. They found her that night in the bay.

And that was the night I was born. Which should explain a lot of things, not that I can explain them, or not that I would if I could.

So Bush held me in her arms that night next to Helen's bed, and Helen thought about the night her father died, and she thought about the night Red left San Diego for Midway, though at the time she didn't know it was Midway, she just knew subliminally it was some big male experiment with deaf, and now, that night, Dee was dead and Bush held Helen's first baby, and Bush said, "Red's still alive, you have your first son, things could be worse."

Helen hadn't been praying fervently for quite some time, she'd said her usual prayers and gone to mass on Sunday but she hadn't really prayed fervently for quite some time, but now almost everything she did was a prayer, everything she said, half of it was to God, and she said, "God, I don't understand why things turn out the way they do."

And Bush held me in her arms and said, "He flips a coin."

Nom de Père

AND THAT'S how I got named Jarvis even though Red didn't want anybody else in the world including himself but especially his son named Jarvis. I guess the psychology of it all is pretty clear, though it never quite got explained just right to Red. I suppose I should be happy I didn't get named Derk Delco Jr.

Because Red came back from the war a little ashamed he didn't get enough fighting in and capable of killing anything that moved, unfortunately all he had around him were those he loved, and went back to the Erie Forge worrying about missing lunch and picking up where he left off with the Union Dirty Man only to find out the Union Dirty Man had eventually found a way to get into the Marine Corps and had been shipped to Midway where he died in action. Red found out from Whitey.

In fact there was a joke that he died in his underwear.

And another story that was pretty heroic about how the Union Dirty Man went down following some maniac who kept leading charges against an overwhelming Japanese attack, first out of the camp and then back in, and the Union Dirty Man followed him the whole way, and even at the end when the Japanese were swarming the last Marines, just before the reinforcements came, and the maniac hero led a charge into the swarm, it was the

Union Dirty Man who went in behind him, going down like a buzz saw in a cattle stampede. Died in his underwear in that story too. Of course the government denied all that.

"That so?" said Red.

"Heh, heh, that's so," said Whitey. He really didn't give a shit what the truth was.

Yes I suppose I'm lucky I didn't get named after the Union Dirty Man.

Though it was bad enough that when Red finally got out of the Marines and came home I was already four years old and calling everything in sight Jarvis. I had a pet turtle named Jarvis, called my chair Jarvis, my bowl and spoon Jarvis, the baby chicks and ducks I got for Easter, I called them all Jarvis. I caught bugs and dragged in worms and called them Jarvis and when they died I buried them in the backyard in a little cemetery under cute little cardboard headstones that said Jarvis-Jarvis-Jarvis-Jarvis. Red brought me home a rocking horse that he made for me in the Marines and I called it Jarvis. I called Red Jarvis. I called Helen Jarvis. It was all Jarvis to me.

Back then Red only had two emotions, he felt like killing things or he didn't, and it was about fifty-fifty. He felt lousy about me being named Jarvis and he felt sorry for me and hated me for it, after all, there was a limit how much he was going to hate Helen for it, for obvious reasons, and that made him feel bad about hating me, which only made it worse. Deep down in he probably liked the idea or else he would have changed my name or called me something else, which he never did. Maybe it might have been better if I looked like him. I didn't look like a shovel and a pickax like Helen's brothers but I didn't look like Red either; my hair wasn't wavy and I didn't have big bones nor the temperament to try and hang muscles on them. On top of it all I was mixed up with the legacy of Derk Delco. Red was also afraid that I was going to be smarter than him, he was always afraid people were going to be smarter than him, and I was already giving evidence by my wreaking Jarvis upon the world, which was just the opposite of his reaction.

Poor Helen was caught in between all this, between me flash-
ing my one-word vocabulary at everything other than myself and
Red who only had two emotions and felt the bad one every time
I opened my mouth to remind him what Helen had done. Nonetheless, she did it, and when they got through fighting about that
and Red turned his attention to me, Helen got protective and
they fought about that. It was after one of those fights that Red
decided to make up and brought me and Helen home a collie
puppy.

Boy was he cute.

"We'll call him King," said Red.

"No, Floppy," said Helen.

"Jarvis," I said.

"Sarge," said Red.

"Sammy," said Helen.

"Jarvis," I said.

Red and Helen called him Sandy. I hugged his neck. "Hello
Jarvis," I said to the puppy.

That was it for Red. He pulled me away. "We're gonna have a
talk," Red said to me. He was still in a good mood about bringing
his gift so practiced a lot of control.

That was me and Red's first big talk. Red took me into the
front room and sat down in his big chair next to the Zenith and
made me stand in front of him.

"Okay," said Red. "I'm going to be rational about this." Lately
when he argued with Helen she always accused him of being
irrational. "Red," she yelled at him, "you're so irrational," so now
Red was working hard on being rational, not because he thought
it was important, just because he didn't want there to be anything he couldn't do.

"Now listen," said Red. "You got to stop calling everything
Jarvis."

Well I didn't have nothin to say about that.

"I don't go around calling everybody Red," said Red. He touched
both my arms. Boy was he being rational. "Your Mom doesn't

go around calling everything Mom or Helen. Why you think we all got different names, so we can keep things straight."

As if I couldn't keep things straight.

"Listen," said Red. "We got to be rational about this. The next time you call something Jarvis I'm going to smack you. And if you do it again I'm going to smack you again, and I'll smack you till you can't walk if that's what it takes."

So that's when I went into my whispering period. Whispered to my bowl, whispered to my spoon, whispered to my duck. Though sometimes Red gave me tests.

"What you got there," Red said. "Nice bowl, huh."

"Yeah."

"What is it?"

"Jarvis."

Smack.

Red didn't fuck around, he let me have it right on the head. Didn't endear him too much to Helen who was now pregnant with Neda, but I got to admit he got me calling things by the right name. Of course I hated him.

"I'm bringing children into tyranny," said Helen.

"This is benevolent tyranny," said Red.

"You learned that word from me," said Helen.

"I learned it in the Marines," said Red. "America is benevolent."

Of course I had the days to myself while Red was at the forge and Helen let me call everything Jarvis then, even her.

"You'll grow out of it," she'd say to me.

"Yes Jarvis," I told her.

Still, when Red was around I named things right unless I felt really brave and that never lasted long. I had to call my duck Ducky and my turtle Turdy and my bowl Bowly and my spoon Spoony. Called my rocking horse Charley. Though Red decided he should be called Rocky, so that son of a bitch had three names. Power was going to Red's head. I thought Jarvis was a dumb name until I had to start calling everything right. Then Red found my Jarvis bug graveyard out back and rubbed out the last vestige of Jarvis heresy. That's when he decided it was time to make me an athlete.

I learned survival baseball. I never learned to throw or move to a ball but I could catch anything that came at me. I couldn't hit far or fair but if it got near me, as it usually did with Red pitching, I could knock it down. Red told me I was crowding the plate so he tried to back me off and when I backed off I got too far away and Red nailed me while trying to get the ball near my bat. It looked like there was a real fine line between achievement and death. Basketball was worse, and I'd have hands that looked like feet if we'd of had a hoop or cement in the yard. Red had me high jumping without sawdust, running races with brick-wall finish lines, catching shot puts, said he thought that's what you're supposed to do with a shot put, pole vaulting with skinny wooden wash-line poles. My hands looked like porcupines. I don't even want to talk about football.

Afterwards I'd come in the house and Helen gave me a bath that was a close facsimile of an automatic car wash. Helen was a sadist with a washcloth, a de Sade with a clean towel. "You have to understand," she told me, "he just got out of the Marines. All he knows is kill, kill, kill. You think it's easy for me? It's not easy for me. But he'll get better. It's just going to take a decade or so."

Helen was a real optimist.

Meanwhile I'd come out of the bathroom with skin like round steak and head right for Sandy's bed in the corner of the kitchen. That was the only solace I had in life. I knew next year I'd be in kindergarten, I'd just get older and it would get worse. I went into Sandy's corner and dug into his silky warm fur. I hugged the life out of that son of a bitch.

"Goddamn kid," said Red. "Give him a bath and he smells like a wet dog."

"Leave him alone," said Helen.

That's when she stuck up for me, after Red got his licks in and she got hers in; Red got the backyard, Helen got the bathroom, and after that I got the dog. I loved that dog with all my life.

After that we ate supper and then Red and Helen went into

the living room where Helen watched the new black-and-white
Zenith with one big knob on the left that turned it on and one
big knob on the right that got one channel, and Red sat down in
his big chair next to the Zenith where he couldn't see the screen
but he could hear the program and watch Helen's face, and Helen
said, "Why don't you watch?" and Red said, "I can tell what's
happening by your face," they both said the same thing every
time, and I put in a couple minutes in front of the TV and then
left for a drink of water but never came back, instead I went into
the corner of the kitchen and hugged the dog.

I communicated. He licked me, I licked him. He bit my ear, I
bit his ear. We smelled each other's butts. It would have been
perfect symbiosis except that that fucker was smarter than me,
nothing new. He knew where to shit, knew how to keep his trap
shut, could open doors, turn on lights, managed to get pets from
Helen and get ignored by Red, and no matter how many times I
bit his ear he wasn't giving up any information. I started thinking
maybe I was just a warm body to him until the night I slipped
up and called my pot roast Jarvis and Red knocked me out of my
chair. Sandy growled at him and Red beat his butt and made him
spend the night in the shed. After that I started sneaking downstairs at night after Red and Helen went to bed and spending the
night with Sandy on the kitchen floor. I remember, he made a
sound in his chest when you hugged him just like you hear when
you've got your head in between somebody's breasts after you've
done good making love. I learned to wake up ten minutes before
Red and Helen and go back to bed, which only goes to prove
neither of them spent many sleepless nights back then when the
only thing they could do to get to sleep was sneak in my room
and stare over my bed in loving ecstasy. That's not a criticism.
They both loved me. They loved the dog too.

Of course Sandy was just too smart and too good. One Sunday
after church I headed right out from the car for the backyard and
when I opened the gate Sandy ran out and headed for the street.
He ran out into the middle and Red yelled at him which of course
stopped him cold and whammo, some drunk driver came rolling

through and ran right over Sandy's back end, didn't even stop. I'm sure Red would have gone after the guy and killed him if he hadn't been so worried about the dog.

Sandy flopped around like a fish for a while but then stopped. His eyes looked way too big for his head and had turned from brown to gray. Already lots of neighbors gathered around and said, "Franky Gorky, Franky Gorky," who was the last person who was too smart and too good and who didn't look both ways. Then Sandy started to whine. Some blood came out of his ears and nose, it didn't look quite right, it looked a little like raspberry jelly, and Sandy whined, just softly at first, but soon you couldn't hear anything else, only Sandy's whine, high and shrill and constant like bomb sirens. And the neighbors slowly went away and Helen went into the house and came out with a blanket that Red wrapped around Sandy and then carried him into the house.

Helen kept trying to call vets but there weren't any vets at their offices on Sunday and Sandy's whining and yelping filled the house like a clay pillow, it suffocated me, it made me want to puke, and Red said to Helen, "He can't live," and Helen didn't say anything, but I figured that was wrong, he wasn't dead so we'd keep him alive till he got better, that's all there was to it, if you're not dead then you're sick and if you're sick you wait till you get better.

But Red said Sandy wasn't going to get better. That's when I started crying. Red put Sandy on his bed in the corner and I kept crying and Helen kept keeping me from running over to hug Sandy and when she wasn't doing that she was talking real quietly with Red. They told me Sandy needed to rest. Helen pulled me out of the kitchen while I tried to drown out Sandy's yelping with my own until it hit me that me and Helen were letting Sandy rest but Red wasn't, Red stayed in the kitchen. And I wasn't really afraid of anything specific, I just didn't want Red alone in there with Sandy, I wanted to be alone with Sandy even if I was screaming blind in my own tears and snot, so when Helen tried to make me sit down on Red's big chair next to the TV I got away and ran for the kitchen and saw Red's broad back over the dog and out the corner his hands around Sandy's neck, his giant hands around that throat, and I heard the snap, the body shuttered and the whining stopped, and as Red stood up and backed away Sandy oozed jelly from his mouth and nose and his back end folded on itself and pushed out piss and shit.

Red never said anything to me about the Marines. He always told me he never did any fighting in World War Two, he got to Midway too late and spent the rest of the war playing handball and pitching horseshoes in Hawaii. He had some souvenirs, a helmet, a dummy rifle, some blank grenade shells, but anytime he talked about the war and anybody asked him did he fight, did he kill anybody, he just said no. Red said he never saw a Jap. Red said he never killed anybody. He said he'd been trained to kill. Said he could kill if he had to, but he didn't have to. He could do it, he said, but he never had to.

About the Author

CHUCK ROSENTHAL was born and raised in Erie, Pennsylvania. He has a PhD in English and American Literature with an emphasis in literary theory, and is currently teaching at Loyola Marymount University in Los Angeles, California. He is at work on a sequel to *Loop's Progress*.